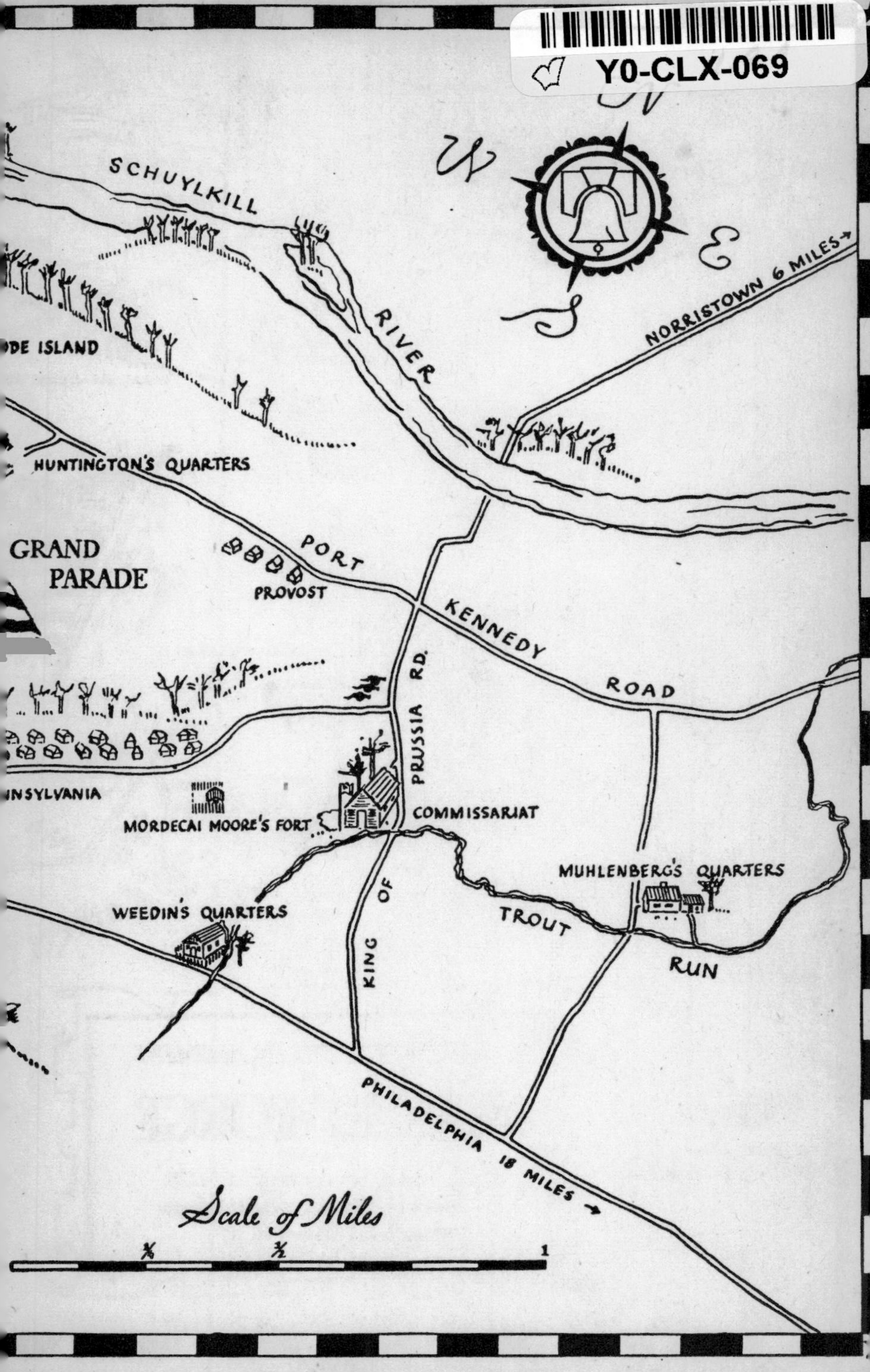
SCHUYLKILL
RIVER
W
E
S
NORRISTOWN 6 MILES
DE ISLAND
HUNTINGTON'S QUARTERS
GRAND
PARADE
PORT
KENNEDY
ROAD
PROVOST
PRUSSIA RD.
KING OF
NSYLVANIA
MORDECAI MOORE'S FORT
COMMISSARIAT
MUHLENBERG'S QUARTERS
WEEDIN'S QUARTERS
TROUT
RUN
PHILADELPHIA 18 MILES
Scale of Miles
¼
½
1

CONCEIVED IN LIBERTY

Books by Howard Fast

PLACE IN THE CITY
CONCEIVED IN LIBERTY
THE LAST FRONTIER
THE UNVANQUISHED
CITIZEN TOM PAINE

Conceived in Liberty

A NOVEL OF VALLEY FORGE

BY HOWARD FAST

CLEVELAND · NEW YORK

THE WORLD PUBLISHING COMPANY

Published by THE WORLD PUBLISHING COMPANY
2231 WEST 110TH STREET · CLEVELAND · OHIO

By arrangement with Duell, Sloan and Pearce

FORUM BOOKS EDITION
First Printing, January 1944

HC
COPYRIGHT 1939 BY HOWARD FAST
All rights reserved, including the right to reproduce this book or portions thereof in any form.

MANUFACTURED IN THE UNITED STATES OF AMERICA

For my Wife

AND HERE
IN THIS PLACE
OF SACRIFICE
IN THIS VALE OF HUMILIATION
IN THIS VALLEY OF THE SHADOW
OF THAT DEATH OUT OF WHICH
THE LIFE OF AMERICA ROSE
REGENERATE AND FREE
LET US BELIEVE
WITH AN ABIDING FAITH
THAT TO THEM
UNION WILL SEEM AS DEAR
AND LIBERTY AS SWEET
AND PROGRESS AS GLORIOUS
AS THEY WERE TO OUR FATHERS
AND ARE TO YOU AND ME
AND THAT THE INSTITUTIONS
WHICH HAVE MADE US HAPPY
PRESERVED BY THE
VIRTUE OF OUR CHILDREN
SHALL BLESS
THE REMOTEST GENERATION
OF THE TIME TO COME

—HENRY ARMITT BROWN

Inscription on the Memorial Arch at Valley Forge

PART ONE
THE VALLEY

I

WE STOP, and the word comes down the line to bivouac. It's early; there's a good hour of daylight left. We are used to march until the light is gone, stumble into camp in the dark, wake up in the morning before the light and go on.

There is a faint sound of a bugle, far up the line, dismount. Jacob Eagen drops his pack. Charley Green sits down at the side of the road. His round, bearded, elf's face attempts a smile. His little form is a punctured bubble of weariness. I look up and down the line. Toward evening, the line is four, five, maybe six miles long.

I crawl out of my pack, say: "Ah, Jesus, I'm tired."

All up and down the road men are dropping to the ground. Their muskets clatter against the frozen road. That's the first idea; get rid of your musket. It weighs twenty pounds. It's twenty pounds of hell with a rusty bayonet.

"Why do we stop?" Jacob asks, but of no one. He alone is tireless. He stands stiff and grim, his dark eyes questioning. He probes face after face, and desires to know why we don't go on. He's a tall, spare man, bearded, his long hair falling loose to his shoulders, his large hooked nose thrusting forth from his face. His lips are a thin line, almost hidden by the hair on his face. He might well have no lips at all, and when his mouth parts to speak, I see his uneven, tobacco-stained teeth. There is something fierce and animal-like about his mouth and teeth, about the sharp, wide-spaced yellow fangs.

"What difference so long as we stop?"

"This ain't a place to stop. You don't have to be a general to know this ain't a fit place to stop." He waves a lean arm to indicate our open, unprotected position.

We are in a great flat space, with a roll of hills to the north of us. The hills mean shelter. We think of what it would be for six miles of army to be caught in this open space. But not too much thinking, because most of us don't care.

I sat down at the side of the road, sighing, stretching my feet, calculating how long I could stay that way, rest without my feet freezing. It was a cold day; half an hour, and my feet would freeze.

Next to me and around me were the men of my regiment. There were eight men besides myself who made up the regiment. We had no officers. You don't need officers for nine men. We had a shred of flag until Ely Jackson covered his feet with it. We were the Fourth New York Regiment. There were three hundred of us at one time, Major Anton, of White Plains; he died at White Plains near his own house. Eeden Sage had been a captain, dead. Lieutenant Ferrel died of dysentery. Now, some day in December in seventeen seventy-seven, we had no officers. I don't know what day it was. When you retreat, the days blend themselves together. Maybe it was the thirteenth of December, or the fourteenth. The thirteenth and Friday, perhaps, which is a rare black day. Charley Green had a song about Friday thirteenth, about witches dancing on Boston Common——

The army spilled off the road onto the fields, a haphazard sort of bivouac. I remember that there was one house, a stone building set back against a fringe of forest. The windows were shuttered; no light and no smoke. We were in a country that hated the rebels.

We climbed off the road, a sunken road. We climbed up to the flat of the meadow. Ely Jackson stopped to fix the cloths on his feet; his feet were always bleeding. A pet staff officer rode by us, a boy in a blue uniform. Jacob Eagen stopped him.

"Tell us, son," Jacob said. "We camp here?"

Jacob Eagen, bearded, filthy, a fringe of ice around his mouth, was not nice to look at. None of us was. The boy shook loose his reins.

"We encamp tomorrow. We're resting the troops."

"That's damn nice of you and the General," Jacob said bitterly.

The boy spurred away, and Jacob laughed. Jacob hated officers. God knows, none of us loved them, but there was something of madness in Jacob's hatred. He was a rare man for feeling the revolution, not the way the rest of us felt it, hunger and cold, but as a living, burning thing made by the people. He would argue of the officers, If they're of the revolution, they're of us. It's a war of man by man. I'll call God my superior, but no damned man on a horse. Talking that way now, but we didn't listen. Talk of Jacob's was like wind sighing; we had listened until the words meant nothing

—only the bitter growl of his voice. We walked on. We buried ourselves in the troops. There was no army left now, only five or six miles of rabble strung out over the countryside. It was better to be inside than on the outskirts.

We passed the Pennsylvania line. Their general, Wayne, held them in some kind of order. They were camped in brigades and putting out sentries. A sentry stopped us, a tall southland farm boy. We laughed in his face and pushed past him.

He said: "Who the hell are you? What call you got pushing through Pennsylvania land?"

Edward Flagg said gently: "This land deeded to you?" He was a slow man, Edward, a big farmer, slow to anger, but long-burning when his ire was roused.

"We don't want fights," I told the boy. "We're a New York regiment." We walked on. He called after us, "You're a lousy-low regiment, all right."

We got off the Pennsylvania land; we didn't want trouble. You give men guns and drive them mad, then there's hell to pay. "I'll tell you 'bout this war," Kenton Brenner said. "It'll be north fighting south, and east fighting west. I don't hold with no low German Pennsylvania sonovabitch. I don't hold with no German who takes a gun when it ain't no more use. Where, I reckon, they been at Breed's Hill and White Plains?"

"You hold on, Kenton," Moss said. Moss was just a boy. He was eighteen years old, and next on the list. The list was an idea of Moss'. That we were named off to die. Sometimes he would sit for hours, trying to recall the names on the regiment's first muster. A long list, and there was no moving the names. Anyway, he talked about it so much that we got to believe him. You only had to look at Moss to know he was next. He had a cough that kept flecking his lips with blood. When he said something, we all looked at him. Now we were quiet.

The officers' tents were rising, dotting the brown, frozen fields. The brigades were scattered all over the fields, no order, and some of the last ones to march up were set right on the road. You could see brigades sprawled on the hard ground as far as the edge of the woods, and north and south until the fields touched the horizon.

"A lot of men," Jacob said.

"Ten, eleven thousand," I nodded.

"They'll go."

"I'm tired," Moss said simply. "I been thinking of going along home."

We came to where there were a few fruit trees, and no brigades nearer than thirty paces. We dropped our packs and slumped down on the earth. Kenton Brenner began to stack the muskets, working automatically and moving slowly. We watched him with quiet curiosity. We were very tired.

The kind of weariness that comes from too little food and no real rest. It goes into every joint and every limb of the body. It eats deep. It saturates and brings a vision into the mind, and the vision persists above everything else. That's a vision of a bed, a broad down bed. The down would take you into itself and eat the weariness out of your bones. Sometimes, too, you think of a trundle bed, a child in a trundle bed. Or a hot Dutch oven with bread cooking. Things of home.

We stretched and crouched on the cold ground. Someone would have to start the fire. We looked at each other, but nobody moved. Then Charley Green got up and walked away. We followed him with our eyes, but didn't call him back. I stood up, took a hand axe out of my pack, and began to hack at the fruit tree. It was an apple or plum tree; I don't remember. It was hard wood.

They watched me with deep, significant pain in their eyes, pain that understood the decades of anticipation that made up the growing of the tree. Someone had planted it and watched it grow. Someone had picked the ripe fruit in the heat of Indian summer.

Clark opened his mouth to speak, then stopped himself. They waited until I leaned on the branch and tore it down. Then Ely Jackson stood up and began to break it apart.

"I call to mind the wonderful fruit of a summer," Moss whispered.

I paused; I was hacking on a second branch. I filled myself with the single impulse that every man in the army had. One more summer. Only one more summer with hot sun to make the sweat pour from you. Only one more summer with the juice of fruit bursting its skin.

Then I beat the branch down.

Ely was working with flint and steel. Ely was the oldest, older than Jacob even, and Jacob was a man past forty. Ely was our voice, when a soft voice was needed. Ely was water on fire when we fought in anger among ourselves, and God knows we fought enough of late. He had a loose fleshless body and big hands. I watched the hands now, their sure, tireless motion. Tinder was rare and precious. Kenton shredded it from the inside of his hat. I looked at them and told myself that I had probed deep. I was twenty-one years old. But there were eight men whose souls I knew and whose bodies I knew.

An officer galloped up, reined in his horse, and told me to leave off the tree.

"No pillage," he said. I thought I recognized him. He was bearded and wore no uniform. I thought I recognized him as an aide of Washington. He spoke with the slur of a Virginian.

Eagen got up. He walked over to the stacked muskets. The rest of us rose. We stood in a circle round the officer. Our clothes were filthy and torn. We were all bearded, even Moss Fuller who was only eighteen and whose beard was a patched map on his face. We were filthy and lean, our feet bound in sacking. The sacking on Ely Jackson's feet was a mass of caked blood. There was something wrong with his feet, and they wouldn't heal. They bled all the time, draining the lifeblood out of him.

"Who's in command here? What brigade?"

"Fourth New York."

Kenton Brenner took his musket. Jacob too.

There was sullen light in Jacob's eyes. The officer noticed that, and he said to Jacob:

"You're in command? Where is the rest of your regiment?"

"We're all," Jacob said. "No officers."

He leaned over his saddle, pointed to the tree. "You're killing that tree."

We laughed at him. I raised my axe. The officer drew his pistol, aimed it at my head. "There'll be no pillage," he said.

I brought down the axe. I didn't think he would fire. Maybe I didn't care. As in a dream, I heard the pistol roar, and it tore off my hat. I walked forward, the axe in my hand, but Jacob was ahead of me. He struck the pistol down with the barrel of his musket and tore the man from his horse. I saw Jacob's clenched fist lash into the officer's face.

The officer lay on the ground, and we stood there, watching him, not speaking, but just looking at one another. There were Boston men camped near us. They came over, attracted by the shot. They made a crowd around him, and they didn't love officers, not southern officers.

"Oughta killed the swine," one of them said.

"You oughta killed the dirty slave-driving bastard."

The officer groaned and stumbled to his feet. He mounted and rode off. The Boston men left us, and Eagen sat down and put his head in his arms.

We had the fire going. We tore down most of the fruit tree to feed it. Fires were springing up now, gleams that mingled with the twilight. The staff officers rode past, the big form of Washington bulking above the rest. We saw them ride across the fields to the house and hammer at the door. Then the door opened. The shutters were flung back and lights appeared inside.

"A house like that," Moss whispered.

"Quakers. By God, they're warm in their houses," Jacob muttered.

Ely Jackson laughed. We had some potatoes in our packs. We laid them out and roasted them on the points of our bayonets. Ed Flagg had stolen the potatoes the day before. They were a rare thing for men on a diet of corn.

We heard singing. Charley Green walked up to the fire with a woman on his arm. She was a stout, blonde woman, wrapped in a dirty blanket. Her feet were in sacking. She had a broad smile. We watched her hungrily; you watched any fat person with fascination.

"This is Jenny Carter," Charley said. "She's a fine fat piece of woman." Then he began to sing again.

She dropped down by the fire, her fat legs spread toward it. She moved her hands, anxiously fixing her hair. We began to laugh.

"Where did you find her, Charley?"

"I took her from the Pennsylvania men. A sight of women, too many for stinking Dutch farmers. I reckon they have a hundred women there. I took Jenny and told her we were from the Mohawk. I told her a fine, tall lot of men from the Mohawk. I told her men to love a woman, eh, Jenny?"

He sat down next to her and put an arm around her shoulders.

"A filthy lot of beggars," she said, and spat.

"You won't mind a little dirt."

"I won't mind a little bit of money."

Jacob took a fistful of Continental paper out of his sack. He dropped it into her lap. She scattered it and the hot flame of the fire drew it in.

"None of that!"

"Ye're a haggling Dutch skinner," Jacob said.

I tossed her a shilling and she thrust it into

the sacking that covered her feet. We broke the potatoes and added a few shreds of salt meat. We ate slowly, hoarding the food. It was quite dark now. Against the western sky, the dull mass of the brigades was still visible. But in the east, all had blended into the forest and only the fires made spots of light.

North of us, where the fields sloped to a hill, the fires were a pattern, haphazard. As if fireflies had settled themselves in the field and would soon lift away. The glow in the west died out. The wind rose to a whine.

"A cold, bitter night," said Clark Vandeer.

"A night for a woman——"

"For a fat, round woman."

Jenny was giggling and stuffing a piece of potato into her mouth. Then she rolled back in the arms of Charley Green. Some of us watched, but not with too much interest. We spoke in low tones when we spoke at all, but we could hear the woman heaving and sighing. Far over, from where the New Jersey troops were, there came a confused roar of sound.

Ely Jackson fussed with the bindings on his feet. Sometimes I suspected that there was little feeling left in his feet. But no more than that. I couldn't associate death with Ely. I remembered a time, perhaps ten years ago, when the Hurons came down to the Mohawk. They burnt and killed. Ely came to our house. Then we went with him, from house to house, gathering families. We went to the Patroons' fort, an old rotten place, and Ely and six men fought a hundred Indians for two days. He was a great, strong man, Ely.

"They say there'll be shoes along with the army in a time of days," Ely said wistfully.

"The lies of fatback swine in the Congress."

"There's no hate in me for the British as for the Congress," Clark said.

"There's hate in me for both," Jacob said. "For the rotten, guzzling liars who call themselves our Congress—" He stared into the fire a moment, then went on, "Time for Congress—understand me, Clark—time enough for Congress—after the British. After the British," he repeated. His eyes travelled over the sparks that marked the position of the sprawling, defeated army.

"After the British," he said dully.

"They say we'll be going home," Moss Fuller muttered plaintively.

But there was nothing to go to. The Indians

had burnt out the Mohawk. If my people lived, God only knew where they were.

"I'll not go back to the Mohawk," Jacob nodded. "There'll be no safe living in the New York Valleys. They'll fight us from Canada for a hundred years.

"You won't hold a musket a hundred years, Jacob," Kenton laughed.

"I hear of a rare beautiful land in Transylvania, a place they call the Kentuck. A Virginian named Boone sought it out———"

Jacob cried: "Ye're fools—all o' ye. The British way is to play the red men against us. Where is the power of the Six Nations but in Joseph Brant? An' Brant's their tool. Didn' they have him in England, making him into what he is? Mark me—I'll tell you the power an' scheme of the British, to play one force against another. But we're a free people an' no plaything for a King's hand. There'll be peace in the west—when we drive the last King's man back to his dirty hole!"

From where he was with his woman, Charley groaned: "Peace here, Jacob. Let be and damn the British."

Jenny had rolled over. She lay flat on her

back, and Charley Green sat up, shaking his head wearily.

"You've used her up," Kenton said.

Jacob's mood changed. He got up and went over to her. He slapped her back and pinched her cheeks. "Look at a real man."

"You'll kill her," Moss Fuller complained. He wanted his turn. He wanted the little pleasure he could squeeze from her. He was trembling and anxious, with the fear of death in him.

Jacob lay down next to her. We crouched close to the fire. From the New Jersey troops there came a great uproar, shots fired. We stayed close to the fire, hardly moving. With the heat, inertia had come over us.

"Attack?" Ely asked.

No more shots now. It didn't matter whether we were being attacked. Two officers galloped past, their sabres bare and glistening in the firelight.

"More hell to pay."

Silence and Jacob's hoarse breathing. I glanced at them, the man and the woman together. Only a glance. Moss Fuller had buried his head in his arms. He was coughing softly.

Ely hummed a lonely French tune of the Valleys.

I tried to think of a time when it had been different. I tried to think of a time when there had been shame and humility. I tried to think of the fire in our hearts that had sent us out to fight in the beginning.

I speak my name. My name is Allen Hale. I am twenty-one years old. I am a soldier with the Continental army of America. I have come great distances to fight for freedom.

The fire burns low, and Kenton rises to hack at the fruit tree. He comes back and drops the wood on the fire. He says:

"I wouldn't think to destroy a fruit tree. For a matter of ten years I saved the seed of cherry and plum. We thought to make a great planting in the Lake country when we moved westward. After the war we'll move westward—I'll save the seeds again."

The fire burns up. The brigades are quiet; perhaps they sleep. Moss lies with the woman, and his deep, regular breathing tells us that he sleeps. We none of us would take the woman now and rouse Moss from his sleep.

Some Massachusetts men come and stand about the fire. Most of their brigades are without fire. They crowd close to the fire and break the wind from us. One is an officer, a bearded boy in a tattered field dress of grey homespun, carrying a rusty sword at his belt.

The talk is soft, because some of the men sleep.

A Massachusetts man says: "I hear the retreat will be in a great circle. I hear the General has in mind to strike south around Philadelphia and march across the mountains. They tell of a rare fair land there in Transylvania, a land surveyed by a man called Boone. We can live there and take our food from the ground and defend the land."

"And our wives—children?"

"A man with bonds is no man for an army."

"There's no army now," Kenton muttered.

"If there are five thousand men here with bonds, will they lay down their arms and go back for hanging?"

"There won't be hanging after peace."

"There'll be no peace so long as George Washington lives. And there's a hell's broth in Wayne and his Pennsylvania brigades."

Vandeer said, softly: "At Haarlem, we held while Wayne's men ran."

"The ground's fallow two years now. When

the army's gone, they'll take the ground. If there were women in this land of Kentuck——"

"Where do we march tomorrow?" Eagen asked.

The Massachusetts officer answered: "A place to the north and east called the Valley Forge."

"We camp there?"

Later, the Massachusetts men went back. The fire burnt down. There were sparks of dying fires all over the fields.

I tried to sleep. Ely Jackson rose and took his musket.

"Ely?"

"I'll stand guard awhile," he said.

Green began to laugh. It was that strange for a man to stand guard. For what was the point in guarding? Any blow would crumple us. We were no army. Once we had been an army— but not now.

It began to snow, large, dry white flakes. Ely stood there, holding his musket with bare hands. He became a lump of white, motionless, the flakes floating past him.

2

I SAY to myself, oh, give me a long sleep with an end in the hot sun of the long morning. I yearn for a fire, all of my body stretching toward where the fire had been. There is no fire. I realize that my sleep has been broken, on and off through the night. A bugle is trilling. I sit up and the snow falls from me, two or three inches of snow on the ground, Green and Lane and Brenner and Eagen—piles of snow.

I stand up, trembling with cold, my body half numb. The men are dead. I glance around. The brigades are covered with snow. Ely Jackson stirs and Jacob Eagen climbs to his feet, trembling with cold. We blow on our hands, slap them against our sides, dance up and down.

"I had a wild, terrible fancy," I say, "that all the brigades are dead."

Ely smiles. His beard is all white with ice and snow.

"Ye're a strange being for thinking such thoughts," Jacob tells me.

The rest of us wake. We've slept close together, yearning toward each other for the body's heat. Only Moss Fuller still sleeps, the fat woman clutching him close.

"A woman's a good thing for a sleeping man," Edward nods.

Figures of ice and snow: we try to build a fire, but it's a hopeless task. We give it up and crunch the dry corn, chew on the salt meat enough so that we can swallow it. All the time, we move for warmth. The brigades are up, and the broken sound of voices carries over the fields. Officers canter by. Everywhere men are stamping for warmth. Here and there, a fire that was nursed through the night is built up.

"We'll go into camp soon, or we'll die," Vandeer says.

I nod, trying to rub the chill out of my arms and legs. One or two nights like this can be endured, but no more than that. I have never wanted anything so much as I desire heat now.

Ely points to a fire over among the Pennsylvania brigades. "I can get a brand," he suggests. The bugle blows, to arms.

"We march soon."

"To hell with that!"

"I am thinking hell's a rare cold place," Kenton Brenner smiles. His face is blue and purple with frost, the dead flesh breaking on his nose. I wonder how men endure it, how I endure it. But I keep stamping around. Only get warm, I think. The idea of warmth, any warmth, possesses me.

"Wake Moss."

With the toe of his boot, Jacob prods the woman. He says: "High time to be moving, Jenny."

Charley Green grins, standing feet apart, his face dull with sleep, his hands in his armpits for warmth. Ely walks toward the Pennsylvania men, slowly, stiltedly, as if each step pained the bottom of his feet. I can understand how his mind is set only on fire; he'll bring back the fire. He'll talk to them gently; he has a way with him.

We stand round Moss and Jenny. The woman moves and stretches her arms. The cold bites, and her hands seek out Moss. Then she screams and sits up.

"He's cold," she whimpered.

Vandeer laughed. Her nose had turned bright red during the night and her hair had spread all over her face. She was an ugly, fat, gross creature. We were all of us filthy and ugly, broken in one way or another. But I hated her because she reminded me of things that had once been and brought them back to me, because she was a mocking caricature of a woman. The kind of woman I had known, once.

I dragged her to her feet. I held her, her dirty blanket clutched in my hands, shaking her back and forth. The others watched me. Henry Lane was smiling stupidly, but the others didn't move. They just watched.

"You'll kill me!" she cried.

Then I let go of her. "Get out of here," I whispered.

She arranged her blanket, turning round and round, patting the loose strands of her yellow hair into place. "I'm a good woman, I want you to know," she said. "I'm a good, respectable woman."

Vandeer was laughing again. He was a little man; he had been a minister before the war. He had had two brothers who were killed at White Plains. Lately he had been like this. I could understand that. He was forty years old, yet he had become as lightheaded as a boy.

"Better go," Jacob Eagen told her.

She stumbled away, turning every now and then to swear at us and to scream at us that she was a good woman. Jacob bent down next to

Moss, shaking him gently. Jacob was hard and bitter, but now with Moss he was gentle as a woman. He took the hair away from Moss' face, and we saw blood clotted and frozen above his thin beard.

Jacob stood up, said: "He's cold." When he said that, we knew.

The boy's eyes were open. Vandeer had stopped laughing. I bent over Moss and pulled off his thin cloak, scattering snow. I forced my hands to go to his eyes and close them.

"It's a hard man needed to stand many nights like this night," Brenner said softly.

"He's dead?" Jacob asked me, and then demanded, querulously: "Where's Ely? This is no time for Ely to be away from us."

"Ely went for fire," Edward said, dully.

"Why'd he go for fire? It's too late for fire, ain't it? There was a time for fire before, but it's too late for fire now. The fire will not bring Moss alive."

"He went to wheedle a little fire out of those Pennsylvania men—he has a way, Ely——"

"Shut up!"

"We couldn't be starting a fire with flint. Ely'll come with a burning brand. Cold hands can't hold flint."

"There's nothing Ely can do now, Jacob."

Jacob knelt down by Moss. I went over to the fruit tree and sat down with my back against it. The cold was all through me, but it was not such a cold as Moss Fuller knew, nowhere near such a deep and silent cold.

"You're sure he's dead?"

"He's dead," Jacob said.

The bugles were blowing, and all along the line, brigades were picking themselves up and starting to move. The sun came up, showing through the stretch of forest east of us. Along the forest, men were moving in a thin line. They wore the shapeless grey smocks of Virginian riflemen. The officers were prancing their horses, shouting orders. In a long file, McLane's cavalry rode from behind the grey stone house and paraded across the fields. The Massachusetts men were laughing with their women while they formed into ranks.

"He's dead," Jacob said again, covering over Moss' face with the cloak. He said to me: "Come and give me a hand, Allen."

I stood up. The broken branches of the fruit tree brushed my face. Past Jacob, I saw Ely Jackson coming back with a piece of burning wood in his hand. It was a wonder how Ely got things, how he could work men.

"A fine fire soon!" Ely called.

Then he came up, saw how we were standing. He glanced from face to face, puzzled, meanwhile kicking the snow off the ashes of last night's fire. He said:

"Take an axe, Allen, and bleed the tree a little. Just a little, Allen—it's a fine tree."

I didn't move. He said: "Moss is sleeping? Wake him—or he'll not be able to march."

"Moss isn't sleeping," I said.

"He's dead," Jacob said. "The boy's dead, Ely."

"It was a fierce cold last night, and too much for him," Kenton muttered.

Ely stared stupidly, shook his head, and let go the torch. It fell into the snow, spluttered a little, and then went out. Nobody moved to pick it up. Ely went over to Moss and uncovered his face. He knelt there for a while, and I could see how Ely's feet were a frozen mass of ice and blood. The thought came into my mind immediately: Moss had shoes. They were worn thin now, but they were boots nevertheless. Jacob had pulled them off a dead Hessian a month before and given them to Moss. I wondered who would speak about it first. I couldn't understand that Moss was dead; only his shoes mattered now.

Looking at Ely's feet, I told myself: "Ely will have them." I glanced down at my own feet. I told myself that Ely had seen his youth already and that Ely would die soon. That was not true. Ely would live. His feet could become rotten stumps, and still Ely would live. I cursed him, and then I hated myself for cursing him —for his strength.

Ely stood up, but said nothing. He looked at me.

"He was a fine, tall Valley boy," Edward Flagg said. "I wouldn't have thought him to die so soon."

"He had a cough——"

"He died for wanting home. It's a long distance to the Valley country."

We nodded. We stood around, striking our hands together. Clark Vandeer came and stood above Moss. We watched him.

"You'll bury him and I'll say a few words," Vandeer said. His face seemed to be remembering.

"The ground's uncommon hard," Lane muttered.

Ely said: "Go to the Massachusetts men, Charley, and ask for a bugler to sound a call."

We took our bayonets and jabbed at the ground. I chopped with my axe. The ground was frozen, hard as stone. Once Jacob stopped, and I saw him looking at Moss' boots. I knew what was in his mind.

We dug a foot deep, and it seemed to exhaust us. We stood back and waited for Green to come back with the Massachusetts man. We stood there thinking, and maybe we were all thinking the same thing.

Finally, Jacob said: "The boy has an uncommon fine pair of boots——"

"We won't bury him naked," Ely said. "Two years together, so we'll not bury him naked."

"I was thinking only of the boots."

"Let him wear his boots."

"You need a pair of boots, Ely."

"I said he'll wear his boots. I swear to God, Jacob, I'll kill you if you take off his boots."

"There ain't no call to rage, Ely," Jacob said. "He's dead and no more feeling heat and cold. He don't need the boots, and you need them, Ely."

Ely said nothing, only staring at Moss' figure on the ground. Jacob went over and pulled off his boots, every so often glancing back at Ely, but Ely didn't move.

"I'm sorry, Ely."

Now Charley was back with a bugler from the Massachusetts brigade. A good many of the Boston men came with him, out of curiosity. They stood round in a circle, while we lifted Moss' body into the grave. A Massachusetts man said:

"They plough this land come spring. That grave's not deep enough."

We pushed in the dirt, and Vandeer said a few words. Vandeer's voice clogged up.

"A long way home," Ely said.

The bugle call drifted up, fine and clear in the morning air. It was what I would have wanted, if I were in Moss' place. There was a drummer, and he rolled several times. That was nice too. The brigades were moving now, and many of them stopped to watch what we were doing. But it was too common a sight to keep them for long. They marched on. The whole army was moving.

Jacob took Moss' bayonet and thrust it into the head of the grave. The bayonet was rusted and bent, and not much good. We gave the musket to a Massachusetts man. None of us was in any condition to carry two muskets, and a good many of the Massachusetts men were without arms.

The Massachusetts brigades were moving, and their men drifted away. We stood awhile, watching Washington and his aides come out of the grey stone building, mount and ride away to the head of the army.

We walked to the road.

"A long march today," Lane said.

"I don't remember knowing a place called the Valley Forge. An iron smithy, perhaps. This has the look of iron country."

"It rests on the Schuylkill."

"Why march north, if he plans a march southward after?"

"They say he's a rare quiet man to tease the British in his own way."

"He's a great fool if he thinks these an army."

Clark said suddenly: "Where's Moss?" He had forgotten.

We are on the road again. It is the sort of day when the sun makes a mirror of the snow, and after a while the snow can blind you.

The whole army is moving, slowly, but moving nevertheless. I wonder how that is and what makes us move. I seem to lose myself in the common soul of beggars strung out for six miles.

We march behind the Pennsylvania men. And behind us the Massachusetts brigades. Twelve lumbering wagons pass us by. From inside, there is the squalling of women, of the whores who are almost as many as the men. One of them puts her head out between the canvas curtains, and sticks her tongue out from between her teeth.

Charley Green calls: "Come and walk with us, lassie!"

"She's a pretty little wench," Edward nods.

We walk along and we don't think of Moss. There's no use thinking of Moss. We're too near to him. The veil between the dead and the living has been drawn too thin.

The Massachusetts men are singing, and we join in. The song runs, rocking the line, mile after mile:

"*Yankee-Doodle went to London,*
Riding on a pony——"

3

We've come, and there's a feeling now that we'll go no farther. We're not resting; I understand that vaguely, but still I understand it. There is no rest.

Ely Jackson says it. It's a terrible thing to see a strong, proud man die slowly, bit by bit. Ely says:

"There'll be no march to the south. He was a wonderous strong man, that Daniel Boone, to go on all his journeys. But we won't follow over his wilderness road to Transylvania. We're no more an army."

"A tired feeling," I said. "I can't march."

Kenton says: "We make a stand here—to meet the British. I call to mind how it was at Breed's Hill, with their red coats flashing. A proud lot of good men. Moss cried. He was sixteen of age."

"Not a thing for a boy to see," Ely says. "A bitter thing, the way they marched the hill—to be blown to bits. I recall there was a boy drumming for the British. He was shot in the belly, and still he tried to drum. Just a boy——"

That was Breed's Hill—Bunker Hill, they call it now.

"A boy like Moss," Ely went on. "It put iron into his soul, and he was too young, too young."

We sit around a fire, this time a great, roaring fire. But it has no power to warm us. The cold is in our bones. The cold beats down the flames and adds up on itself.

We are camped on the top of a hill, forest to one side of us and a sweep of meadowland on the other. All over the hill and down into the valley fires burn. Westward, in the bed of a creek, the valley drops to the Schuylkill. The place is called the Valley Forge. There was a forge once where the creek enters the river, a few houses there. It goes that the officers are taking up quarters in the houses.

East, across eighteen or twenty miles of the same rolling land, is Philadelphia. We glance again and again in the direction of Philadelphia. We try to picture a British army, correct, uniformed. They sleep in warm houses. At night, they gather in the taverns and toast each other with warm ale. Philadelphia—men, women, and warm beds—is theirs.

We try to understand that this is the end, that we go no farther.

Clark Vandeer shrugs his shoulders. He is crouched close to the fire, so close that his beard singes without his seeming to be aware of it. He has become an old man since Moss died, and many of his former parson's ways have returned to him.

"I'm afraid," Edward says. That's the way with Edward, who was a strong man once, a heavy farmer man, not dreaming and not fearing.

Ely Jackson shakes his head.

"If our orders are to march tomorrow?" Edward says, anxiously.

In each face is the same fear, that we march. We are too worn to march, too tired. We try to see the way out of the place. The slopes are covered with snow and bright in the moonlight. We crowd up to the fire.

Below us, the Pennsylvanians have built their fires in a wide circle. Each fire is an ember. Between half-closed eyes their encampment might be a crown. My mind is full of fancy, caused by hunger. Jacob sought out the commissary at nightfall. He came back bleeding, with a hatful of corn—for eight men.

"You're too quick for blood," Ely said gently.

Jacob is silent through the evening. A strange, deep man, Jacob, hard. When he was a boy, he fought in the French war. He was a revolutionist then—and no halfway man. In his mind, the revolution began with the French war. It was all one and the same—drive out the French first, then the British. A land for the people. That was what Jacob preached— for the people, all of it. The Indian must go. But first the French, then the British. Both had played along with the Indians, played them against us. He had fought to destroy the French, and now he was fighting to destroy the British. He would always fight. The land was not for him, but for them who came after. Jacob would fight until a shot found him; then he would rest. But the land would never be his.

"I call to mind," Ely says, "how Moss spoke about home. They say four brigades of Maryland men walked out of the line with fixed bayonets."

"It's only the beginning."

"They're a strange bad breed, the Maryland

men. Pope-crawlers and sons of thieves," Jacob muttered.

"Only the beginning," I said. "The army's falling to pieces. By God, when I think of that stinking Congress, talking of united states, filling their fat bellies and letting us starve. We fight for Maryland and Maryland walks home. What did Moss die for this morning?"

"Leave him in peace," Clark Vandeer says quietly.

"He spoke of the Mohawk——"

Ely says, simply: "Where would you go, deserting, Allen? We're all of us used up."

"Afraid?"

"I'm not afraid," Ely said. He looked at me. His swollen feet were stretched out towards the fire, his thin hands trying to grasp the heat. His dark eyes looked at me and through me.

Vandeer says, fretfully: "Why—why, Ely? You don't believe any more. There'll be no peace with Virginians hating the Boston men, with the New York brigades feared and hated. Even if we win, there'll be no peace—only battle and more battle."

Ely didn't answer. Jacob raised his dark, shaggy head. Above us, against the forest, shreds of song floated down from the New Jersey line. They were singing a plaintive Dutch melody. I lay down, closed my eyes and tried to sleep. Kenton was talking. He was explaining the thing I had heard a hundred times before, how the colonies could send an army into the New York Valleys and destroy the Six Nations. He was explaining why England would never permit the colonies to overwhelm the Indians.

"The moment we become strong," Kenton says, "we become a nation. It's our destiny." More of abstract destiny. What has that to do with a defeated rabble?

Jacob joins in, his bitter voice marking time to the nodding of his shaggy head. "Ye're right, Kent, and the strength is here—a strength of many. Look you, we could go back to the Mohawk where they're burnin' and killing, so God only knows who lives an' who's dead—but our strength is here. The Indians depend on the British, so it's our fight with the bastard King's men. After we rest, only one more blow. We'll gather strength an' hit them—hit them——"

I try to sleep, my coat drawn up over my face. I think of a woman; I think of little Moss Fuller with Jenny. I finger my beard and scrape the dirt from my face. The cold eats in and I turn my other side to the fire. For a moment, my eyes are open to the sky, and I see the broad stretch of stars. My hunger becomes a gnawing pain. I say to myself, sleep—don't think.

"—or Six Nations—or ten nations. If this man Washington sets himself up for king with his Virginia brigades behind him?"

"You mistake the man," Ely Jackson says.

The stars become sparks in a morning sky, and I lie awake watching the dawn come. The fire still burns, a low smouldering fire. I have slept on and off—a long night. Why have the nights become so long now? Rolling over, closer to the fire, I realize that someone fed it during the night. Wondering who, I think that it might be Ely or Kenton or one of the others. Charley Green, who was a printer in Albany; he was alien and strange for a long time. In the beginning he had been fat and round, but his fat had gone. Edward Flagg, born out of farmers. Or Jacob and Ely, strong men and different. Someone in the night, feeding the fire and making a great sacrifice in the cold.

I stood up; the others slept. They were curled for warmth, and they looked like bundles of rags. I remembered once, years ago, seeing a man dying of a cough, fleshless, but here were men as lean as he and living.

I walked toward the forest for wood. The snow had a crust of ice over it, and it crunched under my feet. As the morning advanced, there was no sign of sun in the sky, only a quilted grey that might turn to snow later on.

In front of the forest, the Jersey brigades lay, men sprawled about their fires. They had flung out sentries who slept now, all huddled over their muskets. I walked past, and the sentries didn't move. The Jersey men were worse than we; bare feet showed and bare skin through their coats. Almost no blankets and only two tents in all the brigades. They were tight, uncomplaining men, Dutch stock, not like the Pennsylvania German.

I gathered wood, went back and built up the fire. The heat of it woke Jacob and Henry. Then the Pennsylvania trumpets shrilled away the morning. The scene was old now, half-naked beggars coming to life, a great rush of movement back and forth to drive off the cold. The brigades were assembling.

"There's to be a review of the brigades today," Jacob said. "A grand review with a flag parade."

Charley, sprawled out, sang, "The beggars

are coming to London Town, London Town..."

"We'll need a flag——"

"A great white flag with a smoked ham painted on it—a roasted ham with gravy dripping for a border to the flag."

We had no food; we stood and looked at the fire. Edward Flagg slowly munched a handful of snow.

"I wouldn't," Ely said. "The snow'll burn yer mouth and belly."

"The Jersey men are eating," I said. I could see a few camp kettles boiling over their fires.

"I'll go to the commissary," Ely said.

"They'll want an officer's requisition."

Ely stumbled off. "He'll not wear Moss' shoes," I said. "His feet are fair gone and shapeless, not to be put inside shoes."

"There was a good coat gone to the grave with Moss. The dead don't feel cold."

"The shoes shouldn't go to waste," I muttered. I sat down and slowly untied the bandages over my feet, holding them close to the fire. Finally, they were bare, blue with frost. I let them warm by the fire. They were covered with sores, unhealed cuts, dirt.

"Rub them with snow, Allen."

I said, laughing: "They'll rot before I make them colder."

Vandeer said: "I call to mind a tract of Bishop Berkeley's I read through. A rare fine philosopher who holds that pain and all material things vanish with the mind that knows them."

"Well, Moss is dead, and we're here. I'd as leave be here as dead and stiff."

"But no cold for Moss," I said. "We can draw for the shoes, Jacob."

"They won't fit me," Edward said sullenly. He was a big man, big hands, big feet. I think he had the largest hands and feet I've ever seen on a man.

Kenton found a pair of dice and rolled them on a crust of snow. Henry drew the shoes with a double six. He held the boots between his knees, fondling them and feeling their softness. Then he unwrapped the bandages from his feet. The bandages clung, and he told us it was the first time in eight days he had bared his feet. When he got to his socks, he found they were crusted with blood. His feet were swollen out of all shape.

We tried to force the boots on. Henry lay down on his back, his feet stretched out, his hands clenched with pain. I had a little tobacco left, and I broke off a piece of it, gave it to him to chew while we worked on his feet. He broke up the tobacco, chewing desperately, his face twisted with pain, the brown stain running over his beard.

When the boots were on, he made no move to rise. "I can't stand it," he whispered. "Take them off."

We bound up Henry's feet after that. Jacob insisted that we wash them, but Henry refused. I wanted the boots. We rolled again, and Kenton drew them. I told Kenton I would fight him for them: I told him man to man, I would stand against him and fight for the boots.

Jacob pushed me away. "Keep yer head, Allen," he said.

"They're Moss' boots," I said. "Where's Moss?"

I sat down on the ground, put my face in my hands. I was hungry and my head was light. I felt a great strength, as if I could fight Kenton and all the rest of them. I felt that I could walk with strides yards long.

Then I began to cry, easily; I kept my hands over my face. When I looked up, they were standing round me. I could see how Clark Vandeer's lower lip trembled. Vandeer was a little man with children of his own. Maybe he was thinking of them now.

"Easy, Allen, easy," Jacob said.

Kenton was still holding the boots in his hand. "I'm not needing shoes, Allen," he whispered.

I cried: "I know what you're thinking—me next! Moss and then me."

"We'll eat soon, Allen."

"Moss wanted to go home. There's no one of you got nerve enough to desert and go home! Jesus Christ, there's nothing left inside of me."

Ely came up. They walked away when Ely came. Only Kenton stood there, still holding the boots in his hand. He said, dully:

"We rolled the dice for Moss' shoes."

Ely didn't answer. He had a piece of fatback in his hands.

"You brought food," Jacob nodded. "Ye're a wonderous quick man, Ely." He walked back slowly and put himself between Ely and Kenton. "Ye're not angered about the shoes, Ely?"

"There will be hell and murder at the commissariat. There's no food to feed ten thousand men. He asked me for papers, and I wheedled the fatback outa him. I said for a regiment. I thought he'd have a little corn. There were Boston and Pennsylvania men there with loaded guns."

"I don't hold with Pennsylvania men," Jacob said. "But I hate the guts of those damned Virginians, lording it over the food."

"They're a quiet, strange race."

I rose and walked away. Inside, I was heaving, and my throat burnt. Beyond the heat of the fire, the cold bit in, through my thin clothes. I resented Ely's way, avoiding mention of me or the shoes. When I turned round, they were grouped over a kettle, cutting up the fatback. Jacob poured the last of his cornmeal into it. The brigades were beginning to move, swarming round the forest and over the brink of the hill.

I went back to the fire. Ely put his arm through mine.

We ate quickly and in silence. We took our muskets and wiped them carefully. That was habit; we didn't love the muskets. We walked along with the brigades, Massachusetts and Vermont men, Pennsylvanians, tall, light-haired Jersey Dutch. The talk was all of the spot we were camped in, of its virtues for defence. There were hills all round the Valley Forge. It was a natural fort.

I heard a man say: "If they attack on the Philadelphia road, it's another Breed's Hill." Apparently he didn't remember that at Bunker Hill we were fresh and new to war. There had been no other victories since then.

We moved in no order. Occasionally you heard an officer's voice, but for the most part the brigades stumbled along as they pleased. A great hatred had grown for the officers, and they were afraid. All aspect of an organized army had disappeared. We had not been paid in weeks; we had not been fed. I think we were kept together only by the fear of the cold spaces that lay between where we were and our homes. It was said that the British ringed us in with their patrols.

We moved around the forest, over the hill northward, and down onto a great open meadowland that stretched to the Schuylkill. Afterwards this became known as the Grand Parade. The brigades streamed over it, slowly forming into a rough kind of order—the Pennsylvania Line, north, the New Jersey Line, the New York Line, the Virginian Riflemen.

Round the field there was a scattering of people who lived in the neighbourhood, mostly Quaker boys, hooting and screaming at the soldiers. The Massachusetts and Pennsylvania brigades still had drummers, and gradually their roll increased, until we were moving to a steady beat of drums. There were old habits hard to break.

The eight of us stood at one end of the Pennsylvania line, near the New York brigades. We leaned on our muskets, speaking little. And the wave of sound all up and down the brigades seemed to be dying away. We could hear women's voices, and we saw officers driving them out of the Pennsylvania troops. The camp followers were formed in a rough line behind the brigades, the women making a pitiful attempt at colour.

"Nigh a thousand women," Jacob said.

"It's hard understanding what a woman'll take to be near a man."

The clouds were piling up, dark grey and white tumbled together. A battery of artillery rolled across the parade.

"Knox's cannon," Ely said.

There must have been almost ten thousand men on the field then. That was before mass desertions had reduced us to half that number, then to less than half. There were a mass of men.

I close my eyes and try to see them as an army. If I close my eyes, look between the frost on my lids, I can forget that half of them are without guns, and all of them in rags. There are no uniforms except among the Virginian troops, who wear grey, homespun hunting shirts. There isn't a decent coat or a good pair of boots. Parts of the body show through, bare, blue buttocks where a man's pants are worn away, bare knees, legs bound in stripped blanket, feet in any material that can be made to cover feet. The feet are most important. Even if an army can't fight, it must be able to march —march day and night or forever.

But if I close my eyes, I can see them as an army, haggard, bearded men who will fight the way wild beasts fight. Only I fear we'll never fight again.

I laugh aloud.

Ely looks at me. Kenton says:

"You're not holding Moss' shoes against me, Allen. We've been together too long for that, Allen. I swear to God I'll never wear the shoes——"

"It's all right."

The trumpets blow a call to arms. We stand on our muskets. For an instant, we are no longer men, only a part of living revolution. We are a force. We are beyond men—only for an instant. The wind is blowing itself into a shrill shriek, and cold and hunger return.

A Pennsylvania man says, stubbornly: "To hell with their parades! Why don't they pay us off?"

Wayne and Scott ride down the Pennsylvania front. Wayne has a cloth bound round his head. His coat is shredded with use. He stoops in his saddle and rides close to Scott. There is a ripple of cheering, because they are both favourites with the Pennsylvania brigades. But neither man takes any notice. They sit on their horses in front of the line.

The flags go by. We don't salute. Very few men salute. We keep shifting about in the cold.

The officers press us together and finally we are in a line about four or five deep. Washington rides out to the centre of the field. He sits big on his horse and he seems oblivious to the wind. He's a strange man whom none of us understand and few of us know. Sometimes, we can build a great hate for him. He's a man without fear.

Hamilton is next to him, sitting the horse like an aristocrat, the lace cuffs of his uniform showing, behind him a little cluster of officers.

The voice of the General doesn't carry; it rises and fades out entirely in the wind.

". . . have come a long way . . . a bitter cup to drink . . . to endure . . . the British suffer equally, without our faith . . ."

Someone shouts: "Where do they suffer—in Philadelphia?"

"We must endure all wrong—hate . . ."

"Where is our pay? By God, your stinking Continental money———"

I glance at Jacob. His dark eyes are burning. His face, blue with cold, working—in pain—in anger.

"Soon, there will be food enough . . . rations of rum . . . a petition to the Congress . . ."

"Lies while we starve!"

A Pennsylvania man says: "He's got his fat bit to sleep with, I'll swear."

"A house and enough food to stuff him like a pig."

". . . when we march out of here—to victory . . ."

His voice is drowned out by a deep refrain: Pay us and disband the army! It comes to the thud of rifle butts being stamped against the frozen ground. A thud to the rhythm of a beating drum. Pay us and disband the army! I watch Wayne and Scott, who sit on their horses without moving. Neither does Washington move. His officers crowd round him, but he pushes through them and rides toward the line. Then, close to us, he sits on his horse, motionless. I can see how his face is blue with cold, his lips purple, thin and very tight. I wait for a gun to go off. I can understand how men would kill him now.

Jacob whispers: "There's a man. No officer, but a man to lead men."

"A rare, strange man," Ely agrees.

Then the noise dies away. The General's head drops forward, and his face is twisted with pain.

"A play actor," Charley murmurs.

"You are still my men," he says simply. "I want no more from you than to believe I am still one of you, not your General. We must build houses here—live and endure. We must."

Then he rides away. The brigades break. The parade becomes a seething mass of men, a roar of sound. The women flow forward and mingle with the brigades.

The Pennsylvania men hold some kind of order. Wayne rides down the line and stops in front of our little group. We stand apart.

"You're not my men," he says.

Ely replies: "We're the Fourth New York, sir."

He takes a little book out of his pocket and thumbs through it. The pages flutter in the wind and try to tear loose. "Disbanded?" he asks Ely.

"There are eight of us left."

"I'll list you with the Fourteenth Pennsylvania. You'll take orders from Captain Muller."

"We'll not become a Pennsylvania regiment," Jacob says sullenly.

"You'll obey orders!"

"To hell with your orders!"

"Who's in command among you?" Wayne says coldly.

"We have no officers," I say. "They were killed."

"You'll join the Fourteenth—or you're under arrest."

Jacob raises his musket. Ely tries to hold him

back, but Jacob shakes loose. He says to Wayne: "You're not talking to a German farmer. By God, I'm half-dead already, and I'd be all dead as soon as to crawl for an officer."

The Pennsylvanians had gathered round us now. An officer pushed through them, and Wayne said to him: "Captain Muller, have your men cover him, and shoot him if he fires."

I felt a single spark like that would set the field on fire. I felt that I was looking then at the finale of the revolution. But Ely put his arms around Jacob and forced the musket down.

"They're your men, Captain," Wayne said. Then he rode away, and I stood there with the rest of them, feeling all sick and hot inside. I felt sick the way I had been sick at Breed's Hill, and not since then. I pushed close to Jacob.

The Pennsylvania men were laughing. There were some women there, giggling and making eyes at us.

"I'll have no mutiny in my ranks," Muller said. "You'll take orders, my fine beggars, or you'll stump along."

"You can go to hell, sir," Ely told him, gently.

He couldn't fight Ely's eyes. He turned around, bawling for them to form their ranks.

We form to march back. Jacob is still trembling, and his face is black. Ely holds onto his arm. Kenton has his arm round a tall, thin woman, whose face is a mockery of any decent woman's face. A Pennsylvanian pushes through and claims the woman.

"She's my wife," he said.

"She's a slut and I'm paying her," Kenton says.

"She's my wife——"

The other women are laughing. Kenton's wench spits in her husband's face. A deep roar of laughter goes up.

"A rare lot of women these Pennsylvanians have," Charley Green says.

We march back. The sky breaks open, and it begins to snow. We stumble on through the snow.

4

A DEEP peace and a great stillness, and a wind to wash clear the skies and show the stars. There is a great silence over the face of the world, and it is Christmas Eve.

We have been here days—or weeks. We lose count of days until the word goes round that Christmas is a day away and there will be extra rations of rum. The word goes round that there will be chickens, that Captain Allen McLane and his foragers captured a British convoy train with a thousand chickens. But nobody believes and nobody is very much excited about Christmas. Another lean day. There are enough officers to take care of a thousand chickens.

It's night now, and I have sentry duty. It has snowed three times since we got here. There is six inches of loose, sandy snow on the ground. When you walk, it swirls up and seeps into crevices in your foot-coverings. As long as anybody can remember, there has never been such a winter as this.

I walk one hundred and twenty paces and

back—for two hours. I walk slowly, dragging my musket. At the edge of the forest, where the beat ends, I have a clear view of the frozen Schuylkill, of the King of Prussia Road and of the road to Philadelphia, blue rolling hills that sweep away until they are lost in a mystery of night. A fancy of lights on the horizon— perhaps Philadelphia. Philadelphia is only eighteen miles away.

I wait there for Max Brone. He's a German boy, a weed of a back-country lout from the hills around Harrisburg, who has the beat with me this night. He speaks only a few words of English, and his face is twisted with pain and homesickness and cold. He's better than no one at all. The silence can drive you mad.

I reach the limit of my beat and stop. The moment I stop moving, the cold eats in. It seems that we are here at the edge of the world— with no barrier between us and the cold of outer space. I wear two coats, my own and Kenton Brenner's. But both are worn thin. The snow has crusted around my feet, and they are balls of ice. My hands are wrapped in a piece of blanket; with them and with my elbows I hold my musket. But no keeping out the cold; I try to kick the ice off my feet.

As I wait there, I see Brone toiling up the slope. He is bent over, almost crawling on all-fours. He doesn't see me until he is quite near, and then he starts back.

"All's well," I say.

He straightens up and sighs. His breath comes out in a cloud of frozen moisture. He leans his musket against himself and beats his hands against his sides.

"I vas feard," he says. "*Gott*—it's lonely."

We stand together for a while, silent, only moving in little jerks to keep the cold off. A wolf howls. His howl begins with a quiver, strengthens and climbs into the night. A dog's bark answers. I feel little shivers crawl up and down my spine, and Brone's face drawn taut.

"I'd like to get a shot at that one," I say. "I'd make me a nice cap and a pair of mittens out of his wool."

Brone answers: "I tink—ven I valk alone, dey're vaiting."

There were no wolves here when the army first came. Farming country that has been farmed for years doesn't have wolves. Eighteen miles away, there was a city of twenty thousand people.

"There are more every day," I say.

"At home, tonight, dere vud be a fire. A roasting pig. Ve drink all night—and dance."

We stare at each other, and I nod. I look at him and try to see him, a thin, short boy with a frost-bitten face, a sparse yellow beard and wide-set unintelligent eyes. No imagination and no hope. I say to myself, why? I say to myself, what have you ever dreamed to follow a terrible nightmare of revolution?

He's the same blood as the Hessians. We don't hate the Hessians. But the Pennsylvania Germans do; they bear hate for the Hessians as I have never known men to bear hate. I've seen them torture dying Hessians, kick at them, prod them with bayonets, and taunt them in German.

I turn round and walk back. No words of parting. I glance over my shoulder and see him toiling and sliding down the slope. I see him as a picture of myself, and I try to forget the picture, closing my eyes and stumbling forward.

At the other end of my beat, I stop and stand for a while, leaning heavily on my musket and gradually dozing as I stand. I am falling asleep. A delicious sense of parting with the world creeps through me. Bit by bit, all sense of cold vanishes. Through half-closed eyes I can just make out the half-buried dugouts of Scott's brigades. This night merges with other Christmas Eves, and I hear my father's slow, monotonous voice reading the story of a Man. With that, the whir of my mother's wheel. The lulling hum of the wheel puts me to sleep. Outside is the great flat forest of the Lake country, the mysterious kingdom of the Six Nations where we have made our home. All that is mystery and dread, but foot-thick log walls close it out.

My father's voice: "Allen—" And my mother, gently: "You wouldn't sleep while the Words are being read, Allen?"

I come to myself with a terrible, heart-stabbing fear that I am freezing. I try to move and I lack all power of movement. The fear runs through me and exhausts itself. I give way, and the delicious apathy creeps over me.

Then a hand, stabbing from the far outside, beats down my shoulders. I give way and crumple forward in the snow, bruising my face on the hammer head of my musket. The snow in my face brings me awake. I roll over and Edward helps me to my feet. He's big and strong, and it's a relief to feel his wide hands under my arm.

"I was sleeping," I say.

Edward spits on his sleeve, and we watch fascinated as the bit of water freezes.

Edward shakes his head. "A cold wild night—get in to the fire." He shivers and shakes himself, like a huge, tired dog. "Get in to the fire," he repeats.

I nod and stumble away. He stops me and gives me my musket. Mechanically gripping it, I make my way toward the dugouts. Tears come easily; I feel them on my lids, freezing.

The Pennsylvania brigades are quartered on the hilltop facing the road to Philadelphia. A first line of defence; the attack will come from the direction of Philadelphia. We built the dugouts the second and third days at the encampment, half in the earth and half of logs, log fireplaces lined with mud. Ten or twelve men are crowded into each dugout. The doors face the forest, and the forest offers some shelter from a west wind. But the storm winds blow from the east and bite through the spaces between the logs.

I came in and stood with my back against the door. I let go my musket, and it crashed against the dirt floor. The water began to run from my feet in little puddles.

Ely was sitting on the edge of his bunk, watching me. Jacob picked up the musket, wiped it carefully, and put it in its rack. Ely poured me a drink of rum.

"The last, Allen."

I gulped it eagerly. It burnt my throat and warmed me inside. I started for the fire, but Jacob pushed me back.

"You're frozen, Allen."

I dropped to the floor, stretched out my legs before me. Slowly, feeling came back, darting pains in my hands and feet. Ely bent down and peeled the outer layer of bandages from my feet.

Charley Green lay in his bunk with his woman. Charley was no man for fighting; he was the sort of man who is only half of himself without a woman. God knows what took him away from his Boston printer's shop to this hell-hole where we were. When I think of Charley, I think of a small, fat man with children round him, of a small fat wife. But the fat had gone. His skin hung in loose folds. Now he lay in his bunk with his woman, and they must have been asleep, because they didn't move when I came in. Kenton sat on the edge of his bunk, his woman curled behind him. She was a Pennsylvania woman, thin, with light hair and pale blue eyes, speaking a Dutch dialect. She was free with her attentions; it's hard for a woman to be anything else in a dugout with ten men. Vandeer stood in one corner, older than ever, hardly speaking and never smiling, dreaming of a little log parish-house, where the Sabbaths came regularly with six calm days in between. Henry slept. Brone was still on sentry beat. The last was a Polish Jew, a thin, strange man from Philadelphia, tall, hollow-chested, his brown eyes deep sunk in his head. He had been in America only a year, and he spoke no English. But he spoke Dutch, which most of us could understand. He sat next to the fire now, his head bent, his lips moving slowly.

"Praying," Kenton said. "He has no understanding of what night this is." Kenton had never seen a Jew before, and I think he was afraid. "A heathen," Kenton said.

"Edward spat on his sleeve," I said. "It froze before you could count three."

"I call to mind a gypsy at Brandywine—before the battle. He said a winter to freeze the marrow from the land."

Ely had bared my feet. Now, as he knelt over me, his long, grey-streaked beard brushed my hands. He worked my feet slowly. I had to turn my head away, but Ely worked them as if they were his own.

"Feeling, Allen?"

I nodded.

Jacob stood over us, watching with a professional eye. The dugout was hot and close, but draughty, full of body-smell, thick heat and stray curls of cold air. The chimney drew badly, and the log roof was shielded with a layer of blue smoke. The rank odour of bad rum pierced through everything else.

"The foot's a small part of a man," Jacob said.

Kenton's woman sat up and said: "A stinking filthy pair of feet—ye're no more men than pigs!"

"You shut up," Jacob told her. "You Goddamn slut, shut up!"

"Kenton—Kenton, hear his foul tongue?"

Kenton shrugged and smiled foolishly. Kenton was a peaceful, easy-going man.

Charley Green woke up, leaned out of his bunk and looked on, mildly curious. His woman shouted:

"A fine lot of men—to curse a poor woman!"

"It ain't none of your matter," Charley said.
"I'm sicka seeing that slut," Jacob muttered.
"Hear him, Kenton!"
"I'll not have you speaking of that, Jacob," Kenton protested, mildly.

Jacob turned round, his fists tight clenched. I watched them, too drunk with warmth to move. Ely went on kneading my feet, as if he had not heard. The Jew kept his eyes on the ground.

"I speak as I please," Jacob said.

Kenton stood up. Vandeer pushed them apart. "Ye're no men, but beasts," Vandeer muttered. "There's no love or fear of God left in you."

Jacob went to the fire, opposite the Jew, and crouched down. Kenton relaxed on the bed, and when the woman tried to caress him, he pushed her aside. Ely bound up my feet.

"A cold night. I pity Edward," Ely said simply.

Vandeer stood in the middle of the dugout, his arms raised, his mouth half-open, the skin creased loosely in folds about his eyes. Then, abruptly, he dropped his arms and went to his bunk.

Jacob poured some thin corn broth from a pot next to the fire and offered it to me. I drank it slowly, enjoying the warmth of it.

"It's a hard thing to get the cold out of yer bones," Ely said.

The Jew looked up and said, in Dutch: "The cold of Siberia bites deeper——"

"Siberia?"

Green understood no Dutch, but he caught the word. "A frozen land in Asia."

"You were there?" I asked the Jew. "What great journey took you such distances?"

He groped for words, for space that was the length of the world. "Two thousand of us went there—the Czar's prisoners."

"From what land?"

"Poland."

"I knew a Polish man," Jacob said. "He died on Brooklyn Heights."

"You escaped?" Ely asked curiously.

"I escaped——" He opened his coat and shirt, showed us a cross burnt into his breast. "They branded the Jews—said we made the revolution. But I escaped."

I closed my eyes; I tried to see a journey across a world. When I glanced up, the Jew's head was bent over, his lips moving slowly.

"Why were you fighting?" Ely said in English.

The Jew didn't answer. Kenton said: "Tell us, Ely, why are we fighting? I swear, by God, we'll be an army of corpses before this winter's out. I keep saying to myself why—why? I didn't have no call against the British. I never seen a British man before the war that did me a mite of harm. We had two hundred acres clear, and we would have cleared a thousand two years come. We never paid no taxes. All right, I did it. I was a damn-fool kid. I told my paw there was a sight of Boston men making an army to war on the British. I told him I was going, and he laughed in my face. He said he knew Boston men and he'd seen the British fight. He gave two months before they'd hang Adams and Hancock."

"Why'd ye go?" Jacob demanded.

Kenton put his face in his hands.

Jacob said, bitterly: "By God—there's no army to be made outa swine like you."

"Easy, easy, Jacob," Ely whispered.

"On a night like this—Christ was born," Vandeer said tonelessly. "In the name of liberty you're ridden with whores and scum. Ye're a stubborn, hard-necked people, and God's hand is on you."

"To hell with your preaching!" Charley cried.

Kenton's woman screamed: "Shut yer dirty mouth! You ain't no men—ye're a pack of filthy, rotten beggars!"

Jacob rose, took two long strides to the door, and plucked his musket from its rack. He faced Kenton's bunk and said:

"Another word outa her and I'll kill her, Kenton! No damned whore can make mock of me!"

Ely sprang in front of him, pushing the musket to one side. Vandeer said, shrilly:

"If you need to shed blood for the black hate in you—kill me, Jacob!"

Kenton's woman was sobbing hysterically. Ely took Jacob's musket. In Ely's hands, Jacob was like a baby, mouth trembling. All the terror of the past week had come to a head in him—and finally burst. Ely led him to his bunk.

"We're a long time together, Jacob," Ely said softly.

Now there is silence—as if we had used ourselves up for the time. Only the sobbing of

Kenton's woman, and Kenton makes no effort to quiet her. He sits with his head in his hands. The Jew is motionless by the fire.

We hear the wind outside. A wolf howls—mournfully. I look from face to face, bearded faces with long, uncut hair, men who have lost all pride or consideration for their bodies, men in rags, huddled together for warmth. The women are not women any more. I tell myself that; I have to; otherwise I'll go insane. I tell myself that there are beautiful, clean women somewhere, beautiful, clean men. I think of a woman's body the way I used to dream of a woman's body, white and perfect——

Kenton's woman sobs: "We come along with you—you go to hell, but we come along with you."

Nobody answers. We listen for something, the way men listen when the silence is deep and lasting. We hear steps outside in the snow—to the door.

"It's the German lad," Ely says. "Why won't he come in?"

We wait, and then I get up and fling open the door. A rush of snow, and then a figure stumbles into the room.

"Who the hell are you?" Jacob demands.

I force the door shut. She lifts her head, and we see a woman, wrapped in a blanket, barefooted, her feet blue and broken open from the cold.

"Jesus Christ," Green whispers.

She lets fall the blanket; she's half-naked, wearing only an old pair of men's breeches under the blanket. Blue with cold, thin, her breasts the small breasts of a girl, her face sunken, long black hair, curious thin features that might have been lovely once. I stare at her the way we are all staring. Henry Lane wakes and stumbles out of his bunk. He moves toward her, a haggard, bearded, sleep-ridden figure, and she shrinks back against me. I pick up the blanket and cover her shoulders. She gropes toward the fire and crouches next to it.

"Who are you, lass?" Ely asks her.

"Leave me alone," she says. "God's sake—leave me alone."

Kenton's woman says: "I'll tell ye who. She's a fair whore of a Virginian brigade. Her name's Bess Kinley."

"Leave me alone———"

Jacob gets up. He goes to her directly and takes hold of her blanket. "Get out," he says hoarsely.

Vandeer joins him. "Get out—there's enough of rotten women in here. You'll make blood flow between us and the Virginians. Get out."

"Leave her alone," I tell them. I force myself in front of Jacob.

"Boy—get away. The woman's no good!"

"She'll stay," I tell Jacob. "Her feet are bleeding. Let her stay and warm by the fire."

Jacob grips my shoulder, raises his hand to strike. Ely's sharp voice stops him. He stands there, watching the girl.

"They're drunk," she says. "They'd kill me. Look at this." She opens the blanket.

Kenton cries: "They're drunk—drunk. That swine Quiller swore there was no rum, but the Virginian brigades are drunk!" Quiller is the commissary.

"Lead her out," Vandeer says tonelessly.

Green's woman says: "You stay there, honey. Let them try to put me out! A man wouldn't put out a dog on a night like this!"

The door opens, and a man stoops through. He wears the long grey hunting shirt of a Virginian. He's bareheaded, panting. There are others behind him. Some of them carry their long rifles. They hold the door open and the cold eats into the room.

"Close the door," Ely tells him.

"I'll have her—she's our woman."

"She's a Virginian woman!" someone behind him yells.

"Close the door."

"You can go to hell!" I say. "You can get to hell out of here!"

He starts across the room, and I fling myself on him, bearing him back. His fist crashes into my face, and then I hear Jacob's roar as he beats the Virginian through the low door. Ely follows with Kenton and Vandeer. I get up and stumble after them, Lane and Green with me. I catch one glimpse of the Jew, sitting by the fire like a figure out of time.

Outside, there is a mad tangle of figures. I direct all my hate and resentment into the fight. Voices break the night's quiet, and the Pennsylvania men pour from their dugouts. Muskets are clubbed—knives.

The cry goes up: "Virginians!"

There aren't many of the Viginians—a dozen perhaps. They're beaten back. They're overwhelmed by numbers. We stand panting— warm even in the cold.

"Drunk," a Pennsylvania man says.

"We're rationed on rum—and those damned Virginians drink."

We go back to the dugout, grumbling, but feeling that the fight has kept us from madness. We crowd in, close the door; body heat and heat of the fire. The Jew stares at us, as if we were things beyond his understanding.

"Ye're Pennsylvania men?" the girl says. "You'll let me stay tonight?"

"We're no Pennsylvania men," Jacob says.

"What's your name?" I ask her.

"Bess Kinley."

"Sit by the fire and warm yourself," I tell her. "No man will drive you from the fire."

I look at her, and something passes between us. I feel bigger than before, different.

"She'll stay," I tell them.

"She'll stay tonight," Ely agrees.

I sit close to her. She doesn't speak. I look at her face, and for once try to read the mystery of a woman who follows the army.

Finally I say, sullenly: "Why don't you get out of the camp? Why don't you get out of here?"

"Where would I go?" she asks me.

Kenton's woman sobs softly; silence takes

hold of us. Occasionally, someone puts a piece of wood on the fire.

"I'm hungry," she says.

We give her some gruel, and she holds the wooden cup with both hands, drinking it slowly. Nobody speaks. Henry Lane is sleeping again. Green and Kenton crawl into their beds. Already they have lost interest.

Edward comes in, blue with cold, shaking off the snow. He stands and looks at the girl.

"She's Allen's woman," Jacob says. Thus our morality. Thus our years of prayer on the hard floors of hard wooden churches. She was mine without marriage, without the word of any man of God. Because I took her, she is mine.

The girl turns and looks at me, her dark eyes biting into mine. I say nothing. Ely tells Edward what has happened.

"They're hard, bitter men, the Virginians," Edward says. "The girl's a slut. Did she expect them to nurse her?"

"Shut up!" I cry.

"I'm not holding for the Virginians, Allen."

"Where's Brone?" Ely asks Edward. "He should have been back already."

"I didn't see him," Edward says. "I thought he was back."

"I forgot," I mutter. "The boy was sick with cold. I forgot and I had no thought for him."

Ely stands up and puts on his coat.

"Ye're a fool to go out," Jacob says.

I crawl into my coat. I'm sick with weariness, but I know about Brone. Deep in my heart, I know.

I followed Ely out. Jacob came behind me. None of us spoke. We walked across the hillside, away from the dugouts, and then down toward the Gulph Road. It was easy to find the path Brone had beaten in the snow, and follow it. When we came near the end, two low shapes shot away across the snow.

"I should have brought my gun," I said miserably. "You should have known to bring a gun, Ely."

We came to Brone. Jacob knelt down. "Wolves," he said. "Wolves," he repeated bitterly, his voice rising, "and the lad was too weak—too weak."

"He was telling me tonight——"

"He didn't know," Ely said. "He was asleep." We knelt around him, our breath making a cloud, as if from candles. I had to look. Ely tried to hold me away, but I had to look.

"We'll bring him back," Ely said.

"The women———"

"We'll bring him back to the fire," Ely said, and he looked at Jacob and me in a way that made us nod and bend to Brone.

We come into the dugout and put the boy down.

"By the fire," Ely says grimly. "Lay him by the fire."

The Jew stands up, his face full of the pain of the world. He bends his head, touches his head simply with his hand.

The girl is crying, as with pain.

We gather around Brone. Vandeer kneels down. He says:

"God—forgive us. Forgive us tonight." He kneels down, and he prays. He prays with words that we haven't heard for a long time. He prays simply, gently, compassionately.

PART TWO
THE WINTER

5

It is the time of the great hunger, in the middle weeks of January, seventeen seventy-eight. The hunger has been on us three days, and for those three days we have eaten nothing. We have eaten nothing that is food.

Snow has drifted up to the roof of the dugout; snow in the valley in drifts twelve and fifteen feet deep. There are no parades, no drills. There has been no parade for two weeks. There is a rumour that much of the army has disappeared, but we have no check on rumours. As our strength goes, we move slowly, fretfully, the way old men move. A path is cut through the snow for sentries. We hate sentry duty, curse it, but it keeps us from going mad.

Today, we lie in bed, huddled close for warmth. The fire gives out no heat. Only Kenton sits close to it, painstakingly carving a rhyme on his powder horn. His big hunting knife glints in the light, his large hands guiding it with difficulty. On and off, for months now, he has been working on the carving of the rhyme and the picture of a child with arms clasped about the end of the horn. He can forget things with his carving, remembering only that he began it in the warmth of the summer. Now and then he asks Charley the spelling of a word. Kenton is not much for writing words or spelling them out.

We wait for Ely, who has gone to the commissary. The light from the fire lingers in the centre of the dugout; the bunks are in the shadow.

With Bess beside me, I lie in a broken dream. Sometimes I speak aloud, and then Bess says: "Allen—Allen, what are you saying?"

I don't know. I try to explain a figment of a dream. I try to explain that my mother's name was Anna, that if we have a child, her name will be Anna too.

"A girl?" Bess asks me.

"A boy and then a girl."

I sleep again; I wake and my hands grope for her body, frantically. I say: "You slut—you God-damned little slut, you'll go back to the Virginians. You're no fit woman for a man."

"Allen—what are you saying?"

I close my eyes, and my lightheadedness takes my mind away. I am at all places at once.

I am out in the snow, pacing a sentry beat. I am in the deep lush, bottom valleys of the Mohawk. With her hands, Bess tries to reassure me. Her hands travel over my torn clothes, seeking out parts of me. Her hands unravel my beard.

I sink into sleep, and I dream, and I dream that I am a child. It is the morning of a hot, sunny day, and we are moving westward. Where we came from is not very clear to the child in the dream, from some place many marches to the east—Connecticut, perhaps. There are four wagons, four narrow, old, swaybacked wagons. Brown canvas covers them, stretched over bent hickory hoops. The road is bad, and the wagons surge and rock and threaten to fall apart with every step the horses take. But somehow the wagons hold together. They've held together a long time.

I sit at the back of the first wagon, my feet hanging over the tailboard. The hot sun is in my face. Mr. Apply, driving the second wagon, keeps grinning at me. Now and then he snaps his long whip and cries:

"Gotcha then, Allen!"

We both laugh. It's a standing joke between us, the whip. Mr. Apply is a lean old man who sits on his high seat with a long musket balanced across his knees. Somehow, no matter how the wagon sways, the musket never slips from his knees.

My mother cries: "You, Allen, come in or you'll take a fall under Mr. Apply's horses!"

The whip flicks out again. Half-asleep, I cling to the dream. I want the hot sun. When I know that the dream is over, I close my eyes and still try to feel the sun on my face.

When I awake, I turn to Bess with deep, childlike love. A love that's different from the love of a man for a woman. She's warmth for me; she's something for a weak, dying man to hold onto. She doesn't complain. She has never complained. I know she is dying, but I know she won't die until I am gone.

She married a Virginian farm boy at the outbreak of the war. She tried to follow him to Quebec, in the expedition of Morgan's riflemen. She dropped out, went to Boston, and later heard that her man had never reached Quebec. She fell in with a group of Maryland militia— became a camp follower. It was not difficult to understand.

She tells me about it in a slow, truthful voice. "I don't hide anything, Allen. But I was a good woman once. I swear to God I was a good woman once. I'm nineteen years, Allen, and I'm a slut already. You don't have any call to love me, Allen."

Our tears come together, slow tears of weakness. We cling together, and she clutches desperately at my filthy body. I cry the way no man would cry. Each successive wave of sleep is relief.

What she says, she has said before. We dream about it day and night. "You can desert, Allen——"

I think of Edward. Eight days ago, he walked out. He said, simply—he was going to the Mohawk. He took his gun, and nobody answered him, or tried to stop him. He was a great, strong man. "He'll walk through," Ely said. Jacob raged like a madman. Nobody believes but Jacob. We hate the revolution; we hate our officers and each other. Jacob believes. That you must keep in mind. A man can be parts of many things, or a man can be only one thing. And those who believe in only one thing are like torches; they don't burn forever. That you must keep in mind to know how Jacob is— without weakness, without fear. He hates officers because they are a contradiction. He is not a man for thinking too deeply, and what he believes he believes instinctively. And he believes this—that the people are one. Officers are not of the people; they separate themselves: so he hates them but endures them because they lead the revolution. Yet he refuses to believe that they are part of the revolution they lead. But more than that, he hates weakness. A man is nothing, and the revolution is all. Edward was his friend; for years Edward had been his friend; yet Edward was weak, putting himself before the revolution. For that he cursed Edward—who was dead.

He raged like a madman, and then when he had used himself up, he sat by the fire, sobbing hard, dry sobs for hours.

I would have gone with Edward, but I was afraid. I was afraid of the great distances in front of me.

Some of McLean's foragers brought Edward back. He had gone only a mile. They found him in the snow. Captain Muller came to us and said: "Did he desert?"

"He's dead, isn't he?" Jacob muttered. "What does it matter now? The man's dead."

"He was hunting," Ely said, lying. But even

Ely could lie for a man who had died that way —alone and in the snow.

We went to bury him. He was huddled up, his limbs hard and fixed.

"He was sleeping," Ely said. "I thank God he was sleeping. He didn't know. It's an easy way to die, when a man's sleeping . . ."

I ask Bess: "Where would we go?"

"I'm not dreading dying, Allen. But if you go away without me———"

Ely enters the dugout. He closes the door and stumbles over to the fire. The strength of Ely is no thing that can be measured, it's not the strength of a man's body.

He sits by the fire and stares into it.

We climb out of bed and crowd round him. Our faces are sunken death's-heads. Bones stand out through the clothes. Ely looks at us, but he doesn't speak.

Jacob said: "You brought food, Ely?"

"I walked to his house," Ely said. "It's a wonder to see the fine stone houses the officers have. You go in and you hear no sound of storm outside."

I try to visualize it. The houses where the officers are quartered are a mile away. I try to understand a man beating his way there and back. Ely hasn't eaten in three days. Edward walked a mile in the snow and they brought back a dead man. Ely is here by the fire.

"God damn them," I said.

"They told me a food train comes tonight. They took the name of the regiment and company."

Jacob cursed them. He paced back and forth, screaming his rage until it seemed to fill the dugout full and overflowing.

"Enough—enough!" Clark yelled. "The fruit of sin—do you hear me! You're no men, and you reap no fruits of men, but the fruits of sin! As ye sow, so shall ye reap! You lie with your women without shame. You sport and you have no shame for your sporting. You curse God, and in turn you are cursed by God! You made an idol of freedom, and now the idol's smashed open. Allen there—with a slut in his arms. Kenton sharing his woman among the lot of you. Charles who would look from the face of God to the face of a woman! You whore and murder among yourselves! I call God to blast you for your crimes—I call God!" He fell on his knees; he stretched out his arms. His face grew livid and then deathly pale. Then he crumpled up on the floor.

Ely tried to pick him up. He said: "Help me, Allen." We put him on his bed. His eyes were closed, his chest heaving. Jacob tried to make him hear; Jacob was calmed suddenly.

"We're taking yer words to heart—Clark, you hear me?"

I went to Bess.

She was crying softly, without hysteria, but in an agony of pain. She said to me: "Allen, I'm not a bad woman. He laid a curse of God on me."

"You're not—you're not," I said.

"Allen—I'll sleep no more. Even if I die, I'll not sleep in peace."

Bending over, I tried to kiss her. She pushed me away. "Don't kiss me, Allen."

Charley Green's woman cried: "Who's he to curse me? Who is he, the rotten mock of a man?"

"Ah—be quiet, Annie," Charley groaned.

I took Bess' hand. I turned it over, put it to my lips. "You sleep," I said, "sleep."

I turned to Clark. Jacob had dropped onto his bunk, a mass of helpless bones. Ely stood by Vandeer's bed. The Jew stood just behind him, a bent figure for the ages, as filthy and ragged as any of us—but different.

Ely said: "I'm afraid for him, Allen. We need a doctor."

I looked at Clark. He lay in bed, breathing hoarsely, sweating, his eyes wide open.

"There's no doctor in the Pennsylvania huts. A leech won't come here from the hospital."

"We'll bear him down there," Ely said.

I shook my head. "I can't, Ely. There's no strength left in me."

I watched Ely's eyes pass round the dugout. His shaggy, bearded head turned slowly: Jacob of no use, Charley Green sick and unable to move, Henry Lane with great festering sores on his feet, Kenton by the fire, as if he heard nothing of Clark Vandeer's raving.

"You'll come?" Ely asked the Jew.

"I'll come," I said. "Christ, I'll come, Ely."

We took clothes wherever we could find them. Charley's woman gave a blanket, a petticoat. She lay in bed half-naked, clinging close to him. She called me over.

"If he comes to his senses—plead him to take back the curse."

"There's no curse," Ely said uncertainly.

We picked up Clark, the three of us. Ely, myself, and the Jew. He was skin and bones and he couldn't have weighed more than ninety or a hundred pounds, but he was more than enough for us. We could barely hold his weight.

We went outside and tried to go through the snow. There was a sleet blowing; it was like moving through a morass that sucked in our legs. Sometimes we couldn't move, had to stand still waiting for our bodies to gather the strength to go on. I tried to picture Ely going through this for two miles, to the commissary and back. Coming back empty-handed. Now going out with us again. What is it in Ely? I look at him sometimes, and try to understand. Where is the strength? All of us are thin, but Ely is thinner. Our feet are wretched, but Ely's feet are stumps of mangled flesh. Yet Ely walks without showing the pain. When there is work to be done, Ely does it. When a strong man is needed, Ely draws strength from somewhere. Yet he isn't like Jacob. Jacob is fire, but Ely is spirit. Jacob is hate, but Ely is love. I think, sometimes, that when this is over, Ely will endure. Jacob will burn out, but Ely will endure.

It is about three-quarters of a mile to the hospital, around the shoulder of the hill and down into the valley. Where we stand now, on the top of the hill, we are unprotected, open to every blast of wind that crosses the countryside.

I look back and see the dugouts as heaps of snow. No life. Even the smoke is torn from the chimneys and dissipated. I think of how it would be if the British attacked us now, marched from Philadelphia and walked into our dugouts. No one to stop them or challenge them, only half-naked beggars who would sacrifice pride and honour for a bowl of stew. There would be no shots fired. We would be fed. Then we would go back home.

I look down the white slope, half-imagine it. Why don't they come and make an end?

We went on slowly. It was on to late afternoon now, growing dark already. I kept my head down, but Ely led us; and whenever I glanced at him, his head was up, seeking the way. The Jew was a white, inscrutable figure. I had a feeling that I was walking into darkness—made up of white snow, buried deep in white snow. A sense of lightness overcame me, and I no longer felt my feet or the weight of Vandeer.

We stopped once again, taking strength. Across the road, on the slope of Mount Joy, I saw a sentry. He stood in a lunette, a white cannon showing its head beside him. He stood without moving.

"A short way," Ely said.

We pushed up the winding path that led to the hospital. It was a long log building. The sentry by the door scarcely glanced at us. I guess he was used to parties carrying men.

Ely pounded at the door. An officer opened it, a tall, shaven man who wore epaulettes. I didn't know him.

"Who are you?" he demanded.

"We're of a Pennsylvania brigade. We have a sick man."

"You've a doctor there, haven't you?"

"You know damn well we haven't!" I cried.

"Use a little respect when you speak, sir—or that tongue'll be whipped out of you."

"You can go to hell," I said. "By God, you can go to hell, mister!"

"Take no offense," Ely begged him. "We're half-starved. We're not fit to walk."

I could see the officer calculating how far he could go with us. Lately, they were beginning to wonder about the half-beasts they led.

There had been no parades, just a few inspections by lieutenants and captains, and long days between inspections. A sentry on a hill, huddled over his musket, wrapped in all the clothes his comrades could spare him. They were beginning to have strange doubts when they saw us come out of our holes, like beasts. Only a sense of fear of the greater cold outside kept the beasts together. That and their weakness; their weakness made them afraid of the great distances between this place and their homes. But they had their guns. If they turned the guns on the officers and went off together, that would be the end of it.

He measured us, saw we were unarmed. "The hospital's full," he said. "No beds are left. Try Varnum's hospital at the redoubt." Varnum's hospital was a good mile away.

Ely said nothing; the breath came in thin steam from between his lips. The Jew said, in his curious Amsterdam Dutch: "Give a comrade a place to die. We gave our enemies that. Put a little warm food between his lips."

The officer didn't understand Dutch. "Speak English," he snapped. "The army's too full of your kind."

"We can't walk a mile to the redoubt," I pleaded, hating myself for pleading. "We can't walk that far——"

The two sentries were looking on, dulled by cold, their beards full of the froth of their breath. I wondered whether they would make any move; I wondered how long it would be before each of us in turn came there, like Clark. Clark was groaning now, talking. His words didn't make sense.

"We can't walk a mile now," I said. "We can't walk that far."

"Give him space on your floor," Ely said. "Give him six feet of your floor. The man'll freeze to death if you keep him here."

"Six feet on a gibbet would do the lot of you." He was a New York City man—or English-born; he had the whining, rising inflection.

"We're going in," Ely said. I caught Ely's eyes; I had a rush of sickening fear. I knew that when anger came on Ely, it would destroy him and whoever stood in his way.

I cried: "Ely, damn the swine, and we'll go to the redoubt!"

Ely started forward, bearing Vandeer and the two of us with him. I tried to hold back. The officer wore a sword, and his hand was on the hilt now.

Then a little man pushed the officer aside, crowded him out of the doorway. The little man wore a long grey apron, splattered with blood. He wore spectacles, and he was clean-shaven, his thin hair gathered in a neat bun at the back of his head. He had a long, thin nose and remarkably full red lips.

"What's this?" he demanded. "A sick man out there, Murgot?"

"The hospital's full."

"You'll keep your God-damn nose out of my hospital. Bring him in."

I could see the officer trying to face down the little man. The doctor ignored him, turned his back and walked into the hospital. We carried Vandeer in. The place was a log cabin, thirty feet long at the most, but there must have been more than a hundred men in it. They lay close together on beds built the length of the place.

Some of them slept; most of them moved restlessly, the place was cold. There was a continual groaning; after a while, you ignored that.

"We're a little crowded," the doctor said briskly. "They come and go. About even. We're no warmer here than good mother earth." He led us to a tiny place in the back, partitioned off, and he motioned for us to lay Vandeer down on the bed. We put him down and unwrapped his coverings. There was a small iron heater there. We crowded close to it.

"Filth—my God, it's a wonder to me there's any of you left. Filth, filth—why don't you shave off those beards? Let's have a look at him. Tell me about it."

Ely told him—slow, hard words as he brought the scene back to mind.

"I know—I know," the doctor nodded, before Ely was through. "I know, men go mad. Well, there's no cure I know of for that. What can you expect? It's a wonder to me there's a sane person left here. If there is, I'm the one. I won't be that way long. What do you expect? Can I breathe reason back to him? Am I God?"

The Jew said, softly: "You're God. You see, all of us—we're God. We have to believe that, in the God in us. The nearer we go to the beasts, the more we have to believe. I've starved before. I've seen two thousand men die as they walked to Siberia. You have to believe in man in God. You lose your fear of death; you fear only that the God will go out of you."

The doctor took off his spectacles, wiped them on his apron. "Who are you?" he asked the Jew—in Dutch.

"He's a Jew heathen out of Poland," I said.
"You read Spinoza?" the doctor asked him.
"You'll let him die?" He pointed to Clark.

"All right—give me that basin." Ely held it. The doctor bared Clark's arm, whistled softly at the way the veins showed through. He took a piece of cloth and washed the arm as well as he could. He grumbled: "Can't bathe—give me a hell-hole of an icehouse and call it a hospital. I'm as filthy as you—nice on top, but just as filthy underneath." He picked a tiny object from Vandeer's arm. "See that? Lice—all of you lousy with them. What can you expect?"

He took a lancet and opened a vein in Clark's arm. Then he held out the arm, so that the blood drained into a basin slowly. The blood was dull red. The way it came, so slowly, made me think there was little enough left in Clark. The doctor asked Ely:

"How long since he's eaten?"

"We haven't eaten in three days—any of us."

The doctor whistled again.

"He's weak—he'll bleed to death," Ely said.

"What can I do? I'm not God, in spite of your Jew here. I'll bleed him until his reason comes back. He'd die anyway."

We stood there, grouped round the bed, fascinated by the blood welling out of Clark's arm. Clark began to speak. He asked for Ely. Expertly, the doctor stopped the flow of blood. He pinched the vein together with his fingers, and then quickly bound it over with cloth.

"I'm here, Clark," Ely said.

"Where's Jacob?"

"He was broke by yer words. He had no strength to come. We bore you to the hospital, Clark."

"Who came?"

"Allen and the Jew."

"A great load. Allen's loaded with the blackness of his sin. You'll plead him to give up the wench, Ely?"

Ely didn't answer.

"You'll plead him, Ely!" Clark cried. "I'm a dying man."

Ely nodded. I said: "Clark—you're putting a dreadful black curse on me. I love her."

"Promise me, Allen!"

I shook my head.

Then he closed his eyes. Ely turned away.

"Let him sleep," the doctor said. "Come with me."

We went into a room in back. He had a table there, a bed, and a heat box. The coals in it were dying. He put a wooden plate on the table, took out a pot with a few slices of cold meat in it.

"We don't have much——"

I yearned toward the meat. Ely didn't move. The Jew was smiling sadly.

"That won't feed the army," Ely said.

"Don't be noble," the doctor told him. "It will feed you." Then he saw the Jew's smile. "You can go to hell," the doctor said. "You're a filthy pack of beggars. It's a wonder if the English lay hands on your filth to swing you from their gibbets."

We stood there.

"Drink some rum," he said. He poured three small cups. "Drink it, or by God, you'll die before you reach your quarters."

The rum warmed us up, but made us dizzy. We stood there, sucking in the heat and the comfort of the rum burning our insides. The doctor was sitting on his chair, regarding us as if we were some curious specimens he had picked up.

"You and me," the doctor said, speaking to the Jew and in Dutch, "we're the only civilized men here. You and me—in a land of savages, of filth and ignorance and superstition. They know one thing. They want to be free to cheat themselves and kill each other. They want to be free of the English. They want to be free to cheat and lie and hate. They want to be free to plunge a land into ignorance and misery. I'm here because I'm a fool. But why you?"

The Jew shrugged.

"You came with a great dream of a land for your kind."

"A land for all men."

"It's big enough. But men are the same— here or Europe. If they win—and they won't —but if they win, they'll drive you out. You're a Jew, a heathen."

"They won't drive us out," the Jew said softly. "We've come the length of the world——"

"Driven!"

"No—we've come here. We've come for a dream of a place for all men. This is a new world. The day of the old world is over. A long time—maybe two hundred, maybe three hundred years. But it will make the men who live in it. This is only the beginning. This army is nothing—nothing, only a dream. Do you understand? The army goes; the dream never goes. I stayed at the home of a man in Philadelphia who is making this revolution. His name's Haym Solomon. He came out of Poland too. Poland was a school for us. Poland will go on fighting, but Poland won't be free. A school. Here's the land for the dream of God in man."

The doctor glanced at us. "Not a clean god. Come and talk again. Man can't live by bread alone or without it. No bread. I won't last the winter. If you make your land, tell your children about a man of science who wouldn't believe. Damn lies!"

We went back to Clark. He was still sleeping. His face, where it showed through his beard, was white as snow.

"Will he live?" Ely asked.

"How do I know?" the doctor snapped. Then: "It doesn't make any difference. He won't be far from any of you."

We take the clothes that Clark was wrapped in, two coats and a petticoat. I give a coat to Ely and the other to the Jew. I wrap the petticoat round my neck and face.

We go out, and the cold hits us in the face, like knives ripping. Out of some forlorn curiosity, I spit on my sleeve. The others see me, and watch fascinated. I count, only once, and then the little balls of spittle snap with the frost.

"My God," Ely whispers.

We have never known such cold as this. Ely has been to Canada. I have been, in winter, in the highlands of the upper Hudson. I have seen bitter cold weather, but never such cold as this. Neither has Ely. It is a cold that has come on the face of a planet stripped bare of all protection. It is a cold living and malignant. It is a cold that has become a force to destroy soul and body. In all the memory of men in America, there has never been such cold.

We go on slowly, forcing our way through snow that is like dry sand. We move a step at a time, bringing one foot up to the place where the other has been. It is night already, no moon, but stars that glitter like bright jewels. The snow is a sheet of white—no sentries, no living thing except ourselves.

To go back to the Pennsylvania dugouts, we must climb a hill—not very high, no more than two hundred feet. But the hill is the difference between life and death. The hill is a slope that leads to hell. We make a step, stumble, and slide back two. We roll over in the snow, feel it slide into every crevice of our clothes. We spit it out, and our lips freeze and go numb. We stand up and go on.

I don't think any more. My mind is gone.

Only my body moves, and my body is a machine apart from me. It will go on until the spark of life in it flickers out.

I turn round once, and the Jew is lying in the snow. He doesn't move. Ely calls to me, but his words are lost in the rush of wind. I stand above them and watch Ely go back to the Jew. Suddenly, my mind comes alive. I think to myself, ten steps down, ten steps back. I keep thinking that—ten steps down and ten steps back. The words rush in my mind. I begin to cry, and the tears freeze on my lids.

I go down to Ely. The Jew says: "Leave me. They'll find me soon."

We help him up, and the three of us go on together. We go on into endless night and endless distance. I lose all conception of time and all conception of movement. Someone must be leading us.

Then we are at the dugout. We drop on the floor. The Jew is senseless. Ely stares at the fire with wide, terrible eyes. I cry bitterly.

Bess is rubbing my hands, kissing me, trying to work the cold out of my limbs. She drags me toward the fire. I hear, as from far away, Ely telling Jacob of Clark.

Then I am in bed, and Bess is trying to warm

me. I know how little strength she has, and I wonder how she can work so desperately. But the cold won't leave me. I tremble and my lips flutter. My lips are broken and bleeding.

She says: "Rest—rest, my darling."

I feel for her warm face, for her hands, for her breast. I want life desperately. I cling to her for the sense of life.

Then I sleep.

I wake out of my dream, and speak with it: "Clark put a curse on me—he's dying. I should drive you away. He made me promise."

Her cry of terror was the most terrible thing I had ever heard.

I try to soothe her. I whisper: "No—I was dreaming."

But she lies there, awake, and I can feel her fear of the cold night, of being away from me.

6

WE KEEP alive. Days pass, and days slide into one another, days and nights mingling to form a grey. But we keep alive. A strange knowledge comes to me, a knowledge of the strength in men. I can see how layer after layer of life may be taken from a man; take all the strength that is any man's, and still there is strength underneath.

So we keep alive. How many days pass, I don't know. A new man is in the dugout. His name is Meyer Smith, and he was an innkeeper in Philadelphia once. The Jew is sick. We think of Moss Fuller. The Jew has the same racking cough.

Ely said: "A bite of frost. His lungs are frozen. Maybe in the place he calls Siberia. When a man's lungs are frozen, they never heal."

We sit round now trying not to notice that hacking, incessant cough. When we look at the Jew's face, the bony features rising out of the shadow of his bunk, we are forced to think of something we don't want to remember.

"I call to mind Christ was a Jew," Jacob said—strange words for Jacob.

The Jew's name is Aaron Levy. We are very tender with him. With us, it is different: we are born and bred to the land. But the Jew has come great, shadowy distances. The distances keep us away from him, and he is alone. His loneliness oppresses us. In his sleep, he talks in a language we don't understand.

Smith was in the dugout two days when he learnt that Levy was a Jew. He said:

"I'll not sleep with a bloody Jew. I'll not sleep with any Christ-killing bitch."

Jacob almost throttled him. We had to tear Jacob away, and the marks of Jacob's fingers were on Smith's throat for a week after. Jacob pleaded with us to let him go to let him kill Smith. Jacob cried:

"His death won't sit with me. I've seen too many better than he go."

Smith was afraid. He leaped for the gun-rack, tore out a musket and faced Jacob. "I'll kill you!" he screamed. "Stay off! I'll kill any man who lays a hand on me."

Ely walked up to him and wrenched the

musket from his hands. "You're a low, bitter creature," Ely said quietly.

Smith crawled into his bunk and lay the rest of that night in silence. We pitied him; we were beyond hate. I could see the madness coming in Jacob, in myself, in Smith, in Henry Lane. I began to fear Ely's death. One day, I pleaded with him not to die; I pleaded with him hysterically. We lived in him. Ely smiled; he was the only one who could still smile.

Now we sit and talk a little. Bess crouches by my side, her hands touching me, feeling for me always. They tell me that when I go out on sentry duty, she lives in an agony of fear.

"You'll go out once—and not come back," she told me.

"There are other men."

"No other man," she said.

She sits by me now. We talk of the British attack and what holds it. We are all of us here but Kenton, who is on sentry duty.

"There'll be no attack," I say. "The war's over. In two months, there'll be no army. Why should they attack?"

"Ye're wrong, Allen," Ely says.

Green says: "It goes that there are only five thousand men left in the encampment."

"Lies!" Jacob says bitterly.

"Ye're a crazed man, Jacob. Is John Adams or Sam Adams here in this camp? Is Thomas Jefferson here? Is Dickinson here? Is Sherman here, or Hancock here? They're safe and nursing their fat bellies."

"They'll nurse to a different tune when we've won. By God, they'll sweat blood."

Charley said: "Ye're crazy. It'll be King John Adams—King Sam. I knew Adams—a filthy beggar who never did a day's work in his life. He'd come to my store and say, Charley, I've written a fair beautiful pamphlet—blood and revolution. Print it for the cause, Charley. What cause? Hancock's cause, a dirty cheating pirate. If I'd ask him ten shillings to buy paper, he'd foam and curse me. I'll tell you about Hancock. He was a smuggler, he and his friends. Ye're backwoods men, and you'd not know about that. All smugglers. Let us be forced to buy British goods and they'd run no more contraband from the Indies, from the Dutch. But who bought ours? England, I tell you. So Hancock and his friends made a war, with Adams for their man. I went. I had a fair pretty girl who put a tune in my head. She set me off singing Yankee-Doodle, God damn her. She's not sleeping alone now."

"I'm not fighting Hancock's war," Jacob said. "By God, we've learned what to do with guns, and Hancock's no better than British men I've seen dead."

"All right," Charley nodded. He was flushed now and happy. He was a man of words, for words—a little Boston printer who had read Voltaire and Defoe and Swift and Plato, who knew Paine. Now he was happy, baiting Jacob, driving Jacob's words into his teeth. "All right," he nodded, "make an end of Paul Revere too. He's a great hero. We rot here, but the newspapers make a great hero of their Paul Revere. I'll tell you something about Revere. He made a famous ride and saved the revolution; but where's he now? With Hancock, filling his fat belly, I'll swear. Hancock the pirate and Revere the business man. Revere wanted copper. You damned backwoods louts wouldn't know that, but there's a fortune to be made in working copper. But before Revere could smelt, he had to have a revolution. Drive out the British and their smelting laws: drive out the British and their customs men. Then Hancock becomes an honest citizen, and Revere becomes a rich smelter. But mind you, they only started it—cleverly. You're doing the fighting. God damn you, Jacob, you're a fool. When you're rotting a foot under Valley Forge, they won't talk about Eagen. They won't write in newspapers about Jacob Eagen. They'll write about Paul Revere's ride and they'll dress Sam Adams up for a god. Mind me."

"We're making a land," Jacob insisted sullenly. "There's a great, rich land to the west, and it'll never be ours so long as England holds the country. There'll never be peace in the Mohawk or in the Lake country while England lets the Indians kill and burn. I'm a backwoods lout, Charley, with no learnin' for yer city ways. But by God, it seems to me yer city's a middlin' small thing in a land like this. All outa size, you Boston men are swelled with yer glory. You have no sense of the land to the west. I knew a French trapper once who had walked westward. Come spring, summer, winter an' fall—he had walked westward; a great lot of walking, always with his face to the setting sun, an' still there was no end to the land. A land bigger than all o' Europe with their rotten little lies an' deceits. That's a mistake the Boston men make—to think we're fighting the war for them. They have no knowledge of the land, but we're fighting the war for the knowledge of the land that's ours. All the time of the world, all the years and hundreds of years, men looked for a land to be free. Ask the Jew of that, an' you'll understand the forces in men that make them die or be free. Give Hancock his dirty ships an' Revere his pound o' copper. The land's ours."

"Two years we're gone," I said. "The Valley land's raped. I hear no house stands."

Then we look at each other—with dumb, senseless longing. And even Charley longs for the comfort of Boston town. We look at Ely's feet, and we turn our eyes away quickly. We sit in silence until the door opens.

The doctor enters. He wears a greatcoat and a woollen cap. He stands at the door, stamping his feet and peering at us through the smoke of the fire. We haven't seen him since we were at the hospital. For a moment, I don't recognize him. The others stare.

"He's a doctor from the hospital," Ely says.

"No air," the doctor says. "Even the beasts seek air. This place stinks. It's the fifth stinking hole I've been in. Ah, there's my Jew." He walks forward gingerly, stands in the middle of the room and glances from face to face. The women watch him with hostile fear. The Jew smiles a little. Jacob's face is dark.

"Sullen, silent beasts," the doctor says. "If I were to paint pictures for an Inferno made glorious in the verse of Dante, I would come here. Hell holds no fear; sometimes I envy you, my friends. You have tasted all; you have searched the bottom. You have become beasts——"

"Hold yer tongue," Jacob growls.

"A beast of beasts. There's murder, my friend, in what part of your face shows through that beard."

"The hell is ours! Get out of here!" Jacob cries.

"Easy—let him be," Ely says wearily.

"I wonder why I came up here," the doctor says. "Maybe to speak with my friend the Jew. He's a creature of another world, and that cough may journey him there swiftly. Did he get it from the deed of bringing a comrade to me?"

He saw the hate, the burning resentment in us. He had no fear. I don't think he understood fear, or maybe he was only dulled beyond fear? He grinned at us.

"The man's dead!" he said suddenly, "I

walked a mile and froze my hands to tell you he's dead. There's a lot I don't do that for."

"Clark's dead?" Jacob asked, unbelieving.

"You let him die!" I cried. "You let him die!"

"God and me. Jesus Christ, I'm sick of the lot of you, sick of filthy, whining beggars. That Jew there—he and I are civilized. If I trimmed his beard, I'd make him into a pretty Christ. One of Rembrandt's." He went over and spoke to Levy in New York Dutch:

"You've a fine cough, my Jew friend."

The Jew smiled at him. He watched the smile, and felt the smile's meaning, a deep understanding that the doctor tried to brazen off.

"You and I know," Levy said. "We've seen men die."

"And you're not afraid," the doctor insisted. "Tell me that you're not afraid, my Jew friend." He took off his glasses, wiped them carefully, and put them back on again. He pulled off his gloves.

"Tell me you've conquered fear of death," he insisted.

I listened, and I couldn't take my eyes from the Jew's face. In the back of my mind—Clark Vandeer, who had been a preacher once. Clark was dead. But we had known—we were used to death in others. But death in ourselves...

Even Jacob—whose face was a mask of pain that reflected Clark's death—even Jacob listened. Bess was holding tight to me. Mechanically, my hand covered her ear, as if I didn't want her to know.

"Is there a fear of death?" Levy asked the doctor.

"An Oriental way, always a question with a question."

"I wanted to stay," the Jew said. "I wanted to see the spring come. All my life I dreamed of a day when I'd come to this land. It would be beautiful——"

"Here?" the doctor snorted.

"Here in this place—beauty beyond man's conception. A land of milk and honey."

"You're a dreamer," the doctor smiled.

For the first time, deep anger in the Jew's voice:

"Not romance. You make a mockery of this —to find romance here."

"I'm sorry," the doctor said shortly. "Christ, when you see them come and go—all day long. You can't bury them—the ground's like rock —so you stack them like wood. All day long.

You don't want me to pat your head. It's no use bleeding you. You and me, we're civilized. We're not like these beasts. We don't have to lie. There's a line in Pope, I think—the men who grope and grope. We're past that. You're dying, why should I lie to you?"

Jacob cried: "By God—hold your tongue!"

At his deep, black rage, the doctor turned. The Jew was lost in thought, his eyes half-closed. The doctor smiled. He crawled into his coat and went out.

Panting, Jacob walked to the Jew. But he could find no words. He stood there.

Smith said: "He stinks to hell of rum. They have it, but we've had no drink for weeks now."

We sit in silence, and outside, night comes. The light in the cracks of the door fades and vanishes. The days are shorter now. We wait for Kenton. There is no other event, nothing else to look forward to. Kenton will come back from sentry duty, his story the same: cold—freezing feet. When he bares his feet, perhaps a toe from which all life is gone.

We wait—and we hear Kenton's steps, running. He bursts in, and there's blood on him, blood on his face and hands and all over his coat. A knife in his hands. He stands there, panting, his eyes like a madman's. He says:

"Two buck deer, great, beautiful bucks. I heard their horns clash. They fought on the Philadelphia road, locked with each other. I killed both."

Henry shakes him, frantically. He touches the blood, tastes it. "Deer? Deer?"

"He's lying," I say to Bess. "He's lying."

"By God, the wolves'll have them before you." Kenton brandishes his knife. He's a horrible, grim figure of a man.

We scramble for clothes. We put on whatever we can find. We have forgotten about Vandeer, about the doctor, about the Jew.

We go outside, and for once we are unaware of the cold. Kenton starts off, running, and we string after him. Then he goes down. We stop, and our breath steams; we are weak, sick. We move more slowly. The women are with us. They run with short, hard cries. Bess' arms and head are bare.

Ely warns us: "Slow—slow, you'll have no strength to return."

We are laughing hysterically, laughing and crying at the same time. Then we see the deer, two large buck deer, locked in the snow. Kenton shows us; he cuts fiercely with his knife, drives it to the hilt in one of the deer.

"Like this—they fought and I cut the life from them."

Ely cries: "You'll go mad—leave off the deer." I try to touch the blood, taste it. Ely strikes me, a hard blow on the side of my head. The tears come to my eyes, and I plead with him to forgive me.

We dragged the deer back. Men and women, we fought through the snow, dragging them. Somehow, the word had spread, and men poured out of the Pennsylvania dugouts. We had a hundred hands on each animal, men laughing and singing.

We got the deer up on the hill, and Kenton stood over them. The rest of us formed a little ring to keep off the Pennsylvania men.

"Food for all!"

"You'll not keep it to yourself!"

"We're dying for the want of a bit of fresh meat!"

"There's food and plenty for all!"

Jacob's deep voice rang out: "It's Kenton's spoil—let him say!"

They caught the name. Women tried to break through and reach Kenton.

"Ah—Kenton!"

"He's a fine, good man!"

"You've got the light in yer eyes, Kenton. You'll not keep the meat!"

"I've rum to go with it—meat for rum, Kenton!"

Kenton took on dignity. A lean, bearded wretch, his yellow hair all stained with blood, he took on dignity nevertheless. He waved his arms for silence.

"A haunch for us," he cried. "You'll grant us a haunch. Roast the rest. By God, build a fire—a great, roaring fire!"

They screamed for Kenton. Haggard, death-stricken women clawed through our line to touch him. We cut a haunch from one of the deer, and Henry bore it into the dugout. They were gathering wood for the fire. Weariness gone for a moment, the wood grew into a pile. We strung a log from the top of a dugout to a tree for a spit. Eager hands skinned the deer. We took out the entrails and divided them up for separate roasting. Kenton was drinking rum. Hoarded bits of rum came to him from every side. He did not work; he stood close to the crackling fire, drinking rum and getting good and drunk. A dozen times over, he had to tell the story of how he had killed the deer. He called me over, said:

"Ah, Allen—they're noways such bad men, these Pennsylvanians. I got a little bitch for you who speaks a round, fine German. No arguments."

I laughed and tasted the rum. I was in a mood for laughing. Bess stayed close to me.

"You'll be with me, Allen—all night. You'll not leave me go, Allen, for a German Pennsylvania woman?"

"For no woman," I said.

The deer were pierced by the spit and set to roast. We spread the fire, so that it would give out more heat. We laughed the way we had not laughed for long. Even when the officers' horses sounded on the hill, we laughed.

Muller was there, with two others—Lieutenant Colby and Captain Freestone. They dismounted and pushed through us.

"What's all this?" Muller demanded.

Jacob answered him: "You've eye enough to see we're roasting deer."

"All plunder goes to the commissary. Take that meat down. Colby—have a dozen men carry it to the commissariat."

"To the officers' bellies!" Jacob roared.
"You fat bastards!"
"You bleeding, dirty swine!"

Kenton cried: "Since when's deer plunder? I killed them, free beasts of the open." He held his knife in his hand. "I've good fair use for the knife—better game than deer."

The officers wore small arms. Some of us had muskets. We were a hate-maddened bunch. The women egged us on. They hated the officers not so much as they hated the officers' wives, the well-dressed, well-kept women who lived in the stone houses of the Quakers near by, along with their men. They didn't come to the camp very often; but sometimes they came halfway, to look curiously. To look at beasts, male and female. Our women hated them.

One screamed: "Go on, Kenton—show them the killing of deer! Show them a swift killing of deer."

They had courage, those officers. They stood there, in the middle of us, eyeing us one by one. Muller smiled a little. Ely went up to them.

"You won't be fools," Ely said quietly. "You won't see murder done."

Muller turned and walked through us. The

other two went with him. They were followed by hooting, laughter. I felt that they would remember.

"They're no men to lead us," Ely said to me. "They don't know us."

"They're fools," I said.

The meat was being turned by half a dozen men, roasting slowly, dripping fat that burnt with blue and yellow flame in the fire.

We cut it down when it was still half-raw. We stood close to the fire, gulping the meat. Charley Green sang a parody of a Boston song —"The Jolly Sons of Liberty."

We joined in. It took our fancy, and we sang:

Come jolly sons of liberty, come all with hearts united,
We stink so high we scare the foe, not easily affrighted,
Our angry bowels we must subdue, now is the time or never,
Let each man prove this motto true, and droppings from him sever.

We sang it to the tune of "Glorious First of August." We sang it again and again until the words had no more meaning. We were drunk with fresh meat in empty stomachs. Some of us were sick. Finally we stumbled back into our dugouts.

I go out on sentry duty. It is night—a clear, still night. The Pennsylvania brigades have exhausted themselves; the dugouts, small lumped huts, are quiet.

The cold has eased itself a little; there is almost no wind at all. I walk up and down slowly, and sometimes I turn and look at the glow in trees behind the huts—the embers of our fire. I think of how the Jew's lungs froze when we carried Clark Vandeer to the hospital. But Ely and I are still alive; we are two strong men.

Clark is dead, not even buried. I take my bayonet, and thrust through the snow at the ground. It's hard as rock. I go down on my knees, try to dig, and manage to turn up a little earth.

I must get rid of my fear. I look over the country, and try to see it as it will be in the spring. The Jew's words stay in my mind; he never saw the spring in America.

I attempt to rid myself of the fear that this will be our grave. There's no sound. Are we all dead? I cry out, and my voice comes back, a plaintive echo. I want to fire my musket. It's a great desire, and I have to use all my powers to hold back. How many men on sentry beat fire their guns for the same reason? Break the silence. The day before, a man had been whipped half to death for that.

The moon shows above the far hills. It shows a curved rim of yellow ice. It lights up the countryside, gives a weird, unholy beauty. The moon rises until it looks like half a mouth, laughing.

7

The Jew is dying. Smith suffers from scurvy, and we can do nothing for him. To some degree we all have it, but Smith's face is like a rotten apple, and his teeth have fallen out. He lies in his bed, groaning with pain and cursing the Jew. Or calling back memories of roasts in the kitchen of his inn.

His voice grows stronger as he talks. "—a roast of beef, a prime rib roast of beef. Give it fifteen minutes to the pound, and turn it slowly. Turn it slowly and catch the drippings. Drippings for gravy—"

We can't stand that. We tell him to close his God-damned mouth.

The doctor came twice. Once he brought a slice of potato for Smith. It helped a little, but potatoes are rare. The second time, he asked the Jew if he'd go to the hospital.

"Good mother earth has relieved us," the doctor said. "There's a place to spare. They squabble like chickens—give it to a New Jersey man, give it to a Massachusetts man, give it to a Vermonter. God, a stinking breed, those Vermonters, cold as their mountains and ignorant as pigs. Can I say I'm holding it for a Jew? Can I tell them that? I threaten to walk out, and they let me do what I want with the place, save it for my Jew. They listen to me. I tell them eighteen miles away—in Philadelphia—there's ten golden pounds a week waiting for an army doctor. I take their Continental money and use it for bandages. It doesn't make good bandages even."

"How long have I got?" the Jew asked him.
"Any day now."
"I'll stay here," the Jew said, his smile curious.

The doctor looked at him oddly. He seemed to be really regretful. "I thought we'd talk," the doctor said. "You can go mad, not having anyone to talk to."

"You won't go mad," the Jew said.

Then they looked at each other; there seemed to be a sort of understanding between them.

We sit, now, waiting for the Jew to die. We fear his death, more than he does himself. Of that I'm certain. We know it won't be long. He bled for a long time through his nose and mouth, and after that he lay quiet, hardly breathing. His face is like yellow parchment, old skin stretched over bones. But he can't be very old.

I ask Ely what guess he'd make of the man's age.

"There's no age to him," Ely says slowly.

"He ain't seen thirty winters," Jacob guesses.

"He never spoke of wife or children. He's a strange, silent man."

I say, fretfully: "Why won't he die? He's been a week dying."

"A black magic that struck me," Smith says. "The scurvy comes from the heathen Jew."

I crawl into my bed, and Bess asks me: "He's dead?"

"No—not yet."

"Allen, I can't stand any more of this. I tell you, I can't. Only take me away, Allen. It's better to die outside than to die here. I wake up in the night, sweating—thinking that the place has closed in on me. Only take me away."

"There's no fear," I tell her, "no fear."

"But take me away, Allen."

"It's a long, weary five hundred miles to the Mohawk," I say. "It's a road we could never travel. And the British hold all the country in between."

"We don't have to go to the Mohawk, Allen."

"Then where?"

"The British in Philadelphia pay a price and keep for information, Allen. Food and housing——"

"Christ, you slut!" I cried. "You turning, crawling slut. You'd have me sell Ely—you'd have me sell them all."

"Only for you, Allen, only for you—only for my love of you, Allen. Only for my deep, abiding love of you."

"You're not a fit woman to love a man—to be loved by a man. You're not a fit woman to hold a man's body——"

"Allen, what are you saying?"

"I'm saying the truth! Clark Vandeer put his curse on me when he lay dying. He predicted true. You're a little filthy slut, and you're not a fit woman for a man."

"No, Allen—only my love of you to make me say it. Only my love that put thoughts in my mind. Loving and sleeping, sleeping half the day and night from weakness, dreaming all the time, you dream fancies, Allen. Like I dream I'm not here, but in a place where men and women are real. God forgive me, I think of a dress, Allen, almost go crazy making a dress in my mind, a dress of fine white flax, spun. I spin it myself, Allen. Day and night, I spin the flax. I can spin; I can card and weave and spin. I'm a fair, decent woman, Allen, and no bad woman could card and weave and spin. I make the cloth and cut a dress for myself, and sew it. With yellow thread, a cloth as white as snow. Like the snow outside, Allen—a dress of snow, clean and spotless. No marks on it, Allen —all over it not even a mark. To make me good, Allen, and I'm not a bad woman. Not a bad woman, Allen, only a dress of white to make me good. You wouldn't have to tell them truth, Allen. It's said the British are fair stupid beings. They'll believe you, Allen, whatever you tell them. They'll give us food and shelter to keep the winter——"

"You're no fit woman—let me go!"

"Allen, I'm good—stay by me, Allen. Allen, I could grow strong and round with a winter. Come spring, Allen, we could go to the south-land and over Boone's road into Transylvania. There's no war there in the south, Allen, and I would be strong—a fit woman to weave for a man, to clean and to work for him. You wouldn't have to love me then, Allen—only let me work for you. I wouldn't be holding you down, Allen—only to work for you."

I climbed out of bed, stumbled, and almost sprawled into the fire. I heard Bess' little cry of terror. I stood and watched the flames. Our wood is almost gone—a low fire. I tried to see something in the small flame.

Ely is by the Jew. He says something, and then over his shoulder to me: "Allen—come here."

I go and bend over the bed.

"You've had schooling, Allen. You've read books."

I nod.

"You've come on a fair prayer for a Jew in your reading?"

I shake my head helplessly.

He says a few words. The Jew sighs, and Ely closes his eyes. Ely says: "I'm not a man to think a lot about heaven and hell—but I'll go where he went, and content with that."

I can't speak.

Ely says: "Come and cut a few sticks of wood with me, Allen. The fire's low."

I take up the axe, and we go outside. Ely leads the way into the forest. I cut down a small tree, and then I rest while Ely lops off the branches. The work is good; it takes my mind off things.

We come back loaded with wood and build up the fire. Jacob is kneeling by the Jew's bed. We both look at him, but neither of us speaks.

I go to my bed. Bess touches my face, timidly. I put my head on her breast and sob convulsively.

8

We've decided to desert, Kenton Brenner, Charley Green, and I. Not at once did we come to the decision, but slowly, working our courage, and giving ourselves all the arguments we needed to leave the army. First Kenton and I—then Charley.

Two days after the Jew died, I walked on sentry beat with Kenton. The fresh meat had lifted us, brought back little fires of strength that were all but gone. I came on Kenton at the end of my beat. He leaned on his musket, looking northward over the hills.

I said to him: "I was watching you—you were silent and unmoving here wondrous long. I thought to myself, you're frozen and sleeping on your feet."

"I'm thinking a strong man could walk through the snow."

"Where to?" I asked him. "Where would you be walking?"

"North—a great stretch north to the Mohawk. I'm sick to look at the Valley land."

"For five hundred miles? Edward froze. Stiff as a log of wood. They brought him back and laid him down, and he was all ringed over with ice. I don't forget the sight of Edward, with the ice sealing his lips."

"Edward was alone."

Then I looked at him, and I could feel how the hope was tearing inside of me. "We're like rats in a trap—and lacking all courage," I muttered.

We asked Charley that night. Charley a Boston man, a city man. A curious man who had read many hundreds of books. He had a round face, tiny blue eyes, and a stoutness that days of starving wouldn't rid him of.

"We're enlisted three years," Charley said.

"For three years, and three hundred men in our regiment," I said. "Six of us left. There'll be none of you left for ripe rewards at the end of three years—not enough to hang from an English gibbet."

"I've a woman here," Charley muttered. "I'd be sleeping alone many a night."

"You've a dirty slut who won't hunger for you once ye're gone."

"I'm sick to be home."

"There's food on the way," I told him

eagerly. "There's a country full of food on the way. Rich, good food for our taking."

"We've no money. Our Continental paper wouldn't buy a loaf of bread to the thousand dollars."

"We don't need money. We'll take our muskets. Men with muskets can find food."

"I'm no thief," Charley said stubbornly. "By God, I've become a rotten mock of a man, but I'm no thief."

"No plunder. I'm not meaning plunder, Charley. Old soldiers could find a little bit of food."

Then we sit close to the fire, looking at each other, looking around the tiny smoke-blackened dugout. Ely is out on sentry duty. I try not to think about Ely; I try to think only of freedom—of an end to the awful monotony that's rotting my soul. Jacob lies in his bed, a cloak drawn over him, his feet protruding—ragged, bandaged stumps. His eyes are closed, and he lies without moving. Smith groans softly. Henry Lane is sick with the French disease. He has been sick and silent that way for weeks now—a living dead man lying quietly in his bunk.

We three look at each other and measure each other.

I say: "How long? I'm afraid to die here. Outside—anywhere outside. I'm not afraid to go to sleep in the snow, not wake up—just sleep in the snow. That's easy. There was no pain in Edward's heart for his dying."

"We'd start without food," Charley says.

Kenton grins. "We're used to that."

"You'd go to the Mohawk?"

"Or to Boston until the winter's over."

"No women——"

I stare at them, and they both look at me, and I glance over my shoulder; if Bess is awake.

"No women," Kenton says dully.

I get up, and I go to my bed. Her arms are round me. I watch the fire, pretending not to know that she is awake. I lie there for a long time, not moving, watching the fire, until I think she is asleep.

Ely comes in. Slowly, painfully, he gets out of his clothes. He is very tired; his face is sunken and drawn. Each step he takes draws a grimace of pain from him. I had thought of pleading with Ely to come along with us. But his feet wouldn't carry him a dozen miles.

He puts wood on the fire. He stands there for a little while, wiping the smoke out of his eyes. Then he walks to Jacob's bed. He and

Jacob are both older than the rest of us, both of them apart from us. He watches Jacob, draws the cloak up to Jacob's neck. Smith groans. Ely takes a cup of the thin corn-broth that we keep by the fire—when we have corn— and holds it to Smith's lips. The man drinks a little.

Ely takes something out of his pocket. "A bit of onion," he says to Smith. "I got it from a Massachusetts man for a few Continental papers. A rare good thing for the scurvy."

Ely sits down by the fire, puts out his legs in front of him. He closes his eyes and leans back, his hands spread on his thighs. I look at him until he blurs in front of my eyes, and then I say:

"Ely——"

He turns to me. "Allen? I didn't think you were awake."

I don't say anything now.

"You wanted something, Allen?"

"Nothing—nothing, Ely."

I turn round. Bess is awake. I see her wide-open dark eyes.

She whispers: "When will you be going, Allen?"

"Going? Where would I be going?"

"Allen, when I came to you that night, and my feet were bleeding, like a pain all through me, and you bound them up, Allen, and said that I was your woman——"

"I said it to keep men from putting hands on you."

"However you said it, I swore I would make no claims on you, Allen. I swore I would love you as long as I lived, Allen, but make no claim. What they were all thinking—that I was a bad woman and a slut. But it didn't matter about those Virginian men, Allen. It didn't matter, their having me. After you, there's nobody else, Allen. When you go away, I won't live."

"What do you want me to do?" I demanded hoarsely. "If we were man and wife, you could make a claim on me. I'd not part from any wife of mine."

"I make no claim, Allen."

"I could go mad, staying here—making my insides rot out."

"I don't want you to stay here, Allen. I wouldn't ask you to stay here. It's two years now of bitter fighting, and I cannot make out yet what they're fighting for. Only I've come to hate war, Allen. What is there, Allen, to make a man give up his life and bring an abiding sorrow in a woman?"

"I don't know," I said miserably.

"You're a northland man, Allen, and cold in the way of the northland men."

"I can't take a woman with me——"

"But tonight, Allen. I'm not holding it against you. Put your arms around me and love me tonight."

I lay without sleeping. Half the night, I lay without sleeping. Finally, I said: "I'll not go without you."

The next night, we were ready. When I told Kenton that Bess would come, he shook his head. I argued with him. I told him that having a woman with us would make it easier to get food.

"She won't walk it."

"She's a lean, hard woman," I said.

"But ye're a fool, Allen. She's not fit woman for a man. She's a slut. So why would you be nailing yourself to a slut?"

"You can go to hell without me," I said.

"We won't be fighting over the matter of a woman. If you want the wench, take her with you, Allen."

Now that we are ready to go, Kenton's woman

and Green's woman sit and watch us, but say nothing. Kenton's woman is already glancing at Jacob. There are more than enough men for the women.

Jacob hasn't said a word. He must have known before that we were going, but he doesn't speak. He sits on his bed, a ragged, bearded man, hair streaked with grey, watching us. I try to avoid his eyes.

Henry Lane watches wistfully. He says: "When you come to the Mohawk country—if you see kin of mine, you'll not tell them of my sickness. You'll tell them I had a fair, clean death."

Kenton says: "Ye're not a dying man, Henry. It's just a slow spell of weakness."

"But you'll tell them a quick, clean passing?"

We try to smile at him. We wrap our feet carefully, feeling all eyes in the place upon us. Ely is standing in one corner; he doesn't look at us.

"You won't hold it against us, Ely?" I say to him.

He doesn't answer. We go on with our preparations. We load our muskets carefully. We have about ten rounds of ammunition apiece— no food. If we pause for a moment, the entire hopelessness of our enterprise appears to overwhelm us. When we are ready, we stand round and look at each other. Nobody moves toward the door. We look round the cabin we have lived in for so many weeks now, the smoke-blackened timbers, the beds built against each wall, the dugout floor which has become as hard as rock. Out of our own hands.

Where are we going?

Kenton says: "Time to go———"

I say, desperately: "Come along, Ely. We're not doing any wrong, Ely. There's been no pay for weeks, no rum, no food. Two years we've fought for them. Come along."

Ely shakes his head, doesn't answer.

Jacob cries: "Christ—what are you waiting for? Get to hell outa here! A blessing to be rid of a spineless swine. For once I thought there was the making of a man in you, Allen, but ye're one with that bloodless Boston printer. Kenton's mindless, senseless, but I never thought it of you to follow that Boston man."

"Jacob———"

"I want no words with you. Why don't you go?"

"We're going," I say dully.

Charley moves to the door, opens it. The cold

air rushes in. Charley waves to his woman. Kenton follows him. I take Bess' arm, and we go out after them, closing the door behind us.

We go a few paces into the night, and then we stand and look back at the dugout. As if we expect movement, as if we expect some sign of life. The dugouts stand in a long row, and we walk past them.

I glance down at Bess' face. It's lit with happiness. She walks apart from me, as if she wishes to prove that there's enough strength in her. She says:

"I can walk, Allen. Don't fear for me. I'm a strong walker, Allen."

I try to feel glad. We're free; and there's no going back.

"If we're stopped," Kenton says. "What if we're stopped?"

We grip our muskets. We've passed the Pennsylvania dugouts. On our right is the encampment of General Poor's men. We push through the thin strip of woods and come out into the open. A sentry standing on the hill sees us.

"Shall we make a run for it?" Green asks.

"He'll fire if we run," Kenton says. "He's no officer. We'll talk to him."

"He'll listen to reasonable talk," I say hopefully.

Bess shrinks against me. We go on more slowly. When we come up to the sentry, we stop and stand there. We don't know what to say.

"Where are you going?" he demanded.

"We're Pennsylvania men."

Then he sees that Bess is a woman, and his eyes open. He's like us, bearded, ragged. He can't mistake us for anything but what we are.

I say, desperately: "We're deserters. We won't go back. If you want to die—we'll die along with you." Green is covering him with his gun.

"Deserters—" the man says, oddly.

"Which is it?" Kenton demands.

"Go ahead—Jesus Christ, I'll keep no man here."

We go on, and when I glance back, the sentry is still standing there, where we had left him. We cross the Gulph Road, string out over the parade ground. A moon is in the sky. We throw long shadows in the snow.

Bess is limping, and I see that the wrappings on one of her feet have come undone. I stop to fasten them. Green mutters:

"I told you—about a woman."

The moment I bare my hands, they get numb. There's no wind, but it's mercilessly cold. I fumble with the wrappings, finally manage to fasten them. We go on. A grey stone house looms ahead.

"Varnum's quarters, I think," Kenton says. "We'll go round."

We go back, avoiding the redoubt. We skirt a row of dugouts. At the end, we come across a sentry again. He stands blocking our way, but he makes no move toward us.

"Go on," Kenton says.

We walk past him, and he follows us with his eyes; but he makes no effort to halt us. We begin to run, enter the woods panting, and fling ourselves down. Bess clings to me, sobbing hoarsely.

"How'll we cross the river?" I ask Kenton.

Kenton shrugs. He says: "It's better to die this way, better to be shot clean. We'll freeze to death from the river."

"I made you go, Allen," Bess sobs. "You'll hold it up to me that I made you go."

"Christ—shut up!" Green whispers.

We go on, falling, rolling over, clutching at trees and tearing our clothes. Our muskets are useless, clogged with snow, the powder wet in the firing pans. Our strength is pretty much gone, but somehow we manage to stagger through the woods down to the bank of the Schuylkill. At the bank, we lie in the snow, panting hoarsely, unable to move.

"The bridge is guarded," I mutter. "We can't cross the bridge—it's guarded."

"You damn fool, the river's frozen."

Somehow, none of us had realized that. We laugh like idiots. Bess hugs me. She says: "Allen—Allen, I don't care—we're out of it."

It's terribly cold. As we lie there, I can feel myself growing numb, sleepy. I close my eyes, and almost instantly a deep rush of relaxation overtakes me. I want to sleep. I draw Bess close to me.

Kenton is gripping my shoulder. "Allen— we have to get out of here. Sentries patrol the riverbank."

We stumble to our feet. There is a great drift of snow against the bank, and we flounder through it. Bess almost disappears. Then we are out on the river. Some of the ice has been swept bare by the wind, and we go sprawling. We have no strength left for directed action. Green drops his musket, claws at it, and then creeps after it. And all the time we are in an agony of fear that we will be seen from the bank we left.

Finally, we gain the shore. It takes all our strength to scramble up onto the bank.

We go up slowly, panting, breathing heavily; then through the forest. It's black in the forest. We fall, bruise and cut ourselves. Finally, we come out on a stretch of open fields.

Kenton says: "Ah—I'm used up. We'll make no distance tonight."

"We have to keep going," I pant.

Bess looks at me; her face is drawn with an agony of weariness. As we walk, slow as we are going, she falls behind. She can't keep our pace. Forcing herself to run a little, she'll catch up with us, drop back.

"I told you not to bring the woman," Charley said.

"She's here—leave her be. It was a fair hard run out of camp."

Bess says: "Allen—I'll stay with you. It's easy for me, Allen."

She falls once, lies in the snow. We turn, and I can see her straining to raise herself.

"You shoulda known," Kenton nods.

I go back and lift her up. She clings to my

arm, and says: "Forgive me, Allen. I'm no fit woman."

We walk on. More and more, I feel Bess' weight on me. We've been half-starved for weeks—sick. None of us has shoes. Our feet are bandaged, covered over with cloth, and then bandaged again up to our knees. Our breeches are torn. Our coats are thin as paper. Kenton wears a forlorn cocked hat, two of the cocks down and flapping. Charley and I have no hats. Our heads are bound like Turks'.

We come to a little dirt road, walk along it. I seem to sleep, even while I'm walking. Suddenly, I come awake. Kenton is walking on ahead. Charley has stopped; he stands looking at me. I turn around, and see Bess crumpled in a heap on the snow. I go back to her.

"Go on, Allen," she says.

I draw her up to me, and she clings close, sobbing into my coat. We go on, with Charley and Kenton ahead of us.

We made camp. We couldn't have been much more than a mile or two from the Schuylkill. How far, I don't know, because half the walking was a nightmare. But we couldn't have been very far from the river. Half-frozen, we stopped and tried to build a fire.

All I could think of was Edward Flagg, the skin of ice over his lips when they brought him back. He was a great, strong man, Edward; but they brought him back stiff as a log.

We break branches and gather bits of wood together. Bess crouches close to the ground, trembling.

Charley tries to make a fire. He uses a handflint. For minutes he tries, striking again and again, until the flint drops from his numbed hand. He tries to rub life back into his hands.

I tear a bit of cloth from my leg bindings, drop some powder onto it. Kenton takes the flint, and a spark ignites the powder. We feed the fire carefully, nurse it and blow on it. It grows larger. We build up a great, roaring mass of fire.

"They'll see it," Kenton says.

"We need fire. We'll never live the night out unless we have fire."

As the fire grows, we gather around it and absorb the heat. Bess crowds close; her thin, white face lights a little. Kenton grins. He says:

"Edward made a great mistake, walking alone. It's a wonder to me how any man could think to win northward, walking alone."

"Don't speak of Edward."

"You can speak of a dead fool," he says lightheadedly.

"My belly's tight and empty," Charley says. "By God, I'd give ten years of my life for a steak to feed that fire with."

"There's food—we'll feed well enough tomorrow."

We stayed close to the fire. We arranged for a watch through the night to feed the fire. We wiped our muskets clean and reloaded them.

Kenton stood the first watch. I lay down with Bess in my arms, Charley sprawled by the fire a little distance away. I could see how Charley envied me the having of a woman to spend the night through.

In my arms, Bess still trembled. I couldn't make her warm. I tried to soothe her, tried to tell myself that we wouldn't freeze. But if Kenton slept and the fire went out——

"I'm no fit woman, Allen," Bess said as if repeating a lesson she had learned. "You made a mistake to bring me along, Allen. I'll be nothing else but a drag on you."

"We'll go together," I told her. "We'll find a place where we can rest and warm ourselves. Then we'll go together. It'll be nowhere as hard as tonight."

"You're a good man, Allen. You're a strong, good man to be so tender with me."

"I said you'd go, and I'll care for you," I told her proudly.

"I won't ask any care of you, Allen. I'll fend for myself——"

"I'll fend for you. It'll be like you were wedded to me. I'll fend for you."

"Some day, Allen—you might wed me?"

"There's a fair lot of things I'm thinking to do," I said.

Then she slept. I held her close to me, and I lay looking up at the stars, watching the slow rise and sway of sparks against the dark sky. I thought of Ely and Jacob, and tried to understand that I would not be with them again. For the first time, I recalled how Ely had been when we left.

I must have slept. Kenton was waking me.

"Your watch, Allen," he said.

I got up, feeling the cold eat into me as I moved from Bess. She murmured my name in her sleep.

"You saw anything?"

"Nothing," Kenton said.

He curled up by the fire. I leaned on my musket and watched the flames.

9

IN THE morning, I awake to the sound of bugles from the encampment. We can't be very far away. The bugles are thin, but they sound clear in the morning air.

Bess, opening her eyes, looks at me and smiles. Her smile is a deep, happy awareness of my presence. She touches my face, passes her fingers across my beard.

"You're better?" I ask her.

"Better. A hunger inside of me, but I can stand hunger, Allen. I've no fear of hunger."

Charley is feeding the fire. A moment later, Kenton comes across the field, holding a few frozen ears of corn.

"We'll break our fast on this," he calls.

"I wouldn't think of breaking fast, but of getting out of here," Charley says. "We're too near to the encampment, and far enough away to be deserters."

"They'll not stop us any more," I say. "After last night, they'll not stop us."

"We'll go north and east," Kenton says

thoughtfully. "There are good roads through the Jersey bottoms."

"If we had horses——"

Charley looks at us.

"It's horses—or dying in the snow," I say.

We toast the corn over the fire. It's not fit food for a pig, but we eat it eagerly.

"I dug it under the snow," Kenton says. "It's a wonder it stayed so long. The ground's scraped clean of food."

"We can go east—to Norristown. It's a good farmland over that way."

We finish the corn—close to the husk. We take our guns and look at the priming. Then we start off.

We walk slowly in the direction of the King of Prussia Road. Last night was a lesson. We know how little strength we have, and that we must husband it. It's cold this morning, but not so cold as last night. The sun comes up, clear and bright, making long blue shadows on the snow. The snow glistens, and each crystal shoots a tiny beam of light into our eyes.

A sparkle in Bess' eyes. She turns her face to me, showing me how long her steps are.

"I'm a good walker, Allen—a fine good walker."

"A fine walker," I agree.

We're all of us eager. Kenton steps out ahead, long strides, and confidence in the way he swings his heavy musket. We're content that Kenton leads. He's four years older than I am, a powerful man. Bess is like a boy, thin, her long dark hair twisted into braids. Charley sings snatches of song.

Bess keeps glancing at me. She says: "You've no regrets, Allen?"

"No regrets——"

"I think of Ely," Charley says. "I was never understanding men like Ely. A fearfully tolerant man."

"He might have come——"

"He wouldn't come without Jacob. There's a deep bond between the two of them—for all the black murder in Jacob's heart. There's no other man Jacob ever loved, unless it was the Jew. I cannot make it out, but I've never seen such sorrow as Jacob had when the Jew died."

"I'm fearful of Jews," Bess says. "I had not seen a Jew until I was fifteen. My mother said she'd show me a Jew some time, so I'd have a deeper knowledge of the Book."

"There were a pretty lot of Jews in Boston," Charley says. "Sam Adams was a great one to bleed them. He'd spin them a fine tale of revolution and take their last shilling, and there was more respect for him for bleeding a Jew than for all his wild talk."

"It's said Hamilton's a Jew———"

"He has the look in his eyes."

We're near the road now. Kenton waits for us. He's standing there, listening.

"What is it?" I ask him.

"We're too near the camp. I'm thinking we should bide a while longer in the forest. Ye're safer in the trees."

"We make better time on the road."

"It's Quaker country hereabout. I'd put no trust in any Quaker."

"Or fear them——" I said confidently.

We walk out on the road, Bess close to me. Now, again, seeing the stretch of open road before us, we realize the distances. Distances pile up for hundreds of miles to the snowy mountains that bind the Mohawk. Bess presses close, looks up at my face. I understand now that she knows, as I know, that she won't go that great distance. There is no strength in her for that. She stands like a small, frightened boy, half-grown.

She says: "Sometimes I'm afeard, Allen. Hold me."

"You hear anything?" Kenton demands.

I shake my head. We walk on, along the road towards Norristown. We walk very slowly, feeling the cold more than before. A hundred yards more—we stop.

"I hear horses," Kenton says.

"Not from the camp." I can hear it now—a thudding muffled by the snow.

Bess looks at me, shaking her head.

"Not from the camp," Charley cries. "It's up the road."

"More than one horse."

"Farmers don't ride like that."

"Get out—for the trees!" Kenton shouts.

But there are fields on either side the road, trees only in the direction from which the sounds of horses are coming. A heap of snow on the side of the road suggests a stone wall underneath. Long shadows on the road, and a glare from the snow; it makes a scene to stay in my mind.

We stand there like people who have lost all power of movement. Bess says:

"I brought it on you, Allen. God forgive me——"

Kenton leads the way off the road, Charley after him. Kenton stumbles, and Charley bends to help him to his feet. I take Bess' hand and drag her through the drift against the stone wall. We climb over the wall. Kenton is stumbling along, like a man who has been shot.

I turn round, see a dozen men on horse coming down the road.

"McLane's raiders," Kenton sobs.

A man pulls out in front, and I hear him crying for us to halt. They begin to gallop, and the thud of their horses' hoofs is like a drumbeat in my ears. I drag Bess along.

Kenton and Charley are waiting for me. They see that with Bess I can't reach the woods before the cavalrymen, but nevertheless they wait. They hold their muskets before them.

I cry: "Don't shoot—for God's sake. Run for it!"

We're almost at the trees. I think that we'll make it. I sob with pain of the running.

Some of the horses are floundering in the snow. The man out in front cries: "Stop or we'll fire!"

"The hell with you!" Kenton screams. "Keep a run, Allen! They're lost in the snow!"

I glance back once more. We're almost up to Kenton and Charley. They've lowered their muskets and are starting toward the trees. But the men are dismounting, dropping from their horses.

A blast of musketry crashes behind us. Bess is torn from my hand, crying.

Kenton sees; he runs toward me, cursing, Charley after him. I face round and the cavalrymen are closing in on us. I see it all in a red haze, and I fire. Kenton and Charley too; like machines, their muskets go off. I notice one of the cavalrymen falling, so slowly that the picture is impressed permanently upon my mind. I look at Bess, and try to understand what has happened. Bess lies in the snow in a little heap.

They close in on us, and there's no fight left. I wonder why we fired. They're like us, bearded, ragged, their feet bound in blood-stained cloths. They're like us, thin, worn.

They hold onto us. I strain to get away—to Bess. I say: "Let me go to her! God damn you—you've got us now. Let me go to her!"

McLane stands in front of us. He's a young man, clean-shaven except for a small moustache, wearing white breeches and a good blue coat, sword, pistol, a cocked hat. As he stands there, panting, his breath steams out.

"Deserters?" he asks. Behind him, two men

are carrying the one I saw fall. McLane whirls round. "Who is it?"

"Dave Seely———"

"He's hurt?"

We all see it. The man is shot through the head. Vaguely, I wonder whose bullet it was—thinking of Bess. Whose bullet there?

"You filthy swine!" McLane says to us. "You damned, cowardly swine! You'll hang for this if I have to gibbet you myself."

Kenton stares sullenly. Charley says: "Let him go to his woman. You shot his woman."

I try to tear loose. Some of the men are turning Bess over. I scream: "Hands off her! Christ, leave her alone!"

"It's a woman," one of them says.

I plead: "Let me go to her. You have us now. That's enough, isn't it? Let me go to her."

"Hold your damned tongue!"

"Let me go to her——" I pull loose. I don't know how, but I pull loose, and nobody tries to stop me. I run over to Bess, and the men who are bending over her stand aside. I kneel down next to her. She's shot somewhere in the body, because all the front of her clothes is stained with blood.

I rub her cheeks. She opens her eyes, and I keep rubbing her cheeks.

"Allen," she says.

I can't say anything. You fight in an army for two years, and you know a death wound; you know the sign of it in a man's eyes. She knows; the deep knowledge of it is in her eyes. What can I say?

She says: "Allen—I brought a wrong on you. I'm no fit woman for a man."

I shake my head. Maybe it seems to her that I'm going away, because she whispers:

"Bide with me, Allen—for a while."

Very slowly, I stand up. I say aloud: "I should have known—it was such a distance for a woman to walk."

The cavalrymen take hold of me and lead me back. McLane is watching me, oddly. Kenton's face is despair and nothing else. When I come close to him, Charley Green reaches out a hand for my arm.

"Allen?"

I say to myself, in all the crash of shooting, it might have been someone else. It might have been. I tell myself, We're going back.

"It's no great horror—a dying like that," Charley says softly.

"I'm not sorrowing for her," I say desperately. "I'm not sorrowing for her."

"Easy, Allen."

"Easy, sure—you'll be with her soon enough," McLane says.

Kenton cries: "Leave him alone, God damn you! Leave off taunting him!"

They march us back toward the road. I look round, and see that it's still morning, a glorious cold morning. As we reach the road, we see a brigade coming on the run, panting. They must have heard the shooting in the encampment. The brigade gathers round. They keep telling the story.

"Pennsylvania deserters———"

Two men carrying Bess. They walk alongside of me.

"It's Wayne's boast he has no deserters."

"He'll take off some of his pride, Wayne will."

"We were walking to the Mohawk," Kenton laughs. "God—we were walking to the Mohawk."

McLane hands us over to the officer of the brigade. "Take them to the redoubt," he says, "and hold them. They've murdered one of my men. I'll charge them myself."

"We're no murderers!" Green cried. "We shot after your men fired on us."

"Take these swine away," McLane says.

They marched us back slowly. He was no hard man, the officer of that brigade, a young man whose name was Captain Kennedy. They were Massachusetts men. There were a few there whom Kenton knew, and they made things easier for us.

Their officer saw how weak we were, and he marched us slowly. But it was a long way back, a weary way. Kenton came up and put an arm round me.

"It was a good run last night, Allen," he said. "I didn't think it to end so soon. I didn't think of no cavalry to find us out right away."

"I'm not blaming you, Kenton."

"The lass is dead. You'll be blaming me for that, Allen? Her blood's on my hands."

"No—I'm not putting the blame on any man."

We marched down the King of Prussia Road to the crossroads, then turned right toward the redoubt. As we passed between the dugouts of Varnum's brigades, Kennedy stopped and had them send out a drummer. The men, part of the Pennsylvania and New Jersey line, flocked out of their huts to see us pass. The drummer beat a low, monotonous roll—for the condemned and dead. Some of the men dropped their heads. We went through slowly; I heard one man say:

"Poor, damned devils."

All the time moving—the cold air, the sunlight glinting from the snow, half-blinding us; I didn't think much. I understood that Bess was dead, but she was already part of all my memories of the army. They come and go, like the doctor had said, like Moss Fuller had died. I can't think.

We march into the redoubt. Into a cold, bare log hut, where Colonel Varnum sits at a camp table. Kennedy salutes. The guard stand at attention. But we're used up. We stand limply, our hands hanging at our sides.

"Deserters, sir," Kennedy says. "Taken by Captain McLane. They resisted arrest, and one of Captain McLane's men was killed. I have their muskets, all fired. McLane's man had a ball in his head. They had a woman with them, and she was shot in the breast. McLane's men fired a volley."

"What regiment?" the Colonel asked tonelessly. Too many incidents like ours had occurred for it to matter a great deal.

"Fourteenth Pennsylvania."

"Wayne's men?"

We nodded.

"Your names?"

We gave him our names.

"Ragged, filthy beasts, Kennedy. I'd tame a few of them. Maybe we'll tame these."

Kennedy stood without answering.

"Put them in the guardroom."

They took us into a room about six feet square. It had no windows, but there were chinks between the logs. It had a dirt floor, low roof, no fire.

They barred the door. I heard Kennedy say: "Poor devils——"

We sit on the floor in silence. Light comes in thin bars through the cracks between the logs. It splatters us with gold, gold on Kenton's yellow beard.

We're cold. Unconsciously, we move toward each other. But we don't speak.

My feet pain me. I stretch them out before me, to ease the pain. I find myself trembling, perhaps from the cold.

"I never thought to hang," Charley says—like a child would say it.

10

THE light goes; the bars it made throughout the guardhouse vanish, and a deep dusk replaces it. A slow afternoon, and then quick falling of night, with increasing cold. A wind that blows through the spaces between the logs. The floor is cold as ice. Our arms and legs stiffen. We try to find some relief in movement.

Three times the guard outside changes. We can look through cracks in the door and see him, a ragged, lean soldier.

We are given nothing to eat. At first, the pain of hunger drives us half-mad. That's the way hunger is at the beginning. It eases off afterwards. The dull gnawing in your stomach becomes desire, desire for all things. It's not so hard to bear as the thirst.

We pound on the door. "Guard—guard—for Christ's sake, bring us a little food and water!"

He comes close to the door, looks at us curiously.

"A drink of water———"

He says: "A waste of good food."

"Anything—a little water."

"Do you think I've been eating fine today?" he asks us. "Do you think I've tasted meat in a fortnight?"

"Bring us some water."

He brings us a pot of water, watches us as we drink it. "A sight of wretched men you are," he says. "I heard it was nowhere so bad with Wayne's men."

"Why are they keeping us here?"

"I haven't asked them."

Night comes. I lie on the floor. Kenton's close to me for warmth. Charley stands up against the door, a dark blur. Closing my eyes, dozing, I can imagine the body next to me as Bess. I can imagine the place as the dugout, and I wait for Bess to make a movement, to touch me, to put her hands on my beard. I wait for Bess to speak, her voice breaking through my slumber. Bits of her voice at first, and then more and more.

I shake Kenton, and ask: "Bess? Bess?"

"Allen—you're losing yer mind."

"No—no, I dreamed a little. I'm hungry, Kenton. You don't suppose they'll bring us food? Men can't live long without food. If they're meaning to hang us, they'll bring us some food."

Charley growls: "I'll not hang. By God, Allen, I'm meaning to take my life before I let them put a rope around my neck."

"We shouldn't have fired," Kenton groans. "They were well on to take us, and we shouldn't have fired."

"They shot Bess," I mutter.

"A poor fool to think she could walk through five hundred miles of snow and ice. She was no woman to go walking the length and distance to the Mohawk. I wonder to think that you shoulda brought her along, Allen."

"A man 'comes attached to a woman, sleeping with her night after night. You can't bear away the cold, bitter nights without a woman."

"I had a woman," Kenton says, "but she was no legal wedded wife of mine. If I made my mind to go a great distance over the snow, I would not take a woman to drag on me."

"Leave off Allen," Charley snaps. "He's got sorrow enough. The woman's dead, isn't she?"

"She's dead."

"Then leave off Allen."

"I'm holding no hate for Kenton," I say wearily. "I wouldn't be sorrowing over the woman. She was no lawful wedded wife of mine, and she was no fit woman for a man—" I can't say any more. I put my face in my hands, and in the awful, complete silence of the place, I know they're listening to my sobbing.

There's a long while of silence after that. A crunching in the snow outside where the sentry paces up and down, a wash of the wind over the top of the redoubt. A wolf's howling from down the Schuylkill.

I grope back for a time when we were not in the encampment. There was a battle at Brandywine, where three men of the Fourth New York Regiment were killed. That left nine men. Moss Fuller and Edward Flagg and Clark Vandeer. Six men. Allen Hale; Charles Green; Kenton Brenner. Henry Lane was dying. Clark died, and he put a curse on me as he lay dying. Jacob burning like a fire, a black fire. The Jew had died in peace, with knowingness in his eyes. Suddenly, I hate the Jew, envy him. I make a picture of Jacob kneeling by the Jew's bed. Ely is left, only Ely.

I groan aloud.

Charley says: "Be easy, Allen. There's nothing for men to fear who've seen what we've seen."

"Nothing," I repeat.

Kenton says: "I've no fear of dying—only of hanging. They put a man on Mount Joy to hang, a man who went mad and killed his lieutenant officer. They put him there to hang, and I swear to God that when I stood on sentry duty I saw the wolves leaping for his body."

Charley laughs. "You're a man to see things, Kenton."

"As God is my witness, I saw them—wolves leaping high in the moonlight."

"You don't have to talk about it!" I cry. "You don't have to talk about it."

The silence after that makes a tension; I can see how it is: if they're thinking the way I'm thinking—every move since we left the dugout. Kenton's idea—but without Bess we might have gone miles farther from camp. If her blood is on Kenton's hands, then his is on mine.

It comes to me that if Bess were here this night, she wouldn't be afraid. She'd have no fear; she'd only want to abide with me. Her face would be calm, and I would only have to pass my hands over her face to realize the calm.

I say to Kenton: "Did she die with pain? You saw her fall, Kenton. Did she die with pain?"

"There's no pain in her now," Kenton says.

"I couldn't rest again if I thought she died with a great pain in her heart."

Charley says: "I had a brother die—I was twelve years then. He died of the pox. He said there was no pain to dying—he kept saying there was no pain to dying."

"It's different on the gallows," Kenton says bitterly.

There's a movement at the door; it opens, the sentry and another man bulking against the lighter darkness outside. We watch—wondering who it is. Then I know it's Ely. I don't doubt any more. I feel a restfulness that I haven't felt since I left the dugout. My muscles relax. I sit there on the cold floor, my arms hanging limply by my sides; I feel tears come into my eyes.

Kenton knew. I guess we all knew. Kenton said: "Come in, Ely." His voice was lighter.

"Only a while," the sentry said.

Ely came in and stood by the door. "Allen's here?" he asked.

"All of us, Ely," Kenton said.

It was dark where I sat. I got on my feet and went over to Ely. I went close to him—tried to make out his face. I touched his coat. I said to him:

"Ely, I'm glad to see you. You're not hating or despising us, Ely?"

"I was hoping you wouldn't be brought back," he said slowly.

"Give me your hand, Ely? You won't hold your hand from us?"

He put out his hand, and I clung to it. I put it between mine, and tried to feel the flesh under the mitten he wore.

"It was good of you to come," Charley said. "A long walk through the snow. It was mighty good of you to come, Ely."

"I thought I'd see how you were faring. It's no matter of a walk."

"How'd you know?"

"They brought word that you were taken—one of you shot."

"They shot Bess."

"She's dead?"

"She died out there. She never knew what would happen. She died in my arms, Ely."

"She'll rest easy, poor child."

Kenton had stood back. Now he stood against

the further wall. "Ely," he said, "did you come in hate?"

"No——"

"If you came in hate, Ely, I'll tell you that I was the leader. I made Allen a plan to desert, and the woman said she'd die if Allen didn't take her, and Allen had given me his word to go. The woman's blood is on my hands, Ely."

Ely said, softly: "Don't burn yourself, Kenton. The poor girl could not have the peace she has now."

"We shot a man, Ely. They're going to hang us."

Ely didn't answer.

"They say we murdered a man, Ely," Kenton went on, dully, no heat or feeling in his voice. "There was no murder. We fled across a field and McLane's men loosed a volley at us. Charley and I turned to wait for Allen and the girl. I saw the girl shot, and I saw her fall. Then I killed one of McLane's men——"

I forced myself to say: "He didn't—we don't know whose shot it was killed him."

Kenton went on as if he hadn't heard me. "You know, Ely, I draw a good bead with a musket. There was no man in all the Mohawk country could outshoot me. You've seen me take my mark and bring down my mark, Ely. I shot the man, Ely. I want you to remember that. I swear to God."

"He's lying," Charley whispered.

For a while, Ely stands there and says nothing. I can feel what's going on inside of him, how hard it is for him to make the effort to speak. He takes a few steps toward us.

Finally, he says: "I brought you a few bits of salt meat—I had it from the meat Kenton killed when we built the fire—you'll remember that?"

"I remember," Kenton says mechanically.

Ely puts the meat in my hands. He stands a moment, as if he's trying to see my eyes in the dark. Then he turns around and goes out.

We divide up the meat and eat it slowly. We sit down again, with our backs to the log walls.

Charley says: "You didn't aim to kill, Kenton. You shot from your waist. There's no man can aim to kill shooting from his waist."

Kenton doesn't answer. I reach out, put my hand on his knee. His hand covers mine.

11

Somehow, we endured through the night. Man's power to endure pain is only exceeded by his ability to forget. We had some water left in the pot; it froze into a solid block. The guardhouse was like a sieve; we lay on a cold floor, close to each other for warmth. The morning came, and we were more dead than alive. We tried to rise off the floor, but we couldn't. Our limbs were as stiff as if death had already laid hold of us. We crawled to the door and hammered on it. But nobody answered, and after a while we stopped. We lay there, making the least noise we could of our own pain.

Charley said: "A night more of this—and we won't fear the gallows."

Finally, the door was opened. A guard stood there, and a strange officer. He told us to get up.

"We're fair stiff—we've eaten only a bit of meat in two days."

We managed to crawl to our feet, and they

took us to the same log building where he had spoken to Varnum the day before. We could barely walk. There were some chairs there, and we slumped into them. A fire was going, and the heat of it was like nothing we had ever experienced before; the heat was new and wonderful. We were afraid to go too near the heat at first; we went to it slowly.

"You don't look like you'll wait for the gallows," the officer said. "God, what a sorry mess——" He stared at us. "How long since you've eaten?"

"We had a little meat——"

"I'll have some stew sent in."

The stew was of corn and potatoes, in wooden bowls. We gulped it eagerly.

"I've tasted no food like this in many days," Charley said. "They eat well here."

"It warms you."

We crowded up to the fire, stretched out our feet to bake. We opened our coats.

"A rare, fine fire," Kenton said. He seemed more at ease now, hardly worried.

"They'll hang us today, do you think, Kenton?"

He shrugged. Charley stared into the fire. We sat that way, without talking, until the door opened. A young officer came in, not much more than a boy. I thought I recognized him, but dulled as my mind was, I couldn't recall his name. He came in and stood at the table, studying us. He was remarkably well dressed: some of the officers were as ragged as we. He wore a blue uniform greatcoat with black facings, a silk scarf, a black cocked hat, brown leather breeches and good highboots of black leather. He held a riding crop in his hand; and hooking one leg over the table, he beat the crop against his thigh.

He was tall and thin—deepset dark eyes. He had a way of staring from under dropped lids.

"You're the Pennsylvania men?" he asked us.

Kenton stared at him sullenly. I could see he didn't like the young swell. I didn't have much interest in him; I was forcing myself not to think—not to think at all. I was trying not to see a gibbet on Mount Joy. Charley Green hummed a song.

He asked us again: "You're the three deserters?"

"Colonel Hamilton?" Charley asked. He hated officers the way only Boston men can hate. He smiled a little as he spoke. He had nothing to lose. Not even fear. It made me sick at myself to see how little fear he and Kenton had. As if they had lost all human quality that related them to me, leaving me alone.

The boy nodded, still looking at us curiously. I recognized Washington's favorite, Alexander Hamilton. I might not have hated him in another situation. As it was, I despised his smug, well-dressed complacency. I looked at his fine black boots, and I thought of how we had taken the boots off Moss Fuller when he died.

"If I have the story right," Hamilton said, "you're three deserters from the Fourteenth Pennsylvania. Deserted with arms and killed one of Captain McLane's men. By God, you're a pretty, filthy bunch of beggars. I'd let you desert; I'd see you all in hell before I'd have you in my army."

"You can go to hell, sir," Charley said.

The regular motion of the quirt against the boy's thigh didn't stop. As if he hadn't heard Green. He shifted his gaze to the chimney over our heads.

"You'll be court-martialed this afternoon," he said. "You've raised a fuss. You'll be a shining example on a gibbet on Mount Joy."

"All right," Kenton said. "Get out of here."

Hamilton got off the table; he had control: he walked up to Kenton, and I waited for the quirt to cross Kenton's face. Then the boy shrugged.

"I'm to defend you."

Charley laughed. His laugh was more than words.

"We don't need anyone to defend us," Kenton said.

"My orders are to defend you."

Charley kept on laughing. I stood up and walked to a window. Beyond the walls of the redoubt, I could see the snow stretching away to the trees that lined the bank of the Schuylkill. The morning sun made colours on the snow, delicate colours of yellow and violet, tints of brown, stray bits of green, colours of life and of spring. I thought of the Jew's words before he died. Spring like an awakening; spring like the hand of God reaching down and caressing the earth, spring with a softening of the earth, so that a man could die and go to the bosom of the soil.

When I turned round, Hamilton was lighting a pipe, a long-stemmed, Dutch clay pipe, the kind the burghers smoke, sitting in front of their shops at Albany, the kind you see racked round the wall in any small up-country village tavern. He had bent over to take a burning twig from the blaze, and now he was blowing clouds of blue tobacco smoke toward the ceiling.

It must have been in my eyes, on my face, all the longing of a condemned man for tobacco. For weeks we had not smoked; for weeks we had not tasted the odour of tobacco.

He looked at me, that curious smile coming on his face again. Impulsively, he offered me the pipe.

I hold out my hand. Kenton and Charley are looking at me. Whatever they thought before, I'm open to them now. I take the pipe in my hand. I go forward a step or two, and offer it to Kenton.

He doesn't move.

Charley whispers: "Christ!"—his whisper hoarse, loud, breaking up in his throat. He takes the pipe and puffs on it. He watches the smoke, passes his hand through the smoke, smiles childishly. He gives the pipe back to me.

I smoke slowly, just a puff or two. Kenton nods, and I give it to him. He puffs; then, suddenly, he throws the pipe across the room, shattering the clay bowl and stem to bits.

Hamilton, still smiling, watching us. Kenton with his face in his hands. Charley Green walks back and forth. I say to Hamilton:

"They'll hang us today?"

He shrugs.

"We don't want any pity!" Kenton cries. "By God, what do any of you know, tight in your houses, eating, drinking?"

Hamilton says, slowly: "I had dry bread this morning—two slices. I had a little meat yesterday. It was the General's dinner. He forced me to eat it——"

Charley laughs.

"You don't believe me?"

Kenton says: "Why don't they hang us? Why don't they hang us and get it over with?"

"They'll hang you," Hamilton says. "They'll hang you high enough——"

He goes back to the table, hooks a leg over it, remains there, watching us. I stand by the window. Kenton gets up, awkwardly, painfully, goes over and looks at the shattered pipe.

Hamilton says: "Tell me what happened."

"We deserted," I say. "We're Mohawk men,

and we had it in our minds to walk to the Valley country."

He looks at me, at Charley and Kenton. He sees three men who are as thin as men can be—and remain alive; bearded and ragged, none of us wearing shoes. His eyes go to our feet.

"You were going to make that journey?"

I nod. I walk over, sit down, try to hide my feet from his gaze.

"You had no food to take with you?"

"We are used to that."

"Were there any more—only you three?"

"There was a girl with us—who was shot by McLane's men."

"A girl," he murmured. "That's a point against the dashing Captain McLane. Something to remember. Who was she, a wife to any of you?"

"She was no fit woman to be a man's wife," I say. "She was a follower of the camp."

"Whose woman?" Hamilton asks.

"She was my woman——"

"She was killed instantly?"

"She died in my arms——"

Kenton cries: "Can't you see the pain in him? Leave us alone!"

"You killed one of McLane's men," Hamilton says, ignoring Kenton. "Who fired first, his men or you?"

"We fired after he killed the girl."

"And which one of you killed the man?"

"I did," Kenton says.

Charley breaks in: "We shot from our sides without aim. There's no saying who killed him."

Hamilton stares at Kenton. Again, he seems to be a boy, not more than half-grown at that. The smile goes out of his face. He goes over to Kenton, and holds out his hand.

"You'll take my hand?"

Kenton stands stiffly, not moving. Then Hamilton walks out.

12

We wait, without knowing what we are waiting for. We stare at each other with lifeless eyes. We sit close to the fire, but we don't speak. As if we are used up and all of our words are used up.

Kennedy comes in. Beyond him, through the door, we see a guard of eight men. Kennedy has a long leather thong with him, buckles hanging from it. He avoids our eyes, and he stands by the table, staring out of the window.

"Stand up," he says.

He comes over to us, buckles the strap from neck to neck. When he comes to me, I tear away.

"We're to be drummed like beasts?" I cry.

"My orders——"

"Christ!—I'll not be saddled like a beast. Why don't you draw your sword on me? Why in hell don't you draw your sword on me? You God-damned filthy-bellied swine, why don't you draw your sword and kill me?"

Kenton grips my arm. "Allen—Allen, there's no use making it worse."

"I'm sorry," Kennedy says.

I try to cover my face with my hands. Outside, it's biting cold, but clear, and the snow has the glowing sheen of cold sunshine. The men of the guard move restlessly, trying to warm themselves. Two drummers stand just beyond them. As we come out, they break into the roll for condemned men.

The guard walk behind us with fixed bayonets. They have no identity as men—eight beggars like ourselves, their bayonets rusty and bent. The drummers are in front, beating out their roll. Once, Charley falls, and we all go down in a heap; the band is tearing my neck, choking me.

The guard help us to our feet. One of them is a grey-bearded old man. He says:

"Walk easy, son. We've time."

Kennedy is out in front. He doesn't glance back at us, even when we fall. He walks slowly, his head bent over. We pass the rifle pit, and the men on duty stare at us, but not with too much curiosity.

We go through a line of dugouts, and some of the troops come out to watch us.

"You'd make right fine eating," someone calls.

We march on, until we come to the stone house where Washington has his quarters. It's a fine, tall two-storey house, with a long stable next to it. We go round to the front, and the guard stop before the door, beat their roll to a mounting crescendo, and then rattle their sticks into silence. Kennedy takes us in.

He takes us through the house to the rear righthand room on the first floor. Inside, there are six officers, seated at a large round table near the fire. Hamilton is at a camp table near the window, writing. When we come in, he glances up, nods at us. Another officer stands next to a tall clock. By the door, chairs are placed for us, and Kennedy motions for us to sit down. We sit down awkwardly, the straps drawing us together.

One of the officers stands up. I recognize Anthony Wayne. He says: "Why are those men lashed together?"

"Colonel Varnum's orders, sir," Kennedy replies.

"And who in hell is Varnum? By God, they're Pennsylvania men! Tell Varnum to keep his damned fat nose out of my men."

"But it's customary," one of the men at the table breaks in.

"To hell with your customs. Untie them."

Kennedy unties us, goes out. I glance at Hamilton; he sits by the window, wrapped tight in his coat, smiling. Wayne sits down and stares at the table. I watch the officers; some of them I recognize: Greene, Lord Stirling, Colonel Conway, General Scott. There's an empty chair in the centre; they seem to be waiting for someone. They drum impatiently with their fingers on the top of the table. Wayne fidgets with a sheet of paper he holds in his hands. None of them look at us.

It's cold in the room, in spite of the fire. The rustle of the fire intermingles with the dull ticking of the clock. For a while, I listen to the ticking; then I stare at the clock. It's half an hour past one. I look at the clock curiously, time has disappeared for so long, the time that moves on the face of a clock. It moves with short, nervous jerks. I bring time back; I try to watch the hand move.

Outside the frosted window, a ragged sentry paces back and forth. The clock tinkles out the half-hour.

I look at Charley, at Kenton. They are staring straight ahead. Neither of them has spoken since we left the guardhouse. I feel childish, light-headed, full of interest in the clock, in the shiny table, in the bits of lace at the officers' throats. I stare at a hatrack in one corner, all full to overflowing with cocked hats. One of them has a cock loose, and I wonder whose hat that is.

An orderly enters, bearing a pewter pot of water and some pewter cups. Everyone glances at him. He puts the stuff down on the table, salutes, and goes out.

It was fifteen minutes later on the clock when Washington came in. He came in wearing a long, loose blue cloak, his hat under his arm. The officers rose as he entered; he motioned them back to their seats. He went to the rack in the corner, perched his hat there, and began to unknot the collar of his cloak. Hamilton was next to him; he smiled a bit as Hamilton helped him off with his cloak. Hamilton whispered a few words, and the General nodded. Then he went to his seat at the table.

The presence of Washington seemed to fill the room—a tall man, broad, a big face. He appeared years older since that last time, when he spoke to us on the parade ground. His face had fallen in.

After he had seated himself, Hamilton went to the table and placed a sheaf of papers in front of the General. Washington thumbed through them, took out his glasses, then wiped them slowly and put them on. He read a little —then looked at us.

General Greene said: "Sir—it's damnably cold in here. If we're to get this business over with———"

"I'm aware of the cold, General," he said shortly.

He kept his eyes on us. We had risen when he came in; we were still standing. He studied us carefully; his eyes rested for a long time on our feet. When he spoke, his voice was very low:

"You are here before a military court of your superiors on charges of desertion and murder. If you are found guilty, you will be publicly hanged before the assembled brigades. I want you to understand the gravity of the charges and of the sentence that may be imposed upon you."

We nodded.

He turned to the officer who stood by the clock, and said:

"Read your charges, Colonel Mercer."

Mercer was a tall, bearded man, with small grey eyes. He walked over to the table and began to read:

"A charge brought forward by Captain John Muller, of the Fourteenth Pennsylvania Regiment, that on the night of February sixteenth, seventeen hundred and seventy-eight, three men deserted from his brigade. The names of these men are as follows: Charles Green, Kenton Brenner, and Allen Hale. That they willfully deserted is proven by the fact that they made their way out of the set boundaries of the encampment without reporting their action, taking with them full arms and ammunition, bayonets, and muskets, and being in uniform——"

Kenton laughed. His laugh was hoarse and loud, and he swayed back and forth. I gripped his arm.

Wayne rose, glaring at us. The General stared at us, his thin mouth set tightly. Hamilton rose and went to the table. "Your excellency," he said, "I beg you to ignore this. The men are half-starved, certainly not in uniform."

"We're none of us overfed," Washington said.

"Will you grant them the court's pardon?"

"A dozen lashes would cool that laugh," Conway said.

"Or a gibbet," Lord Stirling added.

The General nodded. He said to Mercer: "Go on."

"In the following order, they confessed the fact that they were deserters to Captain Allen McLane, Captain Kennedy, and Colonel Varnum."

To Hamilton, Washington said: "Have you anything to say, Mr. Hamilton?"

"Nothing."

"If you desire," Colonel Mercer said, "I can call any of the officers I have mentioned. They hold themselves at my disposal."

"That will not be necessary. Do you wish to call any witnesses, Mr. Hamilton?"

Hamilton shook his head.

To us: "Do you dispute the truth of these charges?"

We stood as we were. There was no heart in us to say anything.

"The prisoners will answer the court."

Kenton said, shrilly: "The muskets were ours

—mine from my father, and Allen's from his. We had no uniforms and we had no money to buy clothes for our backs or shoes for our feet. We were noways doing a wrong thing. There's no war, and we thought of the Valley land..." His voice died way.

Charley said: "He has no thought to offend these men, Mr. Hamilton."

Wayne said, coldly: "You will address your advocate as Colonel Hamilton."

We stand there, silent again. We feel helpless. We move our feet uneasily, glance down at the filthy wrappings that cover them.

Washington said: "Mr. Wayne, do you have anything to say in behalf of these men? They are in your command."

"Nothing."

Hamilton said: "Your excellencies, may I ask the court to extend its mercy?"

Washington tapped the top of the table with a quill. Greene was whispering something to him. He said a few words to Wayne, softly, and Wayne shook his head. Finally, Washington said:

"The court finds you guilty of desertion with arms. Out of respect to Mr. Hamilton's request, the court withholds a decision of desertion in face of the enemy. The court sentences you to twenty lashes each before the assembled brigades of the Pennsylvania Line."

Hamilton stepped forward and said: "I thank you for your leniency, sir."

We wait there, still not moving, the strain of standing so long on our feet beginning to tell on us. I glance at Kenton and Charley, and both their faces are set in masks. I wonder what my face is like. I touch my beard. I look at Kenton again. There is a certain dignity about him. His thin yellow beard juts out from his chin; his moustache droops. I say to myself, "He's seen twenty-five winters, only twenty-five." But he has become ageless, old; a marvellous mesh of little lines is etched about his eyes.

We wait, and I wonder what is meant by the first sentence. A sort of hope wells up inside of me. I have no fear of lashes, no fear of pain added to pain: only of a gibbet on Mount Joy, with the wolves leaping for my feet. I never felt life more, wanted life more than I do now, standing here.

They are talking among themselves, heatedly. Wayne rises, kicking back his chair. Across the table Colonel Conway stands facing him.

"I'll have no slurs on my men, sir!" Wayne says.

"I meant none."

Washington says, coldly: "Gentlemen, we are trying men for their lives." He says to Mercer: "Continue."

Mercer reads: "A charge brought by Captain Allen McLane of the First Continental Light Horse, that on the morning of February seventeenth, seventeen hundred and seventy-eight, returning from a foraging expedition, his party intercepted three deserters, who later gave their regiment as the Fourteenth Pennsylvania, and their names as follows: Allen Hale, Kenton Brenner and Charles Green; that these men were in uniform and under arms, and that they ignored repeated commands to halt for examination. That as they were about to be taken, they opened fire, killing one of Captain McLane's men, David Seely. That they were taken on the King of Prussia Road, a mile and a half north of the Schuylkill. That there was a fourth member of their party, a woman, shot and killed by the fire of the light horse."

When he had finished reading, he placed his papers on the table. The officers handed them round. Washington took no notice of the papers; he kept his eyes on us.

He said: "Mr. Hamilton, do you wish to deny any point in the charges?"

Hamilton answered: "I should like to question Captain McLane, sir. I should like to call at least two of Captain McLane's men, who were with him on the morning in question."

"The last will not be necessary. Colonel Mercer—will you have Mr. McLane in here?"

Hamilton said: "As a point of justice, your excellency, I ask the court that it summon two more men to testify along with Captain McLane."

"The court denies your request. Captain McLane's word is enough."

"Sir, I demand this. Captain McLane is prejudiced. Any cavalryman is against the foot."

"You forget yourself, Mr. Hamilton."

"I apologize. May these men be seated until the court calls them to speak?"

"They may."

"I thank the court."

We drop into the chairs gratefully. We stare at our feet. Then our eyes go to the window.

We sit there, men dumb as beasts, staring out the window.

I feel an awful resentment at the whole business—at the trial, at the mockery of their reading our charges, at the well-dressed, warm officers sitting at the table. Who are they? What have they to do with us? What of the weeks when we lay in the dugouts, like diseased animals? How is it that they materialize now, to take hold of our lives, to hang us, as murderers and thieves are hanged? I know that they will hang us; I have no doubt of that. Only to draw it out, to play with something called justice, to make an example.

We desert with arms; whose arms? We desert in uniform. I look at Kenton's uniform. His coat is cut from a blanket, sewed with strips of cloth, shredded all round the bottom. The blue skin of his knees shows through his breeches. His mittens are made of a piece of blanket. His neck is bound with a strip of our old regimental flag. But we desert in uniform.

McLane comes in. He never suffers for food, the dashing Captain McLane. His men plunder the British food trains, the produce that the Quaker farmers haul in to the Philadelphia market. They eat well and they eat first. He comes in with a brisk stride and salutes. He wears a hunting coat of grey felt with red facings. He wears high, polished kneeboots and doeskin breeches. He wears a cocked hat of grey kid.

He wears his sidearms, a sabre and a pistol, a bunched hand of lace where his coat opens. He walks up to the table, salutes and stands at attention. Hamilton has dropped into his chair by the window. He leans his elbow on the window-sill, and lazily rubs away the frost with his fingers. I watch, fascinated, as the scene outside comes into view—a sentry passing, a picket fence coming out of a mound of snow, two women picking their way along the road. Then Hamilton turns to us, watches us a moment, and smiles. His smile is reassurance. He's slight as a girl, but the story goes that he is fearless. He doesn't like McLane; the smile is casual contempt of McLane.

Washington glanced at McLane fondly. "You may be at ease, Mr. McLane," he said.

Hamilton rose, walked across the room slowly, staring at a few sheets of paper he held in his hands. He paid no attention to McLane. He walked across the room to the farther wall, and there he turned, resting against the wall. He never looked directly at McLane; his eyes were shaded by long, girlish lashes.

He said: "Mr. McLane, will you describe to the court the incidents that led up to your intercepting these men? Will you tell just how you happened to be returning along the King of Prussia Road at that hour? I believe it was early morning."

McLane said: "Your excellencies, I resent Colonel Hamilton's implication. I was in the line of my duty."

Hamilton: "There was no implication intended."

The court: "You will answer his questions, Mr. McLane."

McLane: "Your excellencies know the work I have done in providing forage for the army. Lately, I have had information that the Quakers are given to travelling at night. They form their produce wagons into trains, start out at sundown, and trust to reach the British outposts, near Philadelphia, before dawn. I make it my practice to range during the early hours of the morning. On the morning of February seventeenth, I was damnably unlucky. I was returning with forty horses along the road from Norristown, when I noticed four persons on foot, bearing arms. I rode forward to investigate, crying for them to halt and stay where they were. They ran across a field, but luckily were bogged in a drift of snow. My men rode them down, but at the last moment, when they saw that escape was cut off, they turned and deliberately fired into my men, killing a trooper."

Hamilton said: "Thank you, Mr. McLane." He walked over to us, turned his back on McLane, and asked softly: "The girl bore arms?"

"No, sir."

He walked back to the table, rested one hand upon it, and faced McLane. "Mr. McLane," he said, "you speak of four deserters. Were they all men?"

"No, sir. One was a woman."

"Then there were only three deserters. To my knowledge, there are no enlisted women in this army."

"Yes, sir—three men."

"And you spoke of four persons on foot, bearing arms. Did the woman bear arms?"

McLane seemed to hesitate.

"Mr. McLane, I call you to answer! Did the woman bear arms?"

"I don't recall."

"Mr. McLane, what is the weight of the average musket?"

The court: "Mr. Hamilton, will you keep to the point? You are not here to dramatize, but to help formation of a just decision."

Hamilton: "If the court will permit me to go ahead, I can prove this all to be to the point. Please answer my question, Mr. McLane."

McLane: "One stone—more or less."

"Or in pounds—fifteen, or twenty. Wouldn't you say a musket could easily weigh twenty pounds, Mr. McLane?"

"I don't make a practice of weighing muskets."

"But I do. Here is a woman, half-starved, weighing eighty or ninety pounds, and you don't know whether she was armed."

McLane said: "Your excellencies, I object to being baited this way by Colonel Hamilton. I am not on trial here."

"Then you'll admit the woman was not armed?" Hamilton asked.

"Your excellencies——"

"Answer Mr. Hamilton's question."

"The men were armed."

"And the woman wasn't. And the woman is dead, shot by your men. You omitted that from the story, Mr. McLane. Will you explain why you omitted that fact—why your men shot an unarmed woman who was certainly not a deserter?"

"We had no knowledge that she was a woman at the time. She was dressed as they were."

"But unarmed. How many of your men fired, Mr. McLane?"

"I don't know—a dozen perhaps."

"Did you give the command to fire?"

"I did. It was in the line of duty. They were armed men, resisting arrest."

"Yet the one shot that took effect brought down an unarmed woman. How do you account for that?"

"I can't account for the marksmanship of my men, and I see no reason why I have to. They were on horse, firing at moving figures——"

"Mr. McLane, you indicated that the man in your brigade whom these deserters killed was shot before you opened fire. You admit that when twelve moving men, on horse or on foot, fire at targets that are not stationary, one hit out of a dozen attempts is a reasonable score. You indicate that your return fire was given immediately after these deserters opened fire, and that at the time the deserters were moving. Let me make myself clear: three moving men fire at your brigade, and one of their shots takes effect. Does that suggest anything to you?"

"That General Wayne's men are better marksmen than mine? My men are cavalrymen, not marksmen."

"Or that your men fired, killed the woman— that the three men halted and fired from a stationary position."

The court: "Mr. Hamilton—you will not attempt to influence the court by conjecture."

Hamilton turned to McLane, said quietly: "Mr. McLane, who fired first, the deserters or your men?"

McLane said: "Your excellencies, do I have to answer that question?"

"You will answer."

"I gave the order to fire when I saw the men were about to escape in the forest."

"And who fired first?"

"My men."

"Yet you stated, Mr. McLane, that these three men returned your fire simply to resist capture. You said that they returned the fire when they saw their position was hopeless. Also, your implication was that they had fired first.

Deliberately, Mr. McLane, you portrayed these men in an act of treason and murder."

"Your excellencies, must I be baited like a common criminal?"

Washington said: "Mr. Hamilton, you have no right to ascribe intentions to Captain McLane. He is not on trial."

"But these three men are on trial for their lives."

Wayne said: "Your excellency, an act of treason reflects upon my command. I demand that it be substantiated."

Hamilton: "Mr. McLane, did these three men fire deliberately, when about to be taken, or was their action simply a burst of fury at the killing of the woman?"

"They killed one of my men. They were deserters."

Conway leaned across the table and said: "Colonel Hamilton, what are you driving at? We are not trying officers or gentlemen. We are trying three deserters. Look at them. You profane the name of soldier when you call them soldiers."

Wayne cried: "If Colonel Conway desires to indulge in personalities at the expense of my troops, he can answer to me. Whether or not these men are soldiers——"

"Gentlemen," Washington said coldly.

Wayne stood up, trembling, facing Conway. Washington said:

"Be seated, General Wayne. You forget yourself."

Hamilton said: "If Colonel Conway wishes to make any remarks, I'll answer them personally. There are five thousand men like these in camp, and if I can't address them as troops of the line, I'll resign my commission."

Washington's voice was like ice. He said: "Mr. Hamilton, you are not here to engage in personalities. If you are through, you have the court's permission to leave."

Hamilton stood there, biting his lips. For a moment, I thought he'd walk out. Then he said:

"I beg your pardon sir, humbly. I have no interest in these men. I was asked to take up their rights. That's my duty, I think."

Wayne said: "Your excellency, I add my voice to Mr. Hamilton's. I beg your pardon."

"Go ahead, Mr. Hamilton," Washington said shortly.

Hamilton said: "Mr. McLane, if your wife

were shot down and you had a loaded gun in your hand, and the man who committed the crime were before you, what action would you take?"

McLane stood in silence.

Washington said: "Captain McLane will not answer. If you can't confine yourself to facts, Mr. Hamilton, I'll dismiss the witness."

"But, your excellency, what are the facts? I have proven that Captain McLane's men fired first. These men could have escaped. Mr. McLane himself has admitted that they might have escaped. They saw this woman shot———"

Lord Stirling said, wearily: "Are you making out a common camp follower as someone to be compared to an officer's wife? If you are, sir, I am not the only person at this table who will take offence."

"Sir, I made no such comparison. If Lord Stirling wishes to pick a quarrel———"

"I shall not warn you again, Mr. Hamilton," Washington said shortly.

"I'm sorry, sir. I beg you to allow me to go on."

"Very well."

"Mr. McLane, did any of these deserters

show signs of sorrow at the death of the woman?"

"I believe one of them did."

"Would you describe his actions?"

"He tore loose from the men who were holding him and ran over to the woman."

"Could you say which one?"

"I couldn't."

"Would you look at those three men, Mr. McLane? Colonel Conway remarked that they profane the name of soldier. Obviously, they are half-starved, half-naked. They don't look strong enough to tear loose from two or three men. Only a fit of intense feeling could impel them to such strength. You would grant that the feeling was intense, Mr. McLane?"

"I don't know."

"But you must know. You saw it happen."

"Then I grant it."

"Thank you. That will be all, Mr. McLane."

"Have I the court's permission to go?" McLane asked.

Washington asked: "Do any of you gentlemen wish to question Mr. McLane." There was no answer. "You may go," he said.

McLane stalked out. Hamilton walked to the window, walked back slowly. The room was very silent. The ticking of the cloak sounded like a beating drum.

Washington said: "Have you any other witnesses, Mr. Hamilton?"

"Have I the court's permission to examine these men?" Hamilton asked, nodding at us.

"You have."

"Allen Hale," Hamilton said. I stood up. Kenton and Charley were looking at me curiously.

"Come forward," Mercer said.

I went up to the table.

"Your name is Allen Hale?"

"Yes, sir."

"Your regiment?"

"The Fourteenth Pennsylvania."

"Are you a Pennsylvania man?"

"No, sir. I was born in New York."

"Where?"

"The Mohawk Valley."

"And you lived there all your life?"

"There and in the Lake country."

"Where is the Lake country?"

"Westward, near the Finger Lakes. We call it the Valley land."

"How old are you?"

"Twenty-one."

"And when did you enlist in the army?"

"At the end of May, in seventeen seventy-five."

"You've served two and a half years. How long was your enlistment?"

"Three years——"

"And what made you desert, when there were only a few months left to serve?"

I shook my head; it felt heavy, clogged. As out of a dream at the dugout, to find myself standing here, the round table of officers, Hamilton watching me with violet eyes from under long lashes, playing a game.

"I thought I'd desert," I said.

"But why?"

"I thought to desert—I had no thought of living out the winter. I was fair in hell, and sick for the sight of the Valley country. I thought to go away. There were a good lot of men deserting, and talk went that there'd be no army in the spring."

"And you expected to reach the Mohawk Valley?"

I nodded.

Expressively, Hamilton looked at my feet, at the clothes I wore. He said:

"When you enlisted in the army, did you enlist in a Pennsylvania regiment?"

"No, sir. There were few Pennsylvania men outside of Boston. I enlisted in the Fourth New York Regiment."

"Where is that regiment?"

I answered: "Dead."

"You mean there's no one left of that regiment except yourself?"

"Five more men."

"Was there any desertion in the Fourth New York?"

"Some few men. The rest sickened or died in battle."

"I see. When you deserted, three men, why did you decide to take a woman with you? Did you think a woman could make the trip you were planning?"

"I had no thought that a woman could go the distance. She was noways a strong enough woman."

"Then why did you take her?"

"She pleaded to go along. She said she'd take her own life if I left her behind."

"Was she your wife?"

"She was no fit woman to be a man's wife," I said dully. "She was a woman of the camp."

"But she loved you enough to take her own life if you left her?"

"Yes."

"Now, on the morning when you were taken, where were you?"

"On the highroad to Norristown."

"And you saw Captain McLane's men. Did you recognize them immediately?"

"We knew they were part of the army from their number."

"What did you do then?"

"We made across a field—to run for the shelter of the forest."

"Were you together when you crossed the fields?"

"Bess fell, and I was helping her to rise. Charley and Kenton were a dozen paces beyond."

"Then they could have escaped?"

"They might, had they not waited."

"What happened then?"

"Some of the cavalrymen took the ground. They fired a volley at us. They had a bullet in Bess, and she fell from my hand——"

"Some of the cavalrymen dismounted before they fired? They took time to aim?"

"I don't know—they weren't much at shooting."

Hamilton smiled. Then his face sobered, deliberately. He said: "What did you do then?"

"When I saw Bess shot, I guess I went crazy. I guess I didn't care much about anything, and I let go with my gun. Kenton and Charley fired. I guess we were all crazy—thinking about going back."

"And when you fired, did you aim?"

"I reckon no. I shot as I held my musket, at my side. They did too."

"Your friends?"

"Yes."

"Thank you. That's all." I walked back to my chair, slumped into it. Kenton and Charley were sitting like stone figures, staring straight ahead of them, but looking at nothing. They didn't look at me.

Hamilton turned to the table. He said: "Your excellencies, there's nothing I can say more. These men are deserters; but they are not murderers; they did not commit treason. They fired in a fit of passion. Their crime was not premeditated or deliberate. I don't have to tell you what they suffer. God knows, you're aware of it. This is a winter of hell. We're quartered in stone houses; we eat and drink and sleep and wear decent clothes. But you've seen them crowded like beasts in their huts. You know."

Washington said: "Mr. Hamilton, we are not in a civil court. We are trying these men for a military offence. They opened fire in an act of mutiny, and killed a man."

"But their act was self-defence. By all the laws of humanity, they're innocent. They had been starving for weeks. They were half-insane."

"Nevertheless, they killed a man."

"Your excellencies, I am not the court. All I can do is to plead a case you have given me. But I know that in the place of these men, I would have done the same."

He walked to the window then, dropped into his chair, and stared out. The men at the table were talking in low tones. I heard Wayne say: "You're not dealing with soldiers, sir, but with beasts. No discipline. You'll touch off a powder keg."

"Then touch it off I will. If there's one man left, he'll be under my command."

Lord Stirling: "I'd have them drawn. I'd teach them a few of His Majesty's lessons."

"Sir, His Majesty is not commanding my army," Washington snapped.

Kenton and Charley both sat motionless, like men in a dream; they seemed to have no interest in the court-martial. They sat staring at nothing at all. I listened to the clock, watched the pendulum. I counted each movement. I felt drowsy, tired. I felt that I would like to sleep. Gradually, the room had become warmer. There was a rug on the floor. I thought of stretching out full-length on the rug and sleeping. I half-closed my eyes. The drone of voices was like bees humming.

Then the voice of Washington broke through: "Mr. Hamilton, will you inquire which of the three men killed McLane's trooper?"

Hamilton turned to us. Kenton lurched to his feet. He said hoarsely: "I did."

I heard Charley's voice, as from far off: "He's lying."

I found myself saying: "He's lying——"

I find myself crying: "What difference? You want to know who killed him? You made us into beasts! You made life a joke! There's no life in this place—only death, nothing but death! You don't bury us; you pile us in the snow, like logs of wood——" I find myself laughing, sitting there and laughing like an idiot.

Kenton's arm is around me, his voice whispering: "Easy, easy, Allen."

Charley says, clearly: "God damn you—you can all go to hell!"

I sit there, feeling away from them now, beyond any pain or power of theirs. They sit around the table like dolls, a little bewildered. Hamilton's face is drawn and twisted; he doesn't look like a boy any more.

"Take them out, Mr. Hamilton," Washington says, his voice cold, tired.

We stand up. Hamilton moves through the door with us. The guards form round us, and Hamilton leads us into the next room.

"Sit here," he says. "There's no need for you to stand. I'll go back, and maybe they'll let me talk some more. I don't know——" He takes a pipe out of his pocket, a small bag of tobacco, and drops them on the table. "You can smoke."

He goes out. We sit and look at each other. Charley says: "A fair lot of talk——"

"I'm afraid," I whisper. "Christ——"

"It's an awful bitter thing to hang," Kenton says. "I can't call to mind that I ever thought to hang. It's a bitter thing to be out there in the cold, hanging from a gibbet."

"It may be that we'll not hang."

"No. It's in their minds to hang us."

"That man Hamilton made a good plea for us. It's a wonder to me that he spoke so long for us."

"I'm thinking, he hates McLane."

"It was fair talking."

We stare at each other, keep staring, then abruptly turn our eyes away—anywhere. It seems to me that I can hear the clock ticking in the next room. I say:

"Strange to see a clock beating out the time."

The room we sit in is shadowed with twilight. Outside, the early winter night is beginning to fall. A low fire burns in the room. We look around curiously, at the fine furniture, at the rugs on the floor.

Kenton remarks: "They live well, these Quaker people."

I reach out toward the pipe. "He was meaning for us to smoke it," I say.

"I'm sick for food, not for smoking," Charley mutters.

"We could draw on the pipe a spell, pass the time."

"They'll sentence us."

"I'm thinking so."

I stuff the pipe with tobacco, go to the fire and draw a spark to it. The smoke makes me dizzy. I hand the pipe to Charley.

Charley looks at it and says: "Ely was a great one to be puffing on a pipe. Night and day, when we had tobacco, he had a pipe in his teeth. You recall?"

"It seems like years past."

"He could take a quiet enjoyment out of tobacco like no other man I've seen."

"He could."

"It's a strange thing that Ely should watch us die. I think back to how Ely watched me grow," Kenton says.

I say: "If we hang, Kenton, I'll be no man. I'll be sick with fear."

"It's a dreadful thing to hang."

We sit and we smoke. It grows darker in the room. The fire throws mottled shadows over us. We seem to tremble and waver in the firelight.

"God—I'm hungry," Charley whispers.

My throat is dry and numb. I think of drinking a glass of clear water.

"They ought to be through with their talk," I say nervously.

"They're making out to hang us."

"Christ, Kenton, leave be," Charley mutters.

Kenton has the pipe. He says, sadly: "I did a fool's thing to smash the other pipe. He was noways mocking at us, giving us the pipe."

We hear steps outside, and we turn to the door. Hamilton stands there, the guards behind him. "You'll come back with me now," he says tonelessly.

I think we know, all of us. We follow Hamilton back into the room where the court-martial is being held. There are some candles on the table. The faces behind the candles waver, change colour.

"Stand at attention," Mercer says.

Hamilton goes to the window. He stands there, back to the room, hands clasped behind his back. I see Washington's big face. It seems to me that the muscles are relaxed, that the compact coldness has given way to loose lines of pain. Wayne stares at the table. Greene looks over our heads. Lord Stirling bites his nails, his face vacuous. Conway has a sort of smile.

Mercer reads: "It is the decision of this court that Allen Hale, Kenton Brenner, and Charles Green be found guilty of high treason and murder. It is the decision of this court that they be paraded before the assembled brigades of the

Pennsylvania Line, drummed out of their regiment, be publicly stripped of arms and insignia, and then he hanged by the neck until dead."

Kenton laughs softly. Charley Green's hand grips my arm, fingers biting into my flesh. I cry out, in spite of myself, and then my throat chokes up and I can say nothing. The guards press out of the room. They stand round us while the officers file past.

Hamilton says: "God help us all for this. I'm sorry. You believe me?"

We can't answer. He goes, and we fall into step between the guards.

13

WE SIT in the guardroom at Fort Huntingdon. The room has no fire, no window. Four log walls and a flat roof. A space between the roof and the walls for currents of air. No lack of air. The cold of the night seeps in, the eternal, awful cold of this winter.

The commandant had a firebox brought in. He said: "You poor devils'll freeze tonight otherwise. No damned sense letting you freeze before you hang." The firebox is red-hot with glowing coals. It may hold its heat for three or four hours.

We sit round the box. Through a crack in the roof, we can see a bit of the sky, a narrow bit with a single star. I look at the star first, and then the others, and then we sit with our eyes fixed on that single star. We sit, and our dumb longing fills the place; senseless yearning in the cold of outer space.

"Tomorrow—" Kenton starts to say. Then his voice and his thoughts drift from him. Words are an effort for us now, each word a distinct and separate effort. We shiver; close to the box, its heat scorches our shins, leaves our backs cold. Kenton says:

"That was a great lot of talk——"

"I had in mind that we would go back northward," I say. "I had no thought in mind that we'd be taken. I had in mind that spring would come on us in our journeying."

"I had that in mind," Kenton agrees.

"I shouldn't have spoken up to them the way I did," Charley mutters. "I lost hold of my senses."

"It's no matter."

"I'm sick with the thought of going to the gallows. I call to mind that as a child my mother would warn me I was born to be hanged. As a way of joking."

"Your mother's living?" Kenton asks Charley.

"She's an old woman in Boston—if she's living. If she's dead, she'll curse me when I come off the gallows. She had no way with war. Christ, how she hated war! She took a stick to Sam Adams one time when he came to my house to leech me on a matter of printing. She took a stick and beat the dust out of his dirty back. He says, All right, my fine Tory. She answers, All right, my fine beggared bastard. Only keep off from my son and keep your dirty feet outa my house!"

Kenton laughs; he says slowly: "I'm not thinking there's aught after death—no matter for a man to fear, no matter of starving and freezing and whoring."

"I can't," I say. "I had no thought of dying. Now I tell myself, I'm twenty-one years, and I'm going into a great blackness."

Charley says, gently: "There's no matter of going alone, Allen. Look, boy, there's no matter at all of going alone. There's Kenton and me and a fair lot of good men all the way down."

I cover my face with my hands; I feel the chill in my heart. I feel a terror so awful that I want to scream and scream again.

When I look up, our faces glisten dully in the glow of the firebox. Kenton and Charley are regarding me strangely.

"You think I'm afraid—" I whisper.

They shake their heads. I put my face in my hands and stifle my sobs.

It might have been an hour or less after that that Hamilton came in. He stood by the door, wrapped in his blue greatcoat, his breath steaming in a red glow.

"I brought you some meat," he said, holding out a wooden bowl. Kenton took it. Kenton said:

"You made a fine plea for us. We're not ungrateful."

"I'm sorry," he said simply.

"We had no thought that we'd be made free by officers."

"You're not dead. The General said he'd speak with me tonight." He looked at us oddly. "One of you come along. He's no hard man, the General."

"Go along, Allen," Kenton said. Charley nodded. I shook my head.

"Better go," Kenton said gently.

I stood up, holding onto Kenton's shoulder. He stared at me, his thin face old and drawn, his beard ruddy in the light. Charley was nodding, whimsically.

Outside, the sentry stopped us. "I have orders to keep these men, Colonel Hamilton."

"I'll stand for him," Hamilton said. He had a curious way of speaking, as if he wasn't to be doubted. Then he walked on. I followed him, his orderly behind us.

At the door of the stone house, he told the orderly to wait. The sentries came to attention. He walked in, and Hamilton said to me:

"There's no need to fear him. He's a strange, hard man, but there's no need to fear him."

Hamilton tapped on the door of the same room that the court-martial had been held in. Then he went in. Washington was there alone, sitting at the table, writing. He didn't look up when we first came in. He was wrapped in a woollen jacket, a small cap on his head. There were a few candles on the table. I could see how slowly his hand moved writing.

"Who is it?" he asked.

"Colonel Hamilton."

"Come in, my boy. And close the door. There's a draught."

Hamilton said: "Thank you, your excellency." He closed the door softly. We stood there, in front of the door. I could see that Hamilton was nervous, biting his lips and staring down at his hands.

Washington was all intent on his writing, squinting through his spectacles. He looked like an old man in the jacket and the cap. The large spaces of his face were filled with shadows. Finally, he laid aside the quill and looked up, half a smile on his face. The smile went, and a sullen, rigid coldness replaced it.

"What is the meaning of this, Colonel Hamilton?" he demanded.

"I thought, your excellency———"

"By God, you go too far, Colonel Hamilton! What do you mean by bringing this man before me? Where is your authority?" He had risen from the table, his whole being rigid with sudden fury.

"I have none, sir."

"Then take him out of here!"

I moved to go, but Hamilton stood where he was. He had dropped his head. He spoke softly.

"I will, your excellency. I wish to resign my commission at the same time. I no longer have a place here."

I thought for a moment that Washington would hurl the table aside and fling himself on Hamilton. His rage was awful and terrible. Then, in a sudden, it collapsed, like a pricked bladder. He dropped back into his chair, limply, staring at us, his face old and tired. He leant his elbows on the table and put his face in his hands.

"Resign your commission?" he said, unbelievingly.

"I must."

His face was broken. I had never seen a face so broken all in an instant. He spread his hands hopelessly, murmured: "You too—I might have known. Stirling spreads his tales, and Conway plots, and Varnum mocks me, and Wayne is half-mad—and now you too. God, I'm alone. It's too much for me."

I didn't know whether he was acting; if he was acting, then he was a marvellous actor. His hands spread wide on the table, his mouth open just a bit, his eyes staring at Hamilton and unseeing at the same time, his face trembling, he whispered:

"Go on—get out—leave me alone. God knows, I'm alone. Always alone. You're no different. I thought you believed—but you're no different."

I glanced sidewise at Hamilton. His face was a reflection of the General's, pain and a deep sorrow in his half-veiled violet eyes. He stood stiffly, his hands a little in front of him.

"Get out," Washington said hoarsely.

Still Hamilton stood there, for moments; and then he stepped backward toward the door, slowly.

"Wait—" Washington had wilted; he was

an old, old man. He said, tonelessly: "Why are you resigning your commission? Why do you want to leave me?"

"I don't want to leave you, sir. Believe me, as sure as there is a God in heaven, I don't want to leave you, sir. After I leave you, there is no reason for me to live. Sir, I have no other reason to live than you and our cause."

A sort of hope in Washington's face, love and a groping toward Hamilton. He stretched out a hand.

"You won't leave me," he said.

"Sir, if one life is taken unjustly, if one man must die because of jealousy and hate, then a cause is already dishonoured. The cause exists no longer. Men can suffer for it no longer. It marks the limit of all suffering, all——"

Washington rose to his feet, crashing his hand down upon the table. The change in him was sudden and furious, like the change in a man gone suddenly mad. We recoiled from him. I felt suddenly that the room was too small for us. He wrenched out from behind the table, stood panting, cried:

"You talk of suffering! My God, you talk of suffering! What do you know? What have you suffered? Does anyone believe in me? Can I trust anyone? Do you know what it is to be alone—always alone, feared, hated? Whom do they come to? They come to me pleading, crying! Men are starving! Have you seen me touch food today? Do I sleep? Do I rest? Is there any peace for me, ever—until the day I die? Is there anything ahead of me but a rope and a gibbet in England? They talk about ambition, about King Washington. Christ!—don't deny it. I'm cold—I'm ice waiting for a throne! Look out of that window and you'll see my throne! Look out of that window and you'll see my throne in the ice on Mount Joy! Howe swore I'd hang there! Who'll be with me then? Whom can I trust? Can a man go on alone, always, endure——"

He stands there, a pitiful giant, used up with his own fury. His arms drop limply to his sides. His cap has fallen to the floor. He fumbles at his glasses, puts them on the table. He reaches for his chair, then walks across the room to the fire. Trembling, he tries to warm himself at the fire, seemingly unaware of the fact that we are still in the room. Hamilton murmurs:

"Sir—I'm sorry."

"We'll endure," he says quietly. "We'll endure." He has taken hold of himself. He walks back to the table and sits down. He says:

"I'm sorry, Colonel Hamilton. I owe you an apology. If you wish to resign, that is your affair. I can do nothing."

"You can, sir—only say you need me."

"God knows, I do."

"You'll hear me?"

"Go ahead, Colonel Hamilton."

"Sir, this man is condemned to death. You know that. He and two more deserters were condemned to hang for shooting one of Captain McLane's troopers. Sir, I didn't bring him here to mock at your decision; I brought him here to appeal to your mercy. I want you to see what war and suffering can do to a boy of twenty-one. I say that he has already atoned for his crime, that the others have atoned."

"There's no place for mercy in an army."

"But there's a place for justice."

"They confessed to the crime."

"But, your excellency, their act was an act of passion, of self-defence."

"I told you, Colonel Hamilton, that civil law cannot apply to an army in the field. The British hang deserters."

"But we're not the British."

"No—we're a rabble, a caricature of an army. But so long as one man is left, that man will be under my command. If he's naked and without arms, he'll still be under my command."

"Then one man can hang. One is enough. Only one of McLane's men died."

The General shakes his head slowly. He says: "Colonel Hamilton, the only justice I know is the justice I have kept an army together with for three years. We're in hell, and hell is not gentle."

"Sir, we are human beings in hell. Once we are not—then where is the use in going on?"

The candles are burning low. I stand there wearily, trying to keep from hope, trying to forget the pain in my feet. The General becomes a blur in the light of the candles. There is a long time of silence. He sits behind the candles, a bewildered man away from the world, unable to be part of the world, staring ahead of him and looking at nothing. Finally he says, uncertainly:

"I'm writing to the Congress for shoes, Colonel Hamilton. The Congress have shoes. They have a thousand pairs, but I can't plead humbly enough. I can't. You'll write it over for me, Colonel Hamilton?"

"I'll write it, sir."

He looks at me, stares at my feet, at my face. It seems that he is trying to break me apart from five thousand men. "Which one of you fired the shot?" he asks, not ungently.

I shake my head. "We don't know, sir," I say.

"Decide it." He turns to Hamilton. "Write an order for the release of two, Colonel. Have them flogged and sent back to their brigades."

Hamilton is unable to speak. He sits down at the table, takes up a quill, and begins to write. When he is through, he says hoarsely:

"You'll sign it, sir?"

Washington signs, drops the quill. He seems hardly able to hold up the weight of his head. Hamilton goes to the door. As he opens the door, Washington's voice stops him.

"You'll come back, Colonel? I can't sleep. If you come back, we'll talk a while."

"I'll come back, sir. I can't thank you now. I'll come back."

We go outside. Hamilton doesn't speak until he hands me over to one of the sentries, with orders to return to the fort. Then he says: "Try to know before morning. I wish it could have been different."

I want to speak. I'm choked inside. He gives me his hand, and I hold on to it. Then he goes back.

I walk across the snow with the sentry. The air is cold, sharp. I think of life. I feel the the bite of the air, the cold of the snow. I try to think of life, not that one of us must die. I think of going back to the dugout the way I would think of going home.

14

THEY keep staring at me, trying to make me out in the dark, and I don't know how to tell them. I stand at the door. I keep in the shadow.

Kenton says: "Come over and sit, Allen."

Keenly aware of the pain in my feet, I go to the firebox and sit down. Only the pain is life, more an evidence of life than of pain.

Kenton tells me: "We saved a part of the meat for you, Allen. It's good salt ham. I have it warming."

"I'm starved," I say. "I'm starved for some meat." I take the meat, eat it. Kenton hands me water to drink. There's more than enough meat for a man. It occurs to me that they ate little themselves, saving the bulk of the meat for me. They look at me while I eat, but they don't ask any questions.

"It's good meat," I sigh. "It's ripe salt ham."

Charley says: "They have a ham called Boston round; it melts like butter in your mouth."

"They have a hickory cure in the Mohawk——"

"I'll pledge Boston ham against backwoods pig. It makes me fair sick to hear a backwoods man talk like he knew the way of living. You take a grown man who can't write his own name, and he's no better than a red savage."

"Allen here has learning, and he's a backwoods boy for all that," Kenton says. "It's no matter of trouble to learn to read and write. Only I had a hatred for it."

Charley laughs. I finish eating, and put the bowl away. They look at me, still asking no questions. I wonder how they can sit that way, talk, laugh, as if there was no gibbet waiting. I'm afraid to tell them; I don't know how to tell them.

A red glow falls upon us out of the firebox, mottles us, burns in Kenton's beard. I touch my own beard nervously, short curly hair; I tangle my fingers in it.

Charley puts a hand on my arm, says gently: "We had no thought to joke with death, Allen, only to drive off fear."

"We shouldn't have sent you," Kenton says. "God damn them, can't they send us to a gibbet without playing with us?"

"It was Hamilton's thought to save us," I say. "He did what any man could do to save us. He made an honest strong plea to Washington."

"I can't abide a man so stone hard as Washington," Charley says.

"He's a hard man."

"I had no great hope when Allen went——"

"What came of it, Allen?"

I look at them.

"We're to die?"

I say, slowly: "We're to choose among ourselves for one. The other two go free with a flogging. But the one man dies on the gibbet."

They stare at me. "One man?"

"He said he would noway spare the three of us."

"One man," Charley whispers.

I can't stand their eyes; I shake my head, cry: "It was not my doing! You think I had no courage to die along with you!"

"We know, Allen," Kenton says. "We're grateful to you, Allen." His voice had a tone of complete relief in it; he smiled a little as he spoke, almost contentedly.

Charley asks, querulously: "How was it that

they came to spare two men? How was it that way, Allen?"

I try to tell them what happened in the room. I try to tell them how it came about. I find myself sobbing hoarsely.

"It's all right," Kenton says. "It's no matter to sob about, Allen."

"You're thinking it's me. You're thinking I had no thought to be the one. Only one of you. You're thinking I had no courage to stand up on a gibbet. I took a way out that was easy— I told them one of us would die for the other two. You're thinking that. Why are you looking at me like that?"

"Allen, Allen—be easy."

"I'm not fearing."

"Allen, we had no mind to give you pain."

"You're despising me."

"Allen, it's better two of us should live. It's a horrible bad thing for a man to die on the gallows. It's a dreadful thing to think about and dream about."

I say weakly: "Which one? Which man of us to die?"

We sit there for a moment, watching each other. Then Charley Green tears himself up, walks over to the door, and pounds his fists against it. He pounds until the door shakes under the impact, and then he leans against it, panting.

"You'll beat yer hands sore. Come away," Kenton begs him. "Come away, Charley."

"God damn them, are they playing with beasts? Are we no longer men, but beasts to be tortured?"

"Come away——"

Charley whispers: "I'm oldest. I'm a man of thirty years."

He turns round to face us. The coals in the box are almost gone—a dim glow. At the door, Charley is a black figure without form. I look at a black figure that is nothing of a man—a fear in form, groping for death, afraid and unafraid. I think of a man who joined our regiment in Boston, a fat, short man with printer's ink staining his fingers black. A small moustache and red cheeks. A black cocked hat and a black coat. Blue eyes. A man in a round happy form who became a butt for our jokes and contempt. A man fascinated by backwoodsmen who wore green hunting coats. He carried a musket with an ivory stock, a treasure of a musket, small, beautiful. He carried a silver snuffbox worked by Paul Revere. He wore lace cuffs. He tried to be a dandy, but he was more a troll than a dandy. I try to think of him that way, making such a figure out of the black mass at the door.

"I'm a man of thirty years," he says again. "I'm the oldest man of you all." Then he comes toward us, sinks down on the floor, and stares at the firebox. A small man, thin and bearded, filthy.

Kenton's voice is soft, curious, a world of curious wonder in his voice: "You'd go to a gibbet for us, wouldn't you, Charley? You'd have no fear to die for us?"

"I'd have a dreadful, awful fear to die on a gibbet," Charley says simply.

"You're a brave man," Kenton says.

"There's a way of being brave, and I'm noways brave. I'm thinking that if Ely were here, he would see no younger man die in his place."

"Ely is a strange creature—a creature out of fear."

A smile tries on Charley's face; a smile takes his mouth and moves it slowly. He reaches out and touches my hand. I'm afraid to look at him. He holds onto my hand. "A long way," he says. "A great length of marching. Christ, we're like brothers, all the three of us."

Kenton says: "I've no matter of fear any more. I'll be in company, good company. There're no men who've gone already to hold back from me with contempt, to say that a man dead on a gibbet is not a man for their company."

"We'll draw lots," I say desperately.

"We'll draw no lots."

"Why? I'm not afraid! I swear to God I'm not afraid. I'm not afraid——"

"It's no matter of fear, Allen," Kenton said gently. "I couldn't live and think you had died in my place. I couldn't go back to the Mohawk and say that Allen Hale, a boy of twenty-one years, had died on a gibbet so I could live."

"But I'd go back——"

"Allen, I shot the man. Allen, I swear a holy oath by God and Jesus that I shot the man. I aimed with my gun and killed deliberately. The sin is on my soul and the taking of blood was by my hands. Can there be any peace for me, if another suffers for my sin, Allen?"

"You're a liar," Charley whispered. "I stood by your side and you took no aim."

"Would I go to death with a lie?" Kenton asked.

Charley took a coin out of his pocket, a tarnished shilling. He turned it over and over. He said: "You're a strong man, Kenton. You're a rare man for loving and hating. We'll not argue."

"We'll not argue."

"The King's head is life for you."

"Agreed."

He threw up the coin, so that it would fall on the firebox, but Kenton caught it midway. He fingered it a moment, then tossed it over to one side of the room, where it fell in the dark. I sighed deeply. Kenton was smiling.

"You shouldn't have done that," Charley said.

"This tossing a coin for a life is play for children. If a man has it in his mind to die——"

"I can't let you."

Kenton said slowly, thoughtfully: "I made a scheme to desert and go northward. I said to myself, no other man'll pay for my scheming."

I couldn't stand any more of that. I put my face in my hands and sobbed. They didn't stop me. I went away from the firebox and threw myself down on the floor of the room.

Finally, Kenton came over to me. It might have been an hour afterwards, two hours. I don't know. The coals had about burnt out, and the firebox glowed dimly. Kenton knelt down by me and put an arm about my shoulders.

"Allen," he whispered.

I didn't answer.

"Allen, I'll have no fear. I swear that to you, Allen. I'll have no fear or shame or remorse to die on a gibbet."

"Leave me alone!" I cried.

He went on talking, his voice soft and easy: "Allen, a time ago, maybe twelve, thirteen years, you stood up to me and I beat you down. I had it over you by a foot of height, and you swore you would not forget the beating——"

I didn't move. Kenton was far away. I groped for him and held onto his arm. I saw a shadow move across the room; Charley Green came up to us, sat down.

"I had in mind to ask your forgiveness. I had in mind to give you my powder horn—for a thing to remember me by."

Then we sit together. There are no more words. We lie close for warmth.

15

KENTON says goodbye to us. A grey morning with big flakes of snow dropping slowly. Charley's face is all twisted up, and the tears wash the dirt from under his eyes. He won't look at Kenton. He stares at the floor, clenching and unclenching his hands, moving nervously, shivering.

The care is gone from Kenton's face. He puffs on Hamilton's long clay pipe, blowing clouds of blue smoke between us. Kenton says:

"If you're the only man to go back to the Mohawk, Allen—then they won't know I died on a gibbet?"

"They won't know——"

"Not for my shame, Allen: I think it no shame. But they might consider it a matter of shame."

I nod my head; I wipe my eyes and hold a hand over my mouth. We go out. Kenton stands in the centre of the room. He waves his hand.

Outside, Hamilton and the commandant of the fort are waiting. Hamilton avoids our eyes.

A guard of four men forms behind us, and a drummer goes in front. The drummer beats a slow roll. I see how the flakes of snow fall on the drum, splatter under the sticks. Charley plods along next to me, his feet dragging. I feel a wild, insane impulse to run back to Kenton, to stay with Kenton. I look at Charley, and see the same impulse in his eyes. He shakes his head. He keeps on shaking his head, dumbly.

We march up the Baptist Road, and then onto the Grand Parade over to the whipping posts. The snow is falling more heavily now. The men of the Pennsylvania brigades bulk like shadows out of the snow. They march along with their heads down and form into their lines.

They curse the snow and they curse us.

"Did you bastards have to pick a day like this?" they cry. "A hell of a thing to drag men out for!"

They stand round us, not too interested, knowing only the cold and the snow, shivering in the snow. They hold their muskets close to their bodies, their hands in their armpits for warmth. They bend their heads to break the force of the wind. They don't look like soldiers; they don't look like men. I try to find Ely, but there are too many bearded, ragged men. They all look the same, their identities lost in the swirl of snow.

The officers come riding up, close together, bent over on their horses. They ride up and down, beating the men into formation. Wayne sits on his horse, wrapped tight in his cloak; the snow gathers all over him, over his horse.

The drum beats up a crescendo. It dies, and the stillness is broken only by the muttering of the men. The parade stretches away, a plain of snow with walls of snow. A man's voice reciting: "——twenty lashes to be delivered on the bare back, in dishonour——" Charley is a little to the front of me, rigid. He shakes his head. Kenton is sitting in the guardroom, alone. Kenton deep in his loneliness. The drum again, slowly, a beggars' dance, a beggars' ball. I dance with Bess. They are a great company on the other side of the veil of snow, Bess with her husband. Is her love for me or for her husband? Like Kenton's love? The love of a man or the love of a woman?

They strip off our clothes. I stand very still. The fear of cold and pain is a monstrous lump, swelling my heart. The same fear that brought Kenton death. —If I were in Kenton's place?

I'm watching Charley. They peel off his rags. In Boston, Charley was a fat man. A round, fat man. Something to be laughed at by a regiment of backwoodsmen. Tall men in green hunting shirts come out of the Mohawk. My mother sews on the shirt, cloth she wove with her own hands, pleading with me not to go. The planting is done; come winter I'm back. The war will be over. The whole land will rise in arms, and then the war will be over. Four, five months, ten months.

They bare Charley's back; they bare my own. I tremble with the cold, and my skin crawls together. I feel that my blood is freezing.

"The whip will warm you———"

The bones stand out of Charley's flesh, bones with skin stretched tight over them. A winter's filth on the skin; but the snow will wash us. I clench my teeth and bite my lips. The snow melts on my skin; the wind on the wet surface is like knives cutting into me.

They bind us each to a post. Hands bound together and then tied to an iron ring at the top of the post. Charley is stretched like a drawn chicken. I feel an impulse to laugh. Kenton feared the cold; he stayed in the guardhouse.

I strain around to see the brigades. Warm in their clothes. Warm——

The first lash. Charley wilts. I feel a knife drawn over my skin. But no real pain; nothing to compare with the cold. The cold makes a wall round me that nothing can come through. Bess could lie up against me and warm me with her body. Bess is in the dugout—or dead. I could have Kenton's woman, because Kenton is good as dead. Back in the dugout, I'll have Kenton's woman to warm me.

Another—third, fourth: I stare in wonder at the red marks on Charley's back. Too cold for blood to flow.

Are there marks on my back, open spaces on the skin with red in between? The fourth lash brings a cry out of Charley. A low animal cry; his strapped hands wrench back and forth, spasmodically. The fifth lash brings blood flowing over the dirt. Blood to wash him—washed in the blood of lambs.

A sense of pain comes to me, pain out of the distance. The wall of cold around me has been broken. Pain with fire; heat and cold at once. The scream from between my lips comes from another, not from myself. I lose count of the lashes.

Maybe the eighth—or the tenth. Charley's back is no longer human flesh. If I see it clearly? I see a writhing figure; or I see nothing. We tried to desert—a long trip back to the Mohawk Valley. Three men plodding through the snow, and the fourth figure is Bess. A fair good walker for a woman. The strength in a woman is the strength of the earth. She clings to me, crying:

"What did we do? Allen, for the love of God, what did we do?"

I realize that it's Charley's voice, and I'm sane enough to hear and understand. I would tell him, a just punishment, meted out by officers sitting round a table. A big man with a big face talks about an army. Men in dugouts talk about Washington's purpose. He plays for big stakes. No other reason for it. He's put his head in a noose—because he's playing for big stakes. A kingdom, a wilderness stretching away for thousands of miles. Jacob knows, and Jacob has explained it to us again and again. Washington sits at the table in a nightcap. Does he love Hamilton? Who is Hamilton?— eyes like a woman.

The fifteenth lash—or more? Much more. They're giving us twenty or thirty. The pain is gone. A thudding hammer on my back and a cold pain in my lungs. But I stand on my feet. Charley hangs by his hands and feels the pain no more. He's at liberty. A word to make songs of. We're scared boys at Bunker Hill, and we try to strengthen ourselves by saying liberty. Always liberty. The British march up, rank upon rank of scarlet-clad men, the drummers beating a mocking parody of Yankee-Doodle. Yankee-Doodle went to London, riding on a pony. They keep on marching. A bugle pipes up the tune of "Hot Stuff." The officers flash swords in the sunlight. I'll throw down my musket and run away—to Boston, hide in Charley's house. Old Putnam says, Fire and give the red bastards hell. Then we're at liberty —free.

A crisp voice says: "Twenty—cut them down."

Charley first. He falls in the snow, a little mound of human flesh, all cut up and bleeding. He falls there and he doesn't move. But I stand up. Oh, dear God—the strength of me! I stand on my feet. I move my arms and spread them apart. Kenton, look at me, cut and bleeding and standing on my feet, the guts inside of me freezing!

"Brigades—at ease!"

I keep moving my arms.

"Brigades—march!"

I move over to Charley, step by step, until I am right above him. The snow is stained with blood.

"Charley——"

He doesn't move.

"Charley—we've done our punishment. Get up!"

"Charley—get up!"

I say: "Oh—Jesus Christ."

I see Ely walking toward me. Ely is an old man. He walks toward me, and more pain than I ever knew is on his face.

I turn to him. "Ely——"

He begins to clothe me. He picks up my rags, bit by bit, and forces me to get into them.

"I'm noways cold, Ely."

He helps me into my coat. Then he goes to Charley. I don't follow him, only stand where I am, looking round curiously. Some of the men have stopped, and they're watching us. The officers force them on; it doesn't matter a damn if deserters die in the snow. An officer spurs over to Ely. Ely glances up at him, and whatever the officer might have said is left in his throat. I walk to Ely.

"We'll help him back," Ely says.

Charley looks at me and tries to smile. I take hold of one of his arms, Ely the other, and we help him to his feet.

"I should have stayed—not Kenton," Charley whispers. "I'm no man to live out of this."

It was an endless distance to the dugout. We walked slowly. Ahead of us, the brigades disappeared into the wall of falling snow. We plodded on, and always there was more of the grey snow wall ahead of us.

We have to carry Charley. He's a limp thing in our hands. Every few feet we stop to rest.

"I'm sore afraid he'll die of the cold," Ely says.

We climbed the hill. There were some Pennsylvania men there, and they helped us along. They looked at me with wonder. Indeed, it was a wonderful thing that I could still move and talk.

"It's a rare man who could stand a flogging and walk afterwards," one of them said admiringly.

"A rare strong man."

"A freezing bitter day for a flogging. It's a wonder."

They carry Charley into the dugout, lay him in one of the bunks. Ely enters and I come in behind him. I was never gone. I see Jacob standing in one corner, avoiding my eyes. The two women are still there, Smith sitting limply on a bunk, his face a haggard mask from the scurvy. Henry Lane is gone—dead, I suppose.

A Pennsylvania man says: "The blond lad who brought in the deer, where is he?"

I begin to laugh. I am cold suddenly. I stumble over to the fire and huddle close to it. In front I am cold, but my back is burning with pain.

"Where is Kenton?" a woman asks.

I crawl into one of the bunks, put my face in my hands and cry bitterly. Ely approaches me, bends over me.

"Allen—I'll go get the doctor."

"It's no matter."

"I'll go get him."

I move from side to side, trying to ease the pain. I kick at the wooden bed until my toes are bruised and hurt. One of the women brings me a cup of water.

"Here—drink."

I drain it down. I try to sleep, to forget myself, but there's no escaping the pain. I whisper: "Ely—Ely."

"He's gone out, boy."

"Jacob——"

I look up, and Jacob is standing where he was when I entered the dugout.

"Jacob—we've suffered enough to ease your hate for us."

He doesn't move, and his face doesn't change.

"Only forgive me, Jacob. Kenton's to die."

"We're a people at war. A just punishment——"

I groan. I put my face in my hands and sob bitterly.

A long time passed then, or perhaps only a short time made long by pain. Ely came back with the doctor. I must have slept, because they were taking off my clothes when I knew things again. The doctor was saying:

"Civilized—here's their civilization. Here's what they fight wars for. Look at that back."

"They were deserters," Jacob said.

"Deserters? Would any sane man remain in this place? Are any of us sane? Eight hundred men in my hospital, piled up like meat in a butcher's. Naked, frozen, starving. I cut off arms and legs. I'm no doctor; I'm a butcher, a barber, a leech. There are no doctors. False— it's all false, a rotten fabric of lies. I know nothing, nothing. I bleed them. I cut off frozen limbs. And they die—they die like ants. What's your cause worth when men die like ants—like savage beasts—? I'm no better than the rest. We're living in a world of ignorance. Let them die. I don't try to save them. It's better if they die."

He washed my back with warm water, rubbed some sort of fatty paste into it.

"He'll be all right?" Ely asked anxiously.

"This one's strong. By God, it's amazing what a strong man will stand. I don't know about the other. Let me have a look at him."

I twisted my head and watched them go over to Charley. The doctor worked with strong, sure hands. Only his hands were the same. The rest of him had changed. He seemed older than when I saw him before, not so clean. Nor was he shaven.

"He'll be all right?"

"How do I know? You expect me to be God, to give life. Well, I don't know. Doctors are fakes. None of us know anything. And it doesn't matter. There's plenty of room in mother earth—plenty of room for all. Don't give him anything but broth. He has a fever."

"Thank you——" Ely said,

"Don't thank me. This does me good. I'm learning. I'm learning the secret of man. Pain—pain. Eight hundred men in a log cabin. I go back there, and they want me to be God. Christ, I'm sick and tired of the lot of you."

Then he went out, and I called Ely over to me.

"Don't fret now, Allen," he said. "Try to sleep."

"I have to tell you, Ely."

"Tell me later."

"No—now. Of Kenton. They said they'd spare two of us, but that one man should die for the shooting of McLane's trooper. Kenton would have himself the man." I grasped Ely's coat. "I was afraid. It was my doing, my bringing the girl along that got us taken."

Ely looked at me oddly; then he shook his head. "If Kenton wanted it. A man's life is his own."

"Kenton had a fear of the gallows—a bitter, awful fear. He was in no way wanting to die on a gibbet."

"Ye're hurt enough, Allen."

"No——"

"Sleep now."

"No—when the brigades march out to see Kenton hanged, I must be there. I want you to swear to it, Ely, that you'll wake me to be there."

"I'll wake you, Allen."

"You've no hatred of me, Ely?"

"No hatred, Allen."

"When the brigades march——"

I slip away—a long way down into darkness. Sleeping and waking. When the brigades march—to dishonour a man.

A long way back, a surging backwards and forwards, and Bess lives and dies. Bess comes and drifts away. She whispers the secret of her death. Why did I die, Allen? Why did I die? Fair, beautiful men die. Why do men die, oh Allen? What is the making of this war? For the poor to drive out the rich, for the rich to crush the poor—for a freedom that makes no man free? What is the making of war, Allen?

She goes and I wake and I see the fire burning; and Jacob feeding logs onto the fire. Jacob is a man with dreams, but men with dreams lose all semblance of humanity. What kind of dreams has George Washington—dreams of a throne? I try to see the big, hurt face underneath a crown. No dream of a throne. A man groping. Jacob wants the wilderness; he's a wilderness seeker. A new land out of a wilderness. A man with one purpose: drive out the British. Men may die; nothing matters so long as the purpose is left. Drive out the last Englishman. Take the wilderness for ourselves. Drive women into the forest to be killed by savages. Women like Bess. All women like her.

I drift into sleep again, dreaming that Bess is with me: but this time I know she's beyond the veil of death. With the others who died, with the great company who know why we fight, why we struggle, and what will come of our fighting and struggling. She asks me no questions. She's thinking of Kenton. Kenton wakes. One more to a company of men who have gone.

A dream of pirates, of Massachusetts men who made a war so that their ships could rule the seas. Virginian planters who would get better than English prices. Fur traders who would break the great English companies. Only why are we here, farmers, dying and becoming beasts? What have we to do with all that? We were farming men, and we would live in peace so long as we could turn the soil and bring food forth from the ground. What had the Jew to do with it?

I sleep, a troubled, feverish sleep. A sleep broken by the faces of living men and dead men——

The brigades marched out the next day. They marched out to see Kenton hanged. The snow had stopped. A blanket of snow, two feet deep in some places, lay all over the ground. The sun glistened from the snow, made the highlands a place of bizarre, incredible beauty. On every side, away from our encampment, the countryside rolled, a white sheet spread on hills.

The order came to assemble for parade. We knew what it meant. Charley Green lay in his bunk, the pain of a feverish man in his eyes. When I went over to him, he said to me:

"You'll go out on parade, Allen. You'll watch him and honour him."

"I'll honour him."

"He was not meaning to humble you, Allen. He did it out of love."

"I know," thinking only that I hadn't guts enough to die for another.

"I'm thinking it should have been me. Allen,

and that I'll never rise out of this bed. Kenton would have lived. Kenton is a strong man. He would have endured the whipping and lived."

"You'll be better, Charley."

"Try to look into his eyes, if they leave them bare."

"Yes—I'll look into his eyes."

I went out of the dugout slowly. It was still an agony of pain for me to move. My back felt like flesh pressed against hot iron bars. Ely begged me not to go.

"It's no sight to see, Allen. They'll not expect a man who was flogged to get out of his bed."

"I'll have no peace unless I go."

We formed for parade on the road, the pitiful remnant of the Pennsylvania Line. There were some eight or nine hundred of us left, poor, tattered wretches. Wayne's pride. The pick of the army. We bent under the weight of our muskets. We dragged our feet through the snow. We blinked like owls at the light that flashed from the polished surface.

The drums beat out their monotonous roll. Wayne rode a nag with ribs prodding out, a half-starved, broken horse. Most of the officers walked. Their horses were dying from lack of fodder.

Ely and Jacob walked in my rank, Jacob still wrapped in the same stony silence as before. Ely bore the weight of my musket.

We marched down into the valley, past the hospital. The doctor was standing on the steps, watching us, a curious, sardonic smile on his face. We turned up and were drawn into ranks near the fort. On the slope of Mount Joy, a gibbet had been constructed. Kenton stood before the gibbet, a guard of four men round him. He was bareheaded, his yellow hair like gold in the sunlight.

I was weak and sick from the marching. Once I had looked at Kenton, I could not take my eyes away. Yet I felt that I would collapse in the snow if I watched the thing.

I whispered to Ely: "He's not guilty. The three of us shot in a passion. There's no knowing who killed McLane's man."

"God help him," Jacob muttered.

"He'll not be fearing God," I said.

The brigades were sympathetic towards Kenton. No one of us had any love for McLane's raiders. They foraged food, but we saw little enough of it. The brigades were muttering and talking among themselves. They remembered the time Kenton had slain the two deer.

I thought of myself up there with Kenton, three gibbets instead of one. What sort of fear was in Kenton's heart? How could he stand like that—and bear it?

I thought he was looking at me. Then I realized that the sun in his eyes would show him only dark figures of men coming out of the glare on the snow.

I thought of Charley, who would have died instead. Only I was always outside of it. Never had it occurred to either of them that I should be the one to die. I had known it. The moment Washington agreed to Hamilton's request, I had known that it would not be I; I had known that I would live.

I thought of how there had been no word of hate out of Kenton's mouth, no word of resentment, only regret for something he had done to me when we were both children, something I had forgotten already. I thought of the Kenton I had always known; this man——

"He's godlike," I said to Ely.

Ely was crying, unashamed. It was the first time I had ever seen tears in Ely's eyes.

The brigades were muttering with resentment. "Let him live—he's a fair good man—he's guilty of no crime——"

Muller walked up to Kenton, tore a piece of cloth from his ragged coat, turned on his heel and walked away. The act signified the defacing of a uniform. But Kenton wore no uniform. There had never been a uniform for any man in the Continental army. The uniform business was a conceit of the Congress and the officers. Now, for the first time, I took a pride in our rags, a great pride in the fact that we were men together, no soldiers, only men in our own right—beggars with guns.

Watching Kenton, watching Muller striding away smugly, watching the men on either side of me, I had a picture of the revolution as coming from us, part of us, part of the awful resentment against forces that destroyed man's pride in himself. Part of men born into a new world.

It rose like the growl from the brigades, a growl of dumb fury and hate. I wonder whether Muller saw it—saw a new world in us, a world groping blindly to find itself. Kenton saw it; I swear to God that Kenton saw it. I swear to God that Kenton died with that vision in his eyes.

I cried to Ely: "He'll not hang! We'll take him back!"

A moment the brigades surged forward, a moment during which Wayne's ringing voice shouted:

"Brigades attention!"

We fell back, men in arms and in rank. We fell back into the years of war that stretched before us, how many years no man there knew.

They stood him on the scaffold. When they wanted to blindfold him, he shook his head. He stood bareheaded, the rope around his neck, his hair golden with sunlight. Then they shot the trap, and Kenton died.

There was a great sigh from the brigades. Men slumped visibly. Men stood with their heads hanging over, holding their muskets limply.

"He's dead," I whispered.

The drums beat out into the morning air. The brigades began to move. Wayne had become a figure of stone; he rode ahead and looked at no man.

Jacob's face was grey, his eyes black hollows.

I said: "You bear him no hate, Jacob. Leave the hate for me. Hate me, Jacob—but not Kenton."

"I bear him no hate———"

Ely muttered: "The love of a man who gives his life for a man———"

We marched back to the dugouts. I went in, and Charley Green was waiting for me, his face flushed hot.

"Kenton's dead," I told him.

"How?—he wasn't afraid?"

"No. He was smiling."

Charley cried. He lay with his face in his hands, crying bitterly. I went to the fire, sat down close to the flames, and stared into them. I tried to get back what I had seen when Kenton went to the scaffold.

16

I shake my head. The hand I hold the cup of water with trembles, spilling some of it. My hand is a frame of bone with yellow skin stretched over it.

"I've seen a lot of fever," Ely says. "It comes, goes, and leaves you weak. It leaves strange thoughts."

"How many days have I been here, Ely?"

"Six days——"

I consider it thoughtfully—six days. Six days without food. Yet I'm alive. I say:

"Have you ever thought, Ely, about a man's lot after he's died?"

Ely shook his head. "I'm no religious man, Allen. It's a thing for preachers."

"Kenton died for me. He'll hold no hate for me?"

"I'm not thinking he'll hold any hate."

"You'll stay by me, Ely?—When I go, you'll hold me, Ely? I'm afraid."

"I'll stay by you, Allen."

"You're a great, good man, Ely. You're the best man I've ever known."

Ely shakes his head. He wets a rag, wipes my face with it. He covers me. He sits by me, washing the heat from my face.

I relapse into a stupor. The cold and heat alternate again. The fire in the dugout fills all the space taken by my eyes, a roaring blaze of fire that consumes me. I cry for Bess. I wake, sweating, and reach out desperately for her. The days and nights blend into the even smoke-filled grey of the dugout. The dugout is eternal; and we are men doomed to it.

The doctor comes once more. The fever has broken itself, and I lie in bed, weak as a baby. Charley is sitting up already, a thin, wasted figure.

The doctor is different, red-eyed, a straggling beard over his chin, thinner. His smock is dirty with blood. His voice has lost its sharp bite. He comes into the dugout, and Jacob helps him out of his coat. He shakes his head.

"I'll climb that damned hill no more. Doctor's no good here. Let me rest."

He sits down by the fire and stretches his legs. He glances at Charley, then at me.

"Both of you sane again," he says. "I wouldn't have thought it."

Charley laughs. "They'll not pile me in the snow."

"Give them time. I've a thousand men in my hospital. Do you believe me? A thousand men in that shack—a full thousand men between the four walls. No room to walk, and it doesn't matter if you walk on top of them. There's no hell hereafter. Hell's here. Hell's in my hospital. A thousand men and no one of them will walk out of the place. Better that they don't. It's not a thing to remember. But the women live. God knows how, but they live and hold on. They won't put the women into hell with the women. But the women live. Look at those two."

Mary says: "You'll not drag me into your charnel house. You're an evil man."

"Am I? You'd both make a fortune in Philadelphia whoring for the British."

"You're a bad man."

"I'll have a look at those two now. Thought they'd be dead and spare me the trouble."

He examines us wearily, shakes his head.

Jacob says: "You've news? We march soon?"

"You'll live—it's a wonder."

"March? Where? How? There's no army left—maybe a thousand men with the strength to walk out of this place. Maybe less. Three thousand deserted. Maybe half the Maryland line, two New York regiments, a Massachusetts regiment. God only knows how many dead. I've cleared a hundred bodies out of my hospital in one day. I can't stand much more. Drives a man mad. I spoke to Washington—a stubborn, ox-like man. I told him, There'll be no man alive in this encampment, come spring. No one man living. You're sitting in a valley of the dead. He said, Doctor, I'll be alive. I asked for medicine—bandages. I said to him, Here's a fair rich country of two million people. A Congress sitting. What the hell is the Congress sitting for? I don't know, he said. They give us nothing. They complain I demand too much. Then he cried like a baby. I said, Your excellency, I've seen a sight of tears—they won't bring us food. He said, I know—I know."

Jacob shook his head. "No—you're lying."

"I'm lying. Look at me. I don't give two damns for your suffering here. I don't give two damns for your cause. I'm no patriot. I'm a doctor. In the beginning I took it. I said, let them be damned. I'll do my leeching, and I'll learn. Maybe I'll help a poor damned soul. Well, I'm broken."

Jacob said, plaintively: "We can't go back—there's no going back now."

"Why not? General Howe would take his surrender."

Ely said: "If it's like you say, why don't the English attack and make an end of it?"

"They're noways discontented in Philadelphia. Why should they waste a man? Two months more—there'll be no army for them to attack. They'll win the war by sitting on their behinds in Philadelphia and begetting children on the good Philadelphia women."

"There'll be men to fight," Jacob muttered.

"Dead men."

Then he went out. We heard, a few days later, that he had shot himself. A Pennsylvania man, back from the hospital, brought us the news. He said: "The little doctor's dead now."

I remember how we stared at him, shook our heads.

"Blew his head open with a pistol."

Jacob whispered: "He would not do that. He was a good, strong man."

"Well, he's dead. There's no doctor left to care for Pennsylvania men."

After that, we sat around the fire. Each of us was afraid to speak.

Finally, I asked Ely: "What now?"

"I don't know," Ely said.

Jacob takes his musket and goes out for relief sentry. But his steps are slow. Charley Green crawls back into bed, his woman with him. She has taken him back as naturally as if he had never gone. Kenton's woman is looking at me. She smiles.

Ely bends over and begins to unbandage his feet. I go to my bed, and Kenton's woman follows me. It doesn't matter—Kenton is dead. Bess is dead.

A long time later—and Ely still sits by the fire. What does he think? Ely Jackson is a farmer man out of the Mohawk Valley. A simple farmer man; there's no great depth to Ely. What drives him?

I turn over—back to the woman, and try to think that she is Bess. I am getting a strange answer to my longing for Bess. More and more often, she will come back to me. I feel her growing inside of me, becoming a woman. I think of the boy Allen who took the woman from the Virginians. That was long ago. She was no fit woman to be a man's wife. She was a camp follower, and a prize for any man who was strong enough to take her. She was a prize for me. She was a rare, good prize, a slim girl with a body to keep a man warm at night. I took from her, and she wanted nothing, and finally, she died.

I lie with Kenton's woman, and I feel a curious grace from Kenton over me. I would have hated the woman, but I don't hate her now. Somehow, hate has gone out of us.

We heal slowly, Charley and I. At first, Kenton's death hangs over us. I can't get out of my mind the picture of Kenton as he stood in the sunlight, in front of the scaffold, Kenton with his bare head golden in the sunlight. I am as close to Charley Green as one man can be to another.

Finally, I speak of Kenton. I tell Charley how he died, word by word. I watch Charley cry, unashamed. It is a curious thing how strong men come to find a relief in tears.

One day, I go to my musket. A man from the Rhode Island brigades brought back our muskets, Kenton's and Charley's and mine. I clean it carefully and rub off the rust with sand.

I go out on sentry duty. We must fill a quota from our dugout, and it is too much for Jacob and Ely to do alone. I go out on a cold, clear night, when there is a new moon in the sky. I walk slowly, thinking how many times before I've walked this same beat, looking over the snow-covered meadows and hills.

When I meet the Pennsylvania man whose beat intercepts mine, we stand together for a while, talk a little. I have no hate left for Pennsylvania men.

"A cold night," he says.

"The back of the winter's broken, I think."

"It's noways different with the cold."

We stand and listen to the wolves howling. There are more wolves than ever near the camp now.

"I can't call to mind such a lot of wolves in farm country."

"They come after the dead. It's said a wolf in winter can scent meat on twenty miles of wind."

I think of the German boy. I glance down the slope, and in my mind's eye, I can see him crawling up, falling in the snow, stumbling to his feet and crawling on again. A German boy thinking of his home in the Pennsylvania highlands. We are a strange lot, Dutch and German, and Puritan men from the seaboard, and Jews from overseas in Poland, and men from the southland, Scotch and Irish and Swedes, men from the Valley country in the north, black slaves from the Virginias.

I spoke to Ely and Jacob the next night. Jacob had come back from the commissariat with a little rum. We had a gruel of cornmeal. We sat around the fire, eating. Some Pennsylvania men had come in to ask news and to have a little talk.

I said to Ely: "It seemed to me that Kenton knew something when he died——"

"How was that?"

"He was noways afraid."

"He was a strong man," Charley said.

"Not only strength. Why do we go on, Ely? We're not paid. They starve us. We're sick for sight of our homeland."

"We'll be free men," Ely said.

"There's nowhere free men in Europe."

"There'll be free men here," Jacob muttered.

"But we can't win the war. It's said the British have twenty thousand men in Philadelphia. A thousand men can't fight twenty thousand——"

A Pennsylvania man said: "There's a wilderness road over the mountains into the land of Kentuck. It's said that Washington has sworn to take that road before he lays down his command. Beyond the mountains, he can fight on for years."

"For years?" we asked incredulously.

"For years," Jacob muttered, almost to himself. "For years."

"I'm sore tired," I said.

For two days, there is no food, a roaring cold wind out of the north. No sunlight. A sleet that forms a coat of ice over the ground. We crouch in our dugouts, staring about like trapped animals. We eat the leather straps from our muskets, boiling them for hours in water. We tear cloth into fine bits, cook it and eat it. Bark from the trees. The few trees left in the forest are stripped bare of their bark.

We fly into rages easily. A word from Charley has Jacob at his throat. Ely and I tear them apart, while the women fill the dugout with their screams. Charley is weak as a baby. His woman has left him. He's too sick to satisfy her. She goes to Pennsylvania men in other dugouts, and Charley demands her back. She comes into the dugout, and they spit at each other like a pair of cats.

"Let the woman decide," Ely says.

She says: "Ye're no men for a woman to want—filthy, rotten beggars."

"You'll come to one of us——"

"As I please. I'm a free woman."

"A dirty slut."

"You don't call me a slut. I was a good woman once. I had no wish to be dragged around by a rotten rebel army."

Finally, she goes back to the Pennsylvanians. Charley lies in his bunk, sobbing weakly. I offer him my woman, Kenton's.

"No, no—keep her, Allen."

I fall into an insane temper of rage. I threaten the Pennsylvania men. I tell Charley that when my strength comes back, I'll kill them, every one that's had his woman.

Ely cries: "By God—we're no strangers! We're men together through hell. We're no men to be at each other's throats."

Ely keeps the fire going. Ely cuts wood in the forest, goes out into the sleet by himself. Ely nurses us the way he'd nurse children. He humors us . . .

He sits at night, and tries to bear the pain in his feet. He no longer uncovers his feet.

A parade is called on the day of March seventh. The troops crawl out of their dugouts. The brigades assemble. Less men than ever. We march out to hear a message from the Congress read.

Rumours go about. A rumour that we retreat southward.

"They're going to break camp."

"It's over now———"

"A British attack, and we're to defend the forts on Mount Joy."

"Congress would know nothing of a British attack. Congress knows nothing of anything. God damn their souls———"

We stand shivering, waiting. At last, Wayne rides up with his staff. He dismounts and walks up and down our line. He says: "Attention, brigades."

We try to form ourselves erect. He shakes his head, and walks back to his horse slowly. He stands there, looking over the grey hills in the direction of Philadelphia.

A young officer comes forward to read the message. We stand tense, waiting. He reads:

"From the Continental Congress to the

Army of the Republic: In recognition of the men's courage in bearing their privations, we hereby appoint a day of fasting and prayer———"

We laughed. By God, we had not laughed like that in days and weeks. We laughed until we were trembling and weak. Then we turned round and marched back.

I remember how Wayne had not moved through all the reading. He mounted his horse slowly, like an old man, and rode down the hill to his quarters.

PART THREE
THE BATTLE

17

It has been raining all morning. We sit in the dugout and try to understand that rain is falling—not snow but rain. The fire burns low, but we put no wood on it. The dugout is warm. The rain on the roof is like a corps of drummers beating out a roll.

Mary cries. She sits on the edge of a bed, sobbing, her lean figure swaying back and forth.

Curiously, Ely asks: "You've a sorrow, Mary?"

"No——"

"Then why are you weeping?"

"The rain—do you hear? I thought the world was lost in the cold."

"It's rain——"

"Rain," Jacob says, nodding, "rain out of the sky—a beautiful, fair rain."

Anna lies in my bed, her head swaying a little to the beat of the raindrops. Near the bed, the roof is leaking. She holds out a skinny hand and lets the drops splash off it. "I mind," she whispers, "how it was when I was a girl.

We clung to the kitchen in the rain. It was a special day for kitchen work. Baking and sewing and weaving cloth. If I had a loom, I'd weave out a fine cloth to make coats."

I go to the door and open it. Trees are like shadows. Clouds hang low to the earth, and the rain pours out in a great downpour, each drop biting a hole in the snow. Already, the snow is giving away.

When I turn back, I can hardly speak. I say: "Ely, what day is this?"

"A day in March—I can't think of the exact day."

Jacob said: "I call to mind how the Jew spoke of the spring coming. He had no sight of the spring in this country."

I whisper: "We're alive—Charley, me, you —we're alive to see the rains."

"A fair land in spring."

"But we're alive. We're talking, moving."

Ely nods. He walks around aimlessly, touching the rough frames of the beds, reaching up and touching the leaks in the ceiling. He sits down by the fire.

Jacob goes over to him, says gently: "You're disturbed, Ely?"

"I'm noways disturbed. I'm thinking."

"We'll go back to the Mohawk some day, Ely—a free land for people to live in, a green, beautiful land."

"We'll go back," but with no faith in his voice.

I go to the door again. I'm like a child. I cry: "Ely—Ely, the snow melts!" I take my bayonet, stand out in the rain and dig through to the ground.

I come back into the dugout, dripping.

"You'll take cold," Ely says. "Don't be a fool, Allen."

Charley whispers: "You were digging in the ground, Allen. It's not soft so quickly."

"We'll bury them," I say. "They'll lie in peace. All those who died—they'll be no longer unburied and prey for the wolves. We'll dig in the ground and bury them."

"In peace."

I sit down on my bed, laughing.

Jacob says: "I call to mind how it was in the Mohawk, April—a month of rain and soft skies. The blossoms would come out on the apple trees in the month of May. I'll never forget the blossoming of the apple trees."

"There are apple trees in Valley Forge," Charley says eagerly.

The rain is dripping through the ceiling with a steady patter. We sit around and look at it, let it drip from our hands, watch the little puddles of mud it makes on the hard dirt of the floor.

"The cold is in my bones," Charley says sadly. "Come years—I'll never get the cold out of my bones. I'll never get out the cold they flogged into me at the whipping post."

"I dream of a hot sun——"

"I have a dream," I say, "to lie down in soft green grass with the sun on me, with a bit of cloth over my eyes, with a breeze overhead."

"With a lass?" Mary asks.

I shrug my shoulders.

"A hot sun," Charley nods.

Jacob, looking into the fire, says: "The army will come back—there'll be new men. Militia will gather. We'll march . . ."

The door swings open, and Kirk Freeman, a Pennsylvania man, bursts in. He stands there panting, dripping wet.

"What is it?"

"The ice on the Schuylkill—it's breaking up."

We follow him. All along, men are out of

the dugouts, standing in the rain, listening. From far off, a dull booming.

"The ice!"

"It's thunder——"

A ripping crash. Someone laughs shrilly.

"Get back into shelter!" Ely calls. "We're not fit to stand out in the pouring rain!"

We go back inside. Some Pennsylvania men come in, and one of them has some rum. He tells a detailed story of how he came by the rum. Eight Pennsylvania men were on guard at the commissariat. Coming off duty one evening, they intercepted two McLane raiders, with a tub of foraged rum slung between them. The sergeant of the Pennsylvanians signed for the rum, as a captain, and they took it to their brigade and got drunk. For that, the sergeant had ten lashes, the others four apiece. But it was worth it.

The Pennsylvania man has what is left of the rum. There's a long drink for each of us. We heat it over the fire, drink it slowly.

There's a toast to liberty—"To John and Sam Adams, may they be hanged!"

"To the Continental Congress, may they rot in hell!"

"May they have dysentery until their bowels rot out!"

We sit around the fire, tasting our rum, listening to the rain. We are lulled by the steady, even beat of raindrops on the roof.

The Pennsylvania men talk of Kenton. "He was a strong man—a bright flame of a man."

"He was a man to fight and to win—never to know pain or sorrow."

Charley is already a little drunk from the rum. We are not used to hard drink, and there's not enough food inside of us to sop it up. Charley says:

"He died for us. There was no man had such a fear of the gibbet as Kenton. But he died for us."

"God damn Muller's soul. He remembered the deer. He took it out on Kenton."

"There are good Pennsylvania men who won't be forgetting a gift of two fine buck deer."

"Something for Muller to remember."

Ely said: "Let Kenton rest in peace. There's no score in the encampment but has been paid out in blood."

"There's no peace for a man who dies on the gibbet."

"Peace enough."

Some of the Pennsylvania men brought in their women. The women shift from man to man. There's no hate. A man dies, and his woman is left behind. We have suffered too much to be jealous. They're a strange race, these women of the camp. Many a camp follower was a good woman once. Her man was going to war; they married and came along together. Then her man died, or he deserted, leaving her behind. No place for her to go; she fell into the life of the camp. These women went from man to man. What a man needed— They had seen how we were like beasts, but still men. Maybe they kept us being men.

We lie in front of the fire, and we sing sad Dutch songs, songs that were sung along the New York and Pennsylvania rivers for a hundred years.

And the rain beats on the roof.

It rained for two days more, and then, on a grey, wet day, the order went around for a grand review of the entire army. Muller brought the news himself. He came into the dugout and said:

"Come out of your hole—clean up!"

He met our eyes and smiled. He had courage,

that man. "Parade with fixed bayonets. Stump!"

"The army moves?" I asked Ely.

"I don't know."

A while later, General Wayne stepped into the dugout. We stood at attention, in spite of ourselves. There was a simple, natural dignity in Wayne, a spark of fire in his light blue eyes. For Muller we had not moved.

He walked round the hut without speaking, took up our muskets, looked at the flints. He nodded, said:

"You're soldiers. A man may go to hell, but he keeps his musket in firing condition." He looked at our feet, man to man—stopped at Ely's. "You can walk?"

"I can walk, sir," Ely said.

"I pleaded for shoes, God knows. Maybe we'll have them soon."

"Yes, sir, I trust so. But I'm fair afraid no shoes'll fit my feet again."

"I'm sorry," he said softly.

He stopped at the door, said bluntly: "You're New York men, but my troops now. We've all seen hell. I pleaded for you at the court-martial." Then he walked out.

We assemble outside the dugouts in brigade

formation. The snow is a slush, and with each step we sink into it, ankle-deep. The drummers stand around, trying to tighten their drumheads. There is movement, new life in the air. Finally, the order comes to march—eight hundred of the Pennsylvania line.

We go through the trees, the slush falling into our faces. At the Gulph Road, we fall in behind the Massachusetts regiments. The Virginian men join in behind us, cursing in their soft drawl. We curse them back.

We march out onto the parade. Across the meadow, the Rhode Island men face us, next to them the Maryland brigades, then the long stretch of the New Jersey line. Thin, white-faced, bearded, filthy, no man with a whole, decent suit of clothes, we make a strange, nightmarish picture of an army. An army come back from hell, crippled beggars collected from the ends of the earth.

The drummers march out to beat their roll, but the noise is dulled. Their drum-skins are wet. Clouds hang low overhead. We can hear the cracking and rushing of ice in the Schuylkill.

Washington rides out, with his staff. They canter to the centre of the parade, draw in their

horses and dismount. The men stand in the slush
—waiting. With Washington there is a stranger, and all eyes are on him. He wears a blue
and white uniform, gold-trimmed, and a white
cocked hat, high black boots. We ask each
other who he is. Nobody seems to know.

He walks toward the Pennsylvania brigades,
Washington behind him. Wayne comes out,
takes his hand, and they stand in a little group,
talking. They are too far away for us to hear
what they're saying, but suddenly the stranger
breaks out into a roar of laughter—real laughter, the kind we have not heard for months. It
takes effect. We look at each other.

He walks toward the brigades, stiffly. He's
a stocky man, a broad flat face. He kicks his
feet out in front of him, splashing the slush.
When he is a few yards from us, he stops; his
eyes widen. He walks along, his head turned
sidewise, staring at man after man. He comes
to one man who has no breeches, who wears an
improvised sort of kilt instead. Then the stranger stops. For a moment, he stares straight ahead
of him, then turns his head slowly—warily to
look at the man. The head goes back. Still warily, it seeks out General Washington—then
back to the man with the kilt. It takes us. We

begin to smile. The brigades smile. A flurry of rain comes—and still the brigades smile.

Wayne says: "You must understand, Baron—we have suffered a winter of hell."

The stranger answers in German: *"Ja—Ich versteh'."*

"You must allow."

"Ja——"

He turns his head again. Then, slowly, he walks toward the man. I know the man, his name is Enoch Farrer. He's a tall thin man. As the stranger approaches him, he backs away, stooping down to hide his knees.

The stranger stops. "Come here!"

Enoch knows no German.

"Come here and turn round."

I know Dutch well enough to make out the German. Most of the Pennsylvania men can speak a Dutch or German dialect. Farrer is a north Pennsylvania man, of English stock. He backs away from the German, making an effort to draw his kilt down over his knees. Then he drops his musket.

"God-damn thing's wet," he snaps, fumbling for it. "Who the hell are you, mister?"

The stranger roars with laughter. His whole body shakes with laughter. He sways from side to side, clapping his hands together. Washington, Wayne, Greene—they stand and regard him with indignant silence. He turns to them, stumbling through the snow, shaking his big head.

"I'm sorry—sorry—but in Europe I hear of an army. An army that stands the English nation on end. An army they chase all over America———"

"We have muskets, sir," Washington says stiffly.

"I know—I'm sorry. Forgive me." But he stands there laughing. He can't stop himself.

It was the first time we had seen Baron von Steuben. He came to the Pennsylvanians first. He came to us when we were almost finished.

That day, we stood in the rain for three hours, half-frozen, soaked through and through. Nothing else could have kept us there—nothing but the fat German who stamped up and down, cursed us furiously, and then roared with laughter at our blank expressions.

We began to remember. Maybe our thoughts went back to that day at Bunker Hill in Boston, when a rabble suddenly became an army.

He walked up and down our lines impatiently. He would tear a musket from a man's hands, grip it with his own, roar in German: "Like this—God damn your cursed peasant soul, hold it like this! It's a musket—not a log of wood! Like this!"

He would thrust it back at the man, a Massachusetts farmer, and the man would hold it limply—as he held it before.

The Baron would snatch it back, become livid with fury. "Like this—like this—pig—peasant—fool!"

The blank face and a sheepish smile. The Baron would groan, give him back the musket, walk back and forth, groaning and shaking his head.

"An army out of this! God—to make an army out of this!"

Or else he would break out laughing, great, animal-like bursts of laughter that echoed across the parade. Then he would try again.

"A manual of arms—one—two—three—four."

A blank, wondering face.

"Ah, God—God, why can't I speak their accursed tongue? Why can't I speak their miserable, savage tongue?"

He marched us back and forth. He stood in the centre of the parade, roaring out his orders.

When we began to march, he mounted his horse, rode up and down our lines, cursing us, trying to keep the brigades in line.

"In line—in line—eyes right! Wayne—God in heaven, come and speak for me!"

The rain grew harder. For hours we marched back and forth, while Steuben roared and cursed. I could see Washington pleading with him to let us rest. He shook his head, drove us.

Weary to death, we staggered back to the dugouts, through the rain. We built up the fire and crouched close to it, trembling with cold and fatigue.

But Jacob was smiling. He stood by the fire, staring into the flames, smiling. Jacob had found a man and an officer.

18

Rains—a ray of sunlight darting through—a sky of rolling black and grey clouds, an eternity of rain that turns the snow to slush and the slush to black mud. The dugouts leak. The floors are muddy. We become creatures of mud and slime.

Some day, the sun will come out.

Baron von Steuben drives us. It seems that the German is working against time. Who is he? What does he expect? Does he hope to make an army out of the few hundred of us that are left? The army of revolution is learning to laugh again—at itself, at the few hundred pitiful men who make up the ranks.

Eleven thousand men came onto the Valley Forge encampment in December. Today, half the dugouts are empty, their roofs fallen in. In the Pennsylvania line, two and three men make up a regiment.

And Steuben drives us. Out into the pouring rain, onto the grand parade, a mockery of drumsticks threshing over wet skins. Form brigades. We drag our bandaged feet through the mud, back and forth, back and forth—drill. We understand the German for one, two, three, four—manual of arms. Men drop out of the ranks, sprawl on their faces in the mud. Bayonet charge—a thin line of tattered men stumbling against the rain. Re-form ranks, charge back. Back and forth until we can no longer stand. Our beards run water. We stand limply, look at one another—then laugh. We have reached the bottoms of misery, of filth, of wretchedness. We can go no lower—we are beasts of the earth.

Steuben roars his orders, more, more—but we stand limply. You can't ask more of a man when he has no strength left. Steuben pleads with us.

"My children—once more."

He stands in the rain, bareheaded. His uniform no longer sparkles with gold lace and braid. His white breeches have become a dirty grey and brown. He stumps along, man to man, pleading with us, losing himself, roaring out in wrath—and then becoming gentle as a woman. He takes a musket and goes through the drill.

"My children, listen to me. I am not making an army out of you. I am making a nation out of you. You and I, we will march across this country—victorious. You understand?"

We stand limply, beggars.

"All right—go home."

Jacob and Ely and I come back to the dugout. Charley has a fever, perhaps the same fever that took him after the flogging. He coughs continuously, and sometimes there's a splatter of red on his lips.

Tired, wet, we come in and crouch close to the fire. We build it up into a great roaring blaze. The rain is harder, like a steady flow of pebbles onto the roof.

Charley calls to me: "Allen——"

I take a rag and go over to his bed. I sit there, wiping the mud and water from my musket. His woman no longer sleeps with him. But sometimes she comes into the dugout to sit with him. In a way, she must still care for the little printer. Now she sits at the opposite side of the dugout, watching us.

"You're better?" I ask him. "You don't look so bitter hot today, Charley."

"I'm used up, Allen—all used up."

"That's no way for a man to talk—that's a foolish way for a man to talk."

"Allen, I want you to swear that you'll bury me. Deep in the earth, deep as the height of a man standing. I have a great fear of lying out in the cold. I want to be below where the ground freezes—far below."

"You're talking foolish."

"But you'll bury me, Allen?"

I nod, stand up and put away my musket. When I turn back, Charley is lying with his eyes closed, breathing hoarsely. I go to the fire.

"He's no better," Jacob says.

"He's used up by the whipping. Kenton would have lived."

"The rain will stop soon—after that, he'll gain strength."

"We should bleed him."

"Or take him to the hospital. They say there's two new men there, doctors from Boston."

"Not to the hospital," I mutter. "There's no man coming out of that hospital."

"I wouldn't want to live—coming into that hospital."

The next day, Ely went to the hospital. He came back, wet and tired.

"There's no doctor would come up to the dugouts," he said.

"You asked them?"

"They said bring him there. It's like going into hell to go into that hospital. They have the beds built one layer over another, with the men lying so close they can't move. The doctors are Boston men, not caring much one way or another."

"We'll bring him there?"

Ely shook his head. We went over to Charley's bed. He lay there, his eyes closed, speaking softly.

"Bleed him," Mary pleaded.

"I can't bleed a man," Ely muttered. "I don't hold with bleeding."

"Can't you see he's far gone? Bleed him——"

"You'd better," Jacob said. "It will relieve him of the evil sickness in his blood."

Ely nodded. I brought a pan. Jacob sharpened his knife on a stone, and then cut into a vein on the inside of Charley's arm, just above the elbow. Charley didn't seem to feel the pain of the cut; he went on talking to himself, talking nonsense. Jacob found the vein, but he wasn't very skillful at bleeding; he cut almost all through the vein, and the blood poured forth in a thick, red stream. It frightened me, the gush of blood. It didn't seem that a man could lose blood that way and live.

"Give over!" I cried. "He'll bleed to death."

"Till he comes to his senses, Allen," Ely whispered. "Otherwise he'll die in madness. Let him come to his senses."

The pan filled with blood. The flush passed from Charley's face, and his skin became the color of dirty parchment. He sighed and opened his eyes. He glanced from face to face, and he knew us. Somehow, he managed to smile.

Clumsily, we bound up his arm, but we were unable to stop the flow of blood completely. It still seeped through the bandage. For a while —and then he bled no more.

"You'll be a new man in a few days," Ely told him.

"In less time than that," Charley whispered. "Tonight, the rains stop, Ely. I have that in mind. A peace on earth."

We nodded. Charley's woman went to a bed, lay down. We heard her lips moving in a soft prayer.

"I'll be near Kenton," he said. "I should never have taken myself away from Kenton . . ."

I went out on sentry duty that night. A wind

from the west had blown the skies clear. There were stars spread in a great circle over the land.

I walk back and forth slowly. The earth is different, a new land. Most of the snow is gone. In the lee of hills, in places where the drifts were, there is still snow; but most of it is gone. The wind is cool and gentle.

My feet sink into the soft earth. Once, I bend over to touch a patch of withered yellow grass. A blade of the grass, I hold in my fingers.

I come to my contact and two of us stand there. We wait for the third sentry. He walks up, shaking his head like a man in a dream.

"On the wind—the smell of the seasons."

"Spring——"

"There'll be green grass and warm winds. There'll be wheat in the meadows and tall corn."

"It seemed like there would never be a time for growing things again, a time for planting."

"A time for breaking the earth—a time for hitching a horse to a plough. A time for the smell of new earth turned."

"I call to mind how the locusts bloom first. We had a spread of locust trees at home, all along the bank of the river. A good Pennsylvania tree."

"You're a Mohawk man, Allen. Is there good crops and good planting in the Mohawk land?"

I nod. My enlistment will be over soon—mine and Ely's and Jacob's. Three of us left.

"You'll be going home, Allen?"

I look at the Pennsylvania men wonderingly. I say: "It's a great distance for a man to walk—alone."

"There be none to go with you?"

"I don't know . . ."

"There'll be war again with the coming of the flowers," a Pennsylvania man says. "There'll be armies marching."

"They say Howe will attack the camp."

"It's not to my thinking that the old man will keep us here. He'll be out—marching."

"There's little enough army left."

"Mark my word—there'll be more. After the planting, they'll come by the hundred."

"I put no faith in militia."

"There's the German baron to train them."

"Feel the wind———"

"It's warm. It's got a deep, strange warmth in it. It's a wind out of the south and the west."

"There'll be a fair sun tomorrow."

"A ripe sun."

"The ice knocked the bridge out of the river.

The Maryland men were in cold water up to their necks, putting the bridge back."

"I've no love for Maryland men. Swedes or Pope-crawlers——"

"Or envy—for men in icy water."

We separate. We wave our hands and plod back on our beats. My feet make a sucking sound as they part from the earth. At the lunette, I stop and lean against a fieldpiece. Its cold surface feels good to my hands, so much has the change wrought in me that I can enjoy the chill after the cold of winter.

I think about going home. Ely and Jacob and myself. I try to picture the soft green fields of the Mohawk Valley. The realization that it will not be the same forces itself upon me, the realization that we are no longer a part of that life. I picture myself behind a plough, breaking open the land. Then I shake my head. The unrest inside of me won't die. Horror can't kill it—or hate—or suffering. We'll go on and on.

Jacob relieves me. He walks slowly, and he doesn't look at me.

"Go back to the dugout, Allen," he says.

"A clear, beautiful night, Jacob. You feel the wind out of the west?"

He nods.

"A warm breeze. I picked a blade of last summer's grass, Jacob."

"There'll be more grass, new grass with fertile soil to feed it."

"Blue skies, Jacob."

I walk back to the dugout. When I come in, I feel that something has happened. Then I see Charley's woman kneeling by his bed. I go over to the fire and sit down. I look into the curling flames. A fire like this—night after night, all through the winter.

Ely says: "We'll endure, Allen."

I remember Washington's words. How much can a man endure? I stare around the dugout curiously, as if I had never seen it before— smoke-blackened logs, packed dirt on the floor, a double tier of beds, built onto the wall, a few rags hanging from wooden pegs. A musket rack. Moss Fuller's musket is there, Clark Vandeer's, Henry Lane's, Aaron Levy's, Kenton Brenner's, Edward Flagg's, Meyer Smith's, Charley Green's——

A roll call—the muskets answer, each one an individual. Charley has a musket with a silver-inlaid stock, the work of Paul Revere. Clark's is a French piece. There are three long-barrelled Valley-country muskets.

I say to Ely: "The rain has stopped."

"I know," Ely answers softly. He is looking at the muskets, too. His big grey head is bent over.

He comes over to me and sits down. He says: "Best not to keep the women here tonight."

"I'll stay here," she says, not moving from her place by Charley's bed.

I nod to my woman, and she goes to the door.

"Tell them you're Allen Hale's woman. They'll keep you."

She's anxious to go. After she's gone, small as the dugout is, it seems curiously empty.

"Ely," I say, "there were three hundred of us come out of the Valley country."

"I know."

"Will any go back?"

The next day we buried Charley Green. We laid him in the hillside, just away from the abatis. We put a wooden cross as a marker on his grave. We laid him where he could see the blue hills, off to Philadelphia.

19

Job Andrews, a Massachusetts man, crying for us to come and see. He's run up the hillside, laughing like a child. We make a circle round him, and he shows us what he has, a delicate purple flower.

"The first," he says. "A winter flower."

It goes from hand to hand until it falls to pieces. Men hold it close to their noses, trying to sniff its perfume. We handle it tenderly.

"Only one," Job says.

"More later."

"I seen these blossoms come in great banks."

We go to the grand parade under a blue sky that's rolling with clouds. The wind out of the west is cool and clean, and brings a fragrance of spring. We are without our ragged greatcoats.

The brigades form, and the drums beat out their roll. Steuben rides onto the field, and we smile. We've found a man to love, a man like ourselves, coarse, hard, living with the earth, but patient and gentle as a woman.

He dismounts and walks toward the brigades.

He has mastered a broken Enlish, which he delights in using.

"Mine children," he says.

We laugh. He's taught us to laugh again. We're a few hundred broken soldiers, but he respects us. It's a new thing with us.

"Mine children—ve learn to march dis day. *Ja*—ve learn to march vere ve vant, take vat ve vant. Vat der British have, ve take—*ja?*"

We imitate him. "Ya—ya, Baron."

We march back and forth, across the grand parade. We have learned to lift our feet, snap them forward in the Prussian fashion. We have learned to march in close order, ten men moving as one. We have learned about bayonets.

He pleads with us: "Mine children—you vill not use der bayonets to cook food? Please. You vill clean der bayonets?"

He tells us to sit down. The staff officers protest. They tell him that he is mad. These men are beasts—and he is destroying what discipline is left in the army. Men on parade do not sit down.

He doesn't understand, and he shakes his head. "But a democratic country—I thought things would be different," he says in German.

"We are at war, Baron."

"I know, I know—I've seen a little of war. But my own way. Let them sit down."

We sprawl about, watching him curiously. He says: "I make mit der bayonet vat you call a show—*ja?* You vill vatch." He walks through the brigades, seeking a musket and bayonet to suit him. As he walks, his rage mounts. Musket after musket, he examines and throws aside in disgust. Finally, he cries:

"Vat pigs—vat svine! Vy did I come to dis accursed country—to dis land of peasants?" He stamps back and forth in a fury of rage, and we watch him without heat. The rage will cool. We know enough of rage. We were penned up like beasts for a winter; some of us went mad.

He cools. He selects a musket and bayonet, and goes out before us. He salutes us, says:

"Vatch careful, mine children."

A short, fat man, he moves awkwardly as he goes through the drill. Beyond him, a cluster of our officers observe with expressions of mingled amusement and resentment. Steuben walks back, whirls, and runs toward us with fixed bayonet presented. He thrusts at the air, wrenches, and plucks back the bayonet.

"As dis, *ja?* Der British are clumsy fools—*ja?* Der virst—brezent, barry—t'rust!" He lunges again. We roar with laughter. We call out:

"More, Baron!"

"Give us one for General Howe, Baron!"

"Give us the whole thing—over again, Baron!"

He doesn't resent our laughter. He joins in himself, laughing and panting at the same time.

"Now—mine children, mit all. Attention!"

The brigades form. The endless drill goes on again: present bayonets, four steps and lunge. Parry, four steps and lunge. We march up and down the parade. We march endlessly, eternally, until our heads are whirling. We lunge at the air, again and again, long lines of tattered men.

Steuben is tireless. He seems to know only one thing—drill. Morning, noon, and night, he drills us. He comes up to the dugouts alone, examines our muskets. He tells us how to clean our bayonets, how to edge a musket-flint to make it spark, how to divide powder into the proper amounts to make a sure load.

He comes into our dugout once. It is toward evening, and we are resting from the drill, lying in our beds.

He enters, and we stumble to our feet. He says in German: "Be seated—I pray you. You understand German?"

We nod, and he looks round the dugout curiously.

"You lived here all winter?"

"All winter."

He turns to our musket rack, and his lips move as he counts the guns. He says:

"Where are the rest of the men who live here?"

"They're dead."

He shakes his head, walks to the fire and stares into it. "I have seen some terrible things," he mutters. "I have seen men suffer———"

The drills go on. The sky turns a shade of blue taken out of our dreams. The locust trees along the Schuylkill bud green. The brown dirt on Charley Green's grave sends up little shoots of growing things.

20

I AM out with Ely on sentry duty—a cool, clear night. We meet each other and walk slowly toward Charley's grave. I bend over and pick a bit of grass from it.

I hold it out to Ely. He takes it in his hand and stands there looking at it.

"I had in mind that Charley would be with us," I say. "I had no thought that he would die . . ."

Ely says, thoughtfully: "There will never be another winter like this. When you were born, Allen, I stood outside your house with your father. It was a bitter, sad thing to hear your mother scream. All night long, she screamed out in pain. You were born in the morning."

I listen; it comes to me that Ely is an old man, part of a past.

"There'll be something out of this winter, Allen—something from our suffering. I don't know what, I'm not a learned man. But we've given birth—do you understand?"

"I don't know——"

"You're only a boy, Allen. You're making something for yourself. It's not for Jacob or me."

"What, Ely?"

"A way of life—a new world for men. The Jew who came from Poland, a great distance, seeking it. The men who died———"

"For whom?" I demand. "They let us starve here, while they filled their fat bellies."

"When your enlistment's over, Allen, you'll go back?"

I shrug.

"You're looking for something, Allen. Only find it. It needs a strong man."

I'm thinking, a man like Ely, a strong man to take things and hold them. I'm thinking of all who went—Moss, Kenton, Charley . . . My turn sooner or later.

I say to Ely: "God—I'm sick for home."

He nods. "I know how that is, Allen."

"You'll come home with me, Ely?" I ask him eagerly. "You and Jacob—the three of us back to the Mohawk?" I take his hand.

"There's too many died here, Allen," he says, shaking his head.

"But why—why must we keep on? Ely, I'm afraid."

He says, gently: "Go back, Allen. If you wish to go back—then go."

We walk apart, and I turn again and again to watch the lean figure of Ely, Ely an old man already, Ely with a knowingness that frightens me because it's away from me, out of my world.

The next day I go to General Wayne's quarters. I try not to think of what I'm doing. I try not to think of how the green shoots are pushing themselves up through the dirt on Charley Green's grave.

Wayne is sitting at a desk, writing, when the orderly brings me in. He glances up at me, and his brow puckers. I can see that he remembers me.

"What do you want, sir?" he asks me.

"I want to sign papers for re-enlistment."

He stares at me. The orderly leaves me alone, and Wayne sits for what seems a long time, staring at me, looking at my torn, filthy clothes.

He says oddly: "Your name's Allen Hale——"

"Yes, sir."

"What regiment?"

"The Fourteenth Pennsylvania."

He takes a paper from his desk, and looks at it thoughtfully. Then he says to me: "That girl you had with you when you deserted—you loved her?"

I don't answer him; I am strangely aware of myself. I don't want to speak of Bess; she is too close to me now; she will be closer.

"Why are you staying with the army?" Wayne asks.

I can't tell him; I can't put it into words to tell him.

"Haven't you suffered enough?" Wayne demands, his voice rising.

"I haven't suffered," I say quietly. "Those who suffered are dead. I haven't suffered."

Wayne stands up and comes over to me. He holds out his hand, says: "You know me, sir."

I take his hand.

I walk back to the dugouts slowly. As I climb the hill to where the Pennsylvania brigades are encamped, I notice the new grass. New grass—its color the faintest, purest yellow-green. Tiny blossoms of violet.

I come to the top of the hill and look round. A faint illusion of green all over the countryside, rolling hills, a blue sky almost near enough for you to reach up and feel of it.

I come into the dugout. I say to Ely: "I've been to Wayne's quarters."

"You'll be going home soon?"

Jacob is watching me, curiously. His long, dark face has a trace of sadness on it. For once, the hard, inherent cruelty of his tight mouth has relaxed. He has the dignity of a silent king as he stands in the little dugout. It seems that into him—not into Ely or myself—has gone the force of all the men who died there. He stands there alone. There's nothing to endure about Jacob: I see him going out in a magnificent flash of black fury; sooner or later, he'll go that way. Now, as if he had suddenly realized himself, he's alone. As much as on Washington's, the force and weight of the revolution is upon his shoulders. The stiffness of his shoulders makes it all the more marked. All during the winter, those shoulders had never once bowed, never once moved from their tense, upright position. Then I see him as the Jew, and I realize for the first time how close together they were in force and understanding.

"I'm not going home," I say. And dully: "I enlisted again—for a time of three years."

Jacob shakes his head. It is the first time I have ever seen pity for any man in his eyes.

"You shouldn't have done that, Allen," Ely says.

Jacob sits down on the edge of one of the beds. He's terribly alone there—the double row of empty beds behind him. His eyes wander around the dugout slowly, from Ely to me—groping for others when he knows there are no others. His eyes come to rest on the musket rack, and it seems to me that he is counting the muskets.

"You shouldn't have done that," Ely says again, sadly. "It's my fault."

"There was nothing for me to go back to."

"Your people, Allen—come spring planting, they'll be watching for you. It's on me, your enlistment—and my words that kept you here."

I try to explain. And then, suddenly, I'm tired, and I don't want to explain. I want to go outside and lie down in the sun. I say: "All that's gone. None of us can go back, Ely."

Jacob nods. "There will be war for years—God only knows how long."

I go outside, feeling that I am leaving behind me two old men who are strangers. I feel bitter—sad. I'm left alone.

I walk through the trees, and find a little space of meadow where the sun beats through. I lie down there. The ground is cool, but not too cold. The sun is a beating pulse in my eyes.

I lie there for a long time, watching the small, bundled clouds drive through the sky. I think of Bess, not of a person who is dead, but of a woman I will meet again some day. I think a little sadly of the boy Allen, who despised her—but there is no feeling of hate or resentment in me, not for her nor for the boy I was and whom she loved.

21

WE SHAVE our beards. A great amount of hair going away. One man lies flat on his back while another shaves him. The knife scrapes and cuts the skin.

We bare our feet. Bandages fall apart as we unwrap them. Feet that are black knobs of filth. We bare our feet and walk gingerly—barefooted.

About two or three hundred of us lie naked along the Valley Creek—Pennsylvania, Virginia, and Massachusetts men. We wash our clothes with sand and ashes, hang them on the trees to dry. All along, up and down the creek—a beggar's wardrobe, tattered breeches, paper-thin coats. We roll over and over in the icy-cold water and then come out into the sun to dry. We can't get enough of the sun. First it burns us red, blisters our backs; we turn brown slowly. We've become a cult of sun-worshippers. The cold is in our bones. We take long hours in the sun the way we'd take a tonic. The hot, salty sweat is good as it runs into our eyes and our mouths.

We sit on the bank, our feet dangling in the water, and scrub ourselves with curiosity. We pick the lice out of our hair. We investigate each part of our body as the winter accumulation of dirt disappears. We're a curious lot—thin, bony, hollow-eyed. We curse the Virginia men goodnaturedly. The spring has washed away hatred, washed away the differences between the north and the south—the east and the west. We've suffered together for too long.

I wash Ely's feet—and then he stares at them curiously. Somehow, they are healing. Long, raw scars are ingrained with dirt, but the bleeding has stopped. The poor, tortured flesh is knitting itself together once more. Soon the scabs will fall off. The dead white skin will be replaced with new flesh, and new blood will flow through the blue veins that stand out so sharp. He stares at his feet as if he had never seen them before. He takes a few steps through the water—then goes back to the bank and sits down. He attempts to say something to me, and his words choke up. He moves his feet back and forth, watching the water wash over his toes. Finally, he asks me:

"You'll shave my beard, Allen? I'm longing to feel my face clean and smooth."

He lies on his back while I shave him. It's strange to watch his face emerge from under the whiskers. The wind is sighing through the trees, and dogwood blossoms fall over us.

I lie down for my turn. While the knife scrapes over my chin, I close my eyes. I feel the bite of the blade as Ely plucks at my whiskers. Every so often he dips the knife into the cold water to wash it. When it touches my face again, it is chilled and clean. Bit by bit, Ely removes my beard. The years drop from me. I'm a boy again. My skin is firm and clean and hairless. Ely's fingers wander over my face, kneading what's left of my beard to soften it, so that it will come off more easily. Under the lulling play of his fingers, I doze. When I open my eyes, he is finished, looking at me and nodding his head.

Later, we play in the water, lean white men, childish. We throw handfuls of water at each other, duck each other. We find deep holes where we can paddle round. We find two wooden buckets, and a couple of Massachusetts men appoint themselves a bucket squad. We line up and pass between them, and they douse us with water. It's a rare treat, and we keep up until the Massachusetts men are dog-tired. Then we lie in the sun, drying ourselves, telling stories, exchanging the latest jokes about the British, about our officers and their wives.

We put on our tattered clothes and walk back barefooted. We rub our feet into the lush, green grass. When we see flowers, we stoop over to pick them, and then stand and look at them. We put the flowers in our hair and prance round. We become pagans and children: we do foolish things and we are not ashamed.

In between drills, we lie out in the sun. That, we can't get enough of. Our bodies are like sponges. As much sun as we soak in, there is always need for more. We lie about, talking, laughing, rolling dice: but we say little of the winter. It's too near us.

The women try to make themselves pretty. There's no whole dress or hat among them, but they fill their hair with blossoms. They parade back and forth—smiling at us. They even wash, and once we surprise a lot of them bathing in the creek. They try to hide their nakedness in the shallow water, and we stand on the bank laughing at them, like gangling boys. Finally, they seize their clothes and dash away.

We chase them, laughing wildly, roll over in the woods, plaster wet bodies with dead leaves.

Recruits are coming into camp, along with food. A great wagon train from the north brings thousands of pounds of meat. The militia come and sign papers for three-month terms. We have no love for the militia; and for their part, they're awed and a little afraid of the regulars. They stand around and watch us. On the parade, they blunder about, while we go through Steuben's Prussian drills like well-trained troops.

Baron von Steuben is losing weight, but he delights in us the way a father would delight in his children. We're his men. Half of the Pennsylvania line he knows by name.

We let the fire in our dugout go out. Ely stands in front of the empty fireplace, poking at the ashes with a stick. The door to the dugout is open, and a breeze from outside stirs the dry ashes. It is the afternoon, toward twilight, and the two of us are alone in the dugout. The two women are gone. They went after Charley died, and afterwards I saw Anna with a Massachusetts man. It doesn't matter.

"A forlorn place without a fire," Ely says.

"I'm not bemoaning the cold, but there was life in the fire."

"A dull, lonely place."

"I hope we march soon."

"I hated this place at first," I say. "I don't hate it now."

The brigades build fires outside. I ask Ely to go out with me, but he shakes his head. I go out alone. The Pennsylvania men are roasting meat over the fire. We sit round in a circle, drinking, singing.

I find myself with a woman, a round young girl with light hair. Three or four men are playing for her attention, but I manage to draw her off. I take her back from the fire, where there's a bit of grass, and we lie down there.

"Your name's Allen Hale," she says.

"How do you know?"

"I seen you around. I heard tell you deserted and were whipped nigh to death."

"Yes——"

"My name's Bella."

"You've no man?"

"I had a man—he deserted without me. I never heard word of him."

"I'm a fit, fair man for a girl to love."

She giggles, and when I put my arms around

her, she comes to me willingly. We lie there, watching the blaze of the fire, the dark figures moving in front of it. I pass my hands over her body.

"They say you're no man to be without a woman," she says to me. "They say you took a fair woman away from a Virginian brigade——"

"Yes."

"What was her name? Tell me her name? You're not thinking of her now—in my arms?"

"Her name was Bess Kinley."

"Did you love her? Were you pained to see her die?"

I cry, suddenly: "Be quiet, God damn you!" Then, as she draws away in fright, I hold her back. "I'm sorry—I was not meaning to fright you."

I come back to the dugout, and Ely sits where I left him, next to the empty fire. He says:

"Allen?"

"Yes, Ely."

"Allen—make me a promise."

"What?"

"You'll have faith in the revolution. There'll be no peace for many years. There'll be strong men needed."

"You'll be with me, Ely."

"No—you'll be alone, Allen."

I go to my bed, and for a long time afterward Ely sits motionless. I can't sleep—and I watch him.

I sleep, and I wake later and still Ely sits there. The door is open, and a vague moonlight seeps into the dugout. Jacob's long form is stretched out in his bunk.

"Ely?" I say.

He looks up at me. "I thought you to be asleep, Allen."

"You'll not sit all night, Ely, not resting?"

"For a little while, Allen—I'm noways tired."

I go back to sleep, but even in my sleep I see Ely's form, bent over the ashes, stirring them with his stick. A man with a deep knowledge—a knowledge that comes out of his heart. A man with a great heart.

The next day, a May day that is like a benediction. An order comes to the brigades for a grand parade—a review of the entire army. A parade, and then a day of rest and celebration. To celebrate . . .

All sorts of rumours; but Melrose, a Massachusetts man, says that he carried dispatches to headquarters. He says that it's an alliance with France.

The brigades form, and we talk about it eagerly.

"A great country over the water. A country that has warred with England these many hundreds of years."

"It's La Fayette's doing—it's said that he brought about the alliance himself."

"Mark me, Ben Franklin's the man who had a hand in this. Old Ben himself."

"An army they'll send—an army of ten thousand men."

"Washington in tears, crying like a child. That, I saw myself."

Wayne is laughing like a boy. He has rum served out while the brigades are forming. We stick blossoms and green leaves into our jackets and our hair. The drums beat out Yankee-Doodle, and we sing it as we march down to the parade.

> *Yankee-Doodle went to Boston,*
>   *Riding on a pony,*
> *Gave all hell to old man Howe,*
>   *Called it macaroni.*

Yankee-Doodle keep it up,
  Keep the lobsters running,
Let the bastard redcoats know
  Yankee-Doodle's coming!

We roar it out, and it echoes back from the parade. We cheer Wayne as he rides up and down our ranks. We sing verse after verse.

Yankee-Doodle went to hell,
  Claimed it was right chilly,
Take six months in Valley Forge,
  Hell is willy-nilly.

Yankee-Doodle keep it up,
  Keep the lobsters running,
Let the bastard redcoats know
  Yankee-Doodle's coming!

We form on the Grand Parade. Washington rides up with La Fayette and Baron von Steuben. Washington sits on his horse, smiling, his eyes wrinkled up with tears. He waves his hand, awkwardly, and begins to dismount. We break ranks. We press around them, half-mad, trying to touch Washington, to touch Steuben. Steuben is crying, frankly the tears pour down his face. Washington nods his head, like a man in a dream. Steuben says:

"Mine children—mine children———"

We go back to our ranks, staring around us, at the trees, at the green spread of the Grand Parade, at the cloudless blue sky. We are men out of a dream. The winter was a dream. More than one man is weeping quietly as he walks.

On the edge of the parade, the officers' ladies stand; a little away from them, the camp women. They wave at us and nod. They make little splashes of delightful color.

Steuben puts us through a parade drill. Bareheaded, he marches at the front of the Pennsylvania and Massachusetts brigades, waving his sword. He's as happy as a child. He beats his sabre against the ground, in time to our marching. He runs down the line of men, glancing along the ranks, nodding his head with approval. Winded, panting, he stands in the centre of the field, smiling.

He calls Washington at the top of his voice: "Mine commander, vatch—der bayonet movements!"

He walks towards us on his toes, his hands spread out. "*Ja*—mine children, you vill do it for me! Like I teached you."

He calls for the bayonet charge, names out brigades for flank attack, marshals in the brigades one after another as covering bodies, pivots us, rearranges brigade formation, and laughs like a delighted child.

"Such troops—vere in der vorld do you find such troops? *Gott*—dey're splendid!"

Washington speaks a few words. He says: "We have made an alliance with France. What we suffered this winter, you know and I know. Nor shall we forget. I thank you from my heart."

He sits on his horse, nodding at us, swallowing hard. He takes off his hat.

The rest of that day we sprawled over the parade, drinking, eating, or lying quietly, soaking in the heat of the sun . . .

The days go slowly, warm days. Lazy days with blue skies overhead. The heavens are a bowl of blue, and Valley Forge is in blossom. The apple trees are like balls of snow, and under the trees the white blossoms make a carpet for the ground. We walk through the woods and try to understand that this is the same place we came into in December.

We have buried the men who died during the winter, and the crosses make long rows along the Schuylkill. I go there with Ely, and we pick out seven of the graves—mark them for our men. Most of the graves are nameless. We mark a grave for the little doctor, and I carve the rhyme on it very painstakingly.

> *He did his work,*
> *He healed the sick,*
> *He did not shirk*
> *To keep men quick.*
> *God rest his soul,*
> *Forgive his sin.*

"They're fair words," Ely says. "A good rhyme for a man to leave behind him."

"He was a strange, hard man."

Charley's grave is a mat of green grass. I am glad that he lies where he does, looking over the gentle hills toward Philadelphia.

One night, we sit and talk. We sprawl outside the dugout, around a fire, Ely and Jacob and myself and half a dozen Pennsylvania men. It is a warm, cloudy night, and a mist rests in the valleys.

"They won't remember long," Ely says. "They'll forget how this winter was."

"It's something to forget."

"It was a hard, cold winter—no such winter before in all the memory of man."

"My father and my grandfather—take back

a hundred year—I can't call to mind that men ever spoke of such a winter as this one."

"It's something to forget—to have no bitter memory of."

"The chill is in my bones yet."

"There'll be no getting the chill outa your bones."

Ely says, thoughtfully: "I puzzle sometimes to make out what will come of it."

"War's not a thing for simple men to understand."

"It's like death. There's no thinking of war or death."

But I wonder whether I understood it then, long past when Kenton died, with a vision in his eyes. I have enlisted again—for three years. I can't think of that, only believe; whether or not there is anything to believe, I must believe.

The days go on—a lush heat flowing over the land, until men predict a summer as hot as the winter was cold. Valley Forge is ripe with beauty—a grand, flowing beauty, as soft as the hills. The hills are green, except where the Quaker farmers are turning over the land with their ploughs, and there the red-brown furrows make warm gashes.

Rumours come that we will march soon, but nobody knows where.

The British will leave Philadelphia. They won't attack us. Four or five thousand militiamen have already poured into Valley Forge. Our position is too strong.

We drill and drill and drill. We who have stayed through the winter, the battered Pennsylvania and New Jersey and Massachusetts brigades, are Steuben's pets. He makes soldiers of us. We were never soldiers before. We were a rabble of farmers, retreating all over the country before the British, defeated in every battle we fought. For the first time, we drill until we are like machines. Steuben is tireless; we must become men of iron; he is a fanatic about that.

He says: "Soon, soon, mine children. Ve strike dem vun blow—and den der var is over. Vun qvick blow. Soon—soon."

It comes sooner than we expect. A rider on a lathered horse pounding up the Gulph Road. He rides through the sentries, screaming out something. The hoofbeats echo through the camp. He reins up wildly before headquarters.

Word of the rider goes through camp like fire. Nobody knows what word he brings, but it's taken that he comes from Philadelphia. We gather in groups, talking, guessing.

"The British march on camp..."

"They've burned Philadelphia—pulled for New York..."

"They've sailed down the Delaware..."

Night comes. We build our fires. For the first time, I wonder how these fires appear to the Quaker farmers down in the valleys. Strange men-beasts, who call themselves an army; they came out of the night, in the snow. They'll go back. The Quakers will live on, the way they've lived for a hundred years.

I wake in the night, and I grope for Bess. I mutter: "If we leave here—where will you come back to?" I think of three more years with no woman, three more years. I cry out for Bess, childishly, longingly. I am afraid to be alone.

The next day, the camp is curiously uneasy. In the morning, Steuben drills us. But he's a sullen Prussian for once, and he puts us through the drills mechanically. The sun is a hot red blister in the sky. Steuben marches us back and forth until we are wringing wet.

We lie about the dugouts, discuss rumours. It is certain by now that the British troops have left Philadelphia. For a winter they lay there at their ease, filling their bellies, twenty thousand of them. Twenty thousand men, while three thousand sick beggars starved in the hill country, eighteen miles away. Now the word comes that the remaining British troops, ten or twelve thousand, have left Philadelphia to march overland through the Jerseys to New York. The officers say nothing, and we try to piece things out for ourselves. Half the British forces have sailed away. If Washington attacks those who march through Jersey . . .

We look at each other. Only once have American troops defeated the English in battle —that was in Boston, in seventeen-seventy-five, at Bunker Hill, and then we could not hold our ground. Since then, we have been defeated continuously.

"We'll know soon," Ely says. He is oddly calm, as if he had been waiting for this.

"We'll know," Jacob agrees.

The next morning, the order comes for the brigades to march. The order comes to break camp—a place where we have lived for six months.

We are very quiet about it. Working in the dugout, putting our few belongings together, we try to understand that we have lived in this place for half a year. The calm is like a blanket over us. We are breaking camp—going into battle.

I stood in the dugout after Ely and Jacob had gone. I walked around, felt the beds, things we had built with our own hands. I leaned against the low, log walls. I kicked at the few ashes in the fireplace. It was very hot in the dugout then. The morning sun beat down on the roof.

It might have been years ago that we had built it—Clark Vandeer, Henry Lane, Edward Flagg, Kenton Brenner, Charley Green, strong men hewing the life out of trees.

Inside, it had been hell and inferno; inside, I had lain with Bess in my arms—loving a woman. How does a man love a woman and not know?

If I had carved inside, along the logs: Here a soldier of the army, Allen Hale, lay with a girl who was no fit and decent woman—a follower of the camp . . .

The musket rack is empty. One day we had brought the muskets to Wayne, eight muskets. Wayne looked at them. Ely said: "You'll need arms, sir. There's a fair lot of men in camp without arms." Wayne answered, dully: "They belong with the men who used them—they belong— I'll take them. We need arms."

Ely called to me now, and I went outside. I closed the door, threw the latch. It would stay closed; it was a place of the damned, and nobody would molest it. Maybe, after years, a pile of rotten timber covering a mudhole. Men of the revolution lived there—half a year. People would look at it curiously.

"Allen—come," Ely says gently.

We join our brigade. It is a hot day, a burning hot day. The sun is a globe of yellow liquid in a sky of cold blue fire. Wayne walks his horse along our line, smiling, nodding—ragged, lean men, but men drawn fine with suffering. Men who will follow him into hell; men without a fear of hell. No fears left.

He calls out: "Brigades—forward!"

The drums pick up the tune. No other tune. A doggerel and a fit song for an army of beggars. A trumpet joins in, pricking shrill notes at the sky:

> *Yankee-Doodle went to London,*
> *Riding on a pony* . . .

The Pennsylvania brigades step out with the Prussian stiffness Steuben taught them. We march past the assembled Massachusetts and New Jersey lines. We walk past a mass of militia. Sitting on his horse, Steuben nods and nods; his face is twisted up; he can say nothing.

We take up our positions at the head of the army, directly behind Washington's life guard of Virginians. The tall Virginians look back at us and grin:

"Come on, farmers—there's ploughin' tu be done!"

We pick up our song.

Yankee-Doodle went to hell,
Claimed it was right chilly . . .

I look back, and the hills of the encampment are like a lush garden in the summer sun. A little cluster of Quaker farmers and their wives watch us from the parade.

Ely is on one side of me, Jacob on the other. I don't look back again.

22

A CLOUDBURST soaks us, and we march on through the pouring rain. The army is sprawled like a great snake over the hills, each end lost in a mist of rain. When the rain is over, the sun comes out again, stronger than ever. The mud on the road is turned to ripples of hard earth, which gradually powders into a fine dust under our feet. Many of us walk barefooted, and the crumpled dirt of the road feels good to our feet.

The rain soaks our clothes, plastering them to our backs. A film of dust forms all over them; it's unbearable. We drop our coats into the road, then our torn shirts. The musket straps bite into our backs. We strip to the waist, become a strange sight, an army of the naked.

We toil on, and at noon, throw ourselves down wearily. We can't eat much. We're strung too fine, nervous, waiting.

Talk is of the enemy. Where are they?— when will we meet them? We hear that the militia is uneasy with fear. We begin to understand why the Pennsylvania brigades march at the head of the army.

"I put no faith in militia," Jacob says. "Whatever comes, we'll drive into it first. If we stand, the militia will stand. But I put no faith in militia to meet an attack."

I feel a curious chill of fear. Life was never so precious or good—after the winter. I lived; all through that winter I lived.

"There'll be a battle, Jacob?"

"There'll be a battle. He cannot keep the militia with him for more than three months."

"The last battle," Ely says oddly.

We both look at him. Ely says, slowly: "I have no love for battle. There's been enough death. I'm sore tired, and wanting to rest. You and me, Jacob—we're no more young. We'll be wanting a long, quiet rest."

"Time for resting," Jacob says. "There'll be time enough afterwards for rest."

We march on—a forced march. The wagon train and the camp followers are left far in the rear. We're chasing something. We drag along, and the drum-beat seems lost in a fog of dust. Blood begins to speckle the road—from the naked feet. When a rest is called, we drop in our tracks, too weary to talk.

It rains again the next day, a solid wall of water, drawn out of the sodden heat. We cross the Delaware River, and come into a country of tall pines and barren sand dunes. The pine smell is heavy and sickening. The mosquitoes buzz in thick droning flocks, biting us until we are covered all over with welts. Sweat drips into our eyes, into our mouths. We are coated with dust.

Wayne laughs and says: "You'll scare the enemy. There'll be no need to fight."

We're not pretty. We've become haunted by a spectre of battle. No rest until we come up with the enemy. We begin to long for the enemy, for anything that will relieve us.

We camp that night in the dunes, build our fires between the pines. We cook, and then sprawl away from the fires. It's cool nowhere. The sand itself is hot, and it doesn't lose any heat during the night. The heat is burnt into everything.

It's difficult for us to breathe. The heavy air, clouded with pine smell, is like a solid thing. It clings to our lungs.

One of the men, a dispatch rider for Wayne, comes over to where we are lying. He was stationed outside the tent where the staff officers were at council.

We ask him for news. Do we march? Do we ever leave this godforsaken Jersey land?

"They're fighting among themselves, the officers. They've been squabbling for hours. Lee wants no battle."

"He's a fair wise soldier, Charles Lee."

"He's no man for leading; he's a sickening man to look at."

"Washington's nigh mad—sitting and muttering that he's alone—no man but Hamilton and Wayne and Steuben to follow him. He's like a man in a dream, Washington, sitting there and muttering, Why aren't you with me? Do I have to be alone? It's too much to be alone."

"Where are the British?"

"Somewhere in the Jerseys. It's said there's a train of them fifteen miles long—half the people in Philadelphia with them, maybe two thousand Philadelphia wenches to lie with them each night."

"Wayne wants battle———"

"It's Wayne's story that he'll go into battle with the Pennsylvania men. He says the whole army can go to hell and be damned—he'll go into battle with his Pennsylvania men."

"He's no man to plan a battle—too hot."

"He sits muttering, Fight—God damn you, fight. God-damn cowards, the lot of you. Lee says he'll take no words like that, and Wayne says he's a lying bastard if he'll swallow any words of his for Lee. Washington tries to soothe them, and Hamilton swears the lot of them are playing treason. Lee calls Hamilton a Jew—and Hamilton's fair ready to kill Lee. They fight like cats and dogs."

"There's no man among them with his mind made up?"

"It's Washington's idea to fight."

"He can't hold the army together for another battle. We're eight—nine thousand strong now. He'll fight now—or come a month there'll be no army."

We march again the next day. Wayne dismounts and walks with us. He's a man burning with rage—tireless, pacing up and down the line, spurring us on. There's no sign of rain, no cloud in the sky, only a blue fire with a concentrated red fire in the centre of it. We trail between the pines, drag ourselves over sand dunes that give under our feet, curse the swarms of mosquitoes, fight blindly through the dust that rises the length of the army.

There's no rest. Hour after hour—forward. The men who started out barefooted have raw, bleeding feet now. The sand blisters our feet, burns them. Between the sun and the dirt, we are burnt black, our faces stubbled with beard again, our skin welted all over with mosquito bites.

Ely is taking it hard. Jacob, a thin wraith of a man, marches with the smouldering fire of a fanatic in his eyes. Jacob is the soul of the revolution, uncomplaining, tireless, fire that will burn steadily until it is blown out. But Ely's feet are cut to pieces again, swollen. They have never fully healed from the winter. They bleed steadily, in spite of our bandaging.

Once, when dropped to rest, Ely gasped: "This is the last march, Allen."

"No—you've been through a lot worse than this, Ely. We rest soon."

He said, not bitterly: "I'm tired. I've carried a load, Allen—a great deal of a load."

Job Andrews, sitting near us, said: "It's hard, tired marching for an old man."

"An old man," Ely nodded, smiling a little.

"You're noways old."

"Old enough, Allen. I'm thinking to give these poor feet of mine a rest soon. A long rest."

We stumble on. Night, and we drop in our tracks. We have no strength to build fires. We fall asleep in brigade formation, toss on the hot sand, gasp for breath. With dawn, we're up and fighting our way north.

Men drop out of line. They clutch at their eyes, reel, stagger a few steps, and crumple to the sand. They lie in huddled bundles and the brigades crawl past them. We're caked with dirt—horrid black, sunburnt figures.

We come to a Hessian's body. A man dead with heat. What with their seventy pounds of uniform and equipment, the heat is more than they can stand. They die like flies. His bright green uniform is streaked with dirt and slime. He lies on his back, eyes open, face swollen shapeless by mosquito poison. He's a strange, lonely figure, a reminder of the enemy we haven't seen for six months. Some of the men pause to drag his boots off.

We go on, and now we know that they're fleeing from us. It's a fantastic, bizarre thing. For six months they could have wiped us out with a single blow. Now they're fleeing from filthy, naked beggars.

We see more and more Hessians dead of the heat. They sprawl directly on the road, or they lie crumpled to either side of it. Their green uniforms make splotches of colour on the sand. It's difficult to understand how they could have marched even a mile with those heavy uniforms. We tear off their boots. We laugh, and some of the naked Pennsylvania farmers wear the high Hessian hats. But not for long.

We see a Fusilier. We stop and stare at his red coat, at the gold facings. A uniform fit for a king.

"But warm," somebody says. "He could noways carry such a warm coat. Poor fellow's dead of a little bit of heat."

"He should have been at Valley Forge. He'd not be minding a spot of sun."

"I could have used such a pretty red jacket this winter. It fair breaks my heart to pass it by."

Things break out of the haze of dust suddenly. The drums have stopped. We appear to be crawling through a sea of dust. The Virginians have spread out to scout the advance. Their voices come hollowly from nowhere.

"All's well—all's well—all's well——"

"A ravine—a dozen feet deep."

"A ridge of sand."

We come to an overturned cart, one of the

British wagon train. A broken axle threw it on its side, and two broken trunks spill women's clothes onto the sand. We hand the clothes round, lace petticoats, lace and silk jackets, a gown.

"My Annie could wear this."

"Your Annie's back with the militia. They're no men to demand lace petticoats."

More men dead of the heat, horses whimpering as they die in the sand. In one place a dozen Hessians lie together, their glassy eyes rolled upward, no longer afraid of the sun.

The pines are endless, tall bare pines that in some places make a complete roof over our heads. There will be an open space, a hundred paces across, rolling sand dunes grown with weeds, then the pines again. There is no forgetting the hot, languid smell of the pines. The sand has no grasp for our feet. It burns them up. Our feet slip, we sprawl, we pick ourselves up. Next to me, Ely is a dogged machine, his eyes glazed. I give him an arm to help him along. He thanks me in a hoarse whisper.

We camp for the night. A thunderstorm drenches us, puts out the few fires we attempt to build. We lie like animals, dumb in our misery.

Word goes round that the British are near us. Faintly, the sound of a trumpet comes to us. Wayne stalks through the Pennsylvania brigades, putting us in a position to resist an attack if it comes. We drag logs to make breastworks, sleeping on our feet, stumbling over the logs and falling prone.

Not far from us, Washington pitches his tent. We watch the officers from other brigades riding up to the council—Varnum, Steuben, Charles Lee, Greene, Lord Stirling. They crowd into the tent, and their figures move against the light as shadows.

For what seems to be hours their tired voices bicker back and forth. We hear Wayne crying hysterically: "Fight—fight—for the love of God, can't you see it's all over if you don't fight? We'll never have this chance again—fifteen miles of half-dead soldiers and whores strung out across the country! We strike one blow—and the war's over! Only one blow! Look at my men out there! Do you think they'll suffer another winter like the last? Do you think you'll have an army a month from now if you don't fight?"

Washington's voice, soothing him, like a weary father.

And from Hamilton: "Sir—I'm sick of this, sick of this. You can have my commission."

Lee's shrill tones: "You'd ruin everything! Sir, is this an army commanded by children— or by men? I'll have no young whelp like Hamilton instruct me——"

"Sir, you'll answer for that!"

"Please—please—for the sake of your brigades, gentlemen, quietly. There's no need to roar."

Their voices drop to a murmur. We come closer to the tent. We lie in the sand, listening, listening. On and off, I doze. Each time I open my eyes—the voices from the tent. La Fayette's broken English:

"Can eet be? Can anything be so shameful? I weel not weesh to live, sirs, eef we don' strike."

"Strike—strike! By God, with what? With those broken beggars out there?"

"Sir, I'll answer for my brigades!" Wayne cries. "I'll answer for the beggars! I'll go into hell with those beggars! Only give me a chance."

Steuben: "Dey're goot men—by Gott, dey're goot men to fight mit."

Finally, the council breaks up. The officers come out of the tent, mount their horses, and go back to their brigades. Washington stands at the entrance to the tent, talking softly with Wayne and Hamilton. His face is years older, thin, a face of large bones with skin stretched tight over them.

Washington shakes hands with the two officers—goes back to his tent then. Hamilton stands there, his deep violet eyes looking at nothing at all. Wayne walks over to the breastworks, sits on the stump of a tree and stares at the ground.

Captain Muller goes over to him, waits expectantly. "Tomorrow, sir?" he asks.

"Tomorrow will answer a lot of things."

"We fight?"

Wayne nods—without glancing up.

I am on watch with Ely. We walk a little way from the breastworks and stand there, looking into the dark. The night is deep and silent, a hot, windless night.

"A strange forest," Ely says. "A forest of the dead with its roots in sand. I was thinking to look at the Mohawk again, to walk between green, soft trees."

"Maybe we'll go back soon. Maybe after the battle tomorrow . . ."

"You're afraid, Allen," Ely says gently.

I nod.

"You're thinking of Kenton and the rest of them."

"Of Kenton. If Kenton curses me for the shame of dying on a gibbet——"

"Kenton's dead. It seems to me, Allen, that the dead rest in peace. A deep peace back there on the hills where we left them. There's no shame. It's peace and a rest for a tired body."

"When I look forward to it—to battle and more battle, to more winters like this winter past, if the war goes on for years. I'm fair sick of war, Ely. I'm fair longing to have one day come after another without the beat of drums. I think of that little girl who came running to us from the Virginian men. She was no fit woman to be a man's wife, Ely—but that's what she wanted. It seems to me, now, that I had a full love for her, and that I wouldn't have hesitated too much to make her my wife. It would have been a peaceful way of things to make her my wife, Ely, to look for the sun-up as a day of planting, to see brown dirt turn up under the plough and to come back at night to a wife who doesn't ask too much of a man."

"There'll be none of that," Ely says. "I

wouldn't hurt you, Allen—you're all to me. I never had a son, Allen, and I think sometimes that you're a son to me. But there'll be none of that—no rest. I deny you rest, Allen, and I'll be resting soon. But you can't rest. My day is over. Yours is beginning."

I look at him, shaking my head.

"You'll come out of the war, Allen, with broken pieces to put together. There'll be years of war for strong men—and you'll be strong. Then you'll put broken pieces together, and there'll be no rest—no peace."

"What then?"

"Maybe a belief sometimes that the dream is coming true. We're not fighting the British. We're fighting for a great, fair stretch of land —out to the west. A different kind of people on that land, Allen. A free land."

"I don't know," I say. "I'm tired, Ely."

"Believe me," he says.

I try to sleep that night. I try to find Bess and draw her to me. But there's nothing—only a struggle without end, a groping for ideals that are empty. I try to believe, the way Ely believes, the way Jacob believes.

23

We wake with dawn. Wayne seems not to have slept at all; he is walking up and down our line, nodding, looking at our guns, whispering to us, though there is no need to whisper. He's nervous, and the sweat rolls off his face.

We strip for battle—naked to the waist, many of us barefooted and without stockings, many of us wearing no breeches, only a tattered sort of kilt. The brigade captains call monotonously:

"Measure loads—measure out your loads. Dry your powder pans and keep them dry. Any man with less than twenty rounds of ammunition report immediately. Try your guns and see that they spark."

Files are passed up and down, and men put edges on their flints. I spark mine, and it seems to fall dull. My hands are wet and shaking. I take a file and attempt to edge my flint. Ely takes it from me and sharpens my flint with two deft strokes, roughens the steel. Ely is wonderfully calm, his face sad and a little puzzled. Jacob's eyes are hot and burning; he seems to have a fever.

Wayne can't stop moving. "Bayonets," he calls. "Fix your bayonets—bolt your bayonets!" He tries a gun and then throws it aside. He acts like a man gone mad.

We count out our loads. I measure the powder in my horn, mechanically. I sift some of it through my fingers. It's dry, but my fingers are wet. I'm wet all over, my breeches plastered to my legs. A film of water covers my body.

I finger my musket nervously. "Load," Jacob says. "Load her careful, Allen. It's the first load that measures a man's life. If she don't spark the first time, she won't spark."

I load the musket. It's an old musket with a large bore—my father's. I load it with a heavy charge and three balls. I say to Ely anxiously: "Three balls—that's not too much?"

"She's a strong musket, Allen."

"I'm sick, Ely—sick and gone. I feel like sitting down and just resting. I'm in no way to move, Ely."

"It's not your first battle," Jacob says shortly.

"It's seven months since we've been to battle——"

"Easy, boy, easy," Ely murmurs.

"Three balls is a fair heavy load for a musket," I say doubtfully.

We form our lines. The word is still being called: "Dry pans and measure loads . . ."

Some of the men are munching on salt meat. I feel empty, terribly hungry. I go to my pack and get a piece of meat, but Jacob strikes it out of my hand.

"You'll be thirsty enough."

"I'm bitter hungry."

"You don't want to eat," one of the men tells me. "It's a rotten thing to have a bullet in your belly after you eat."

The officers are clustered around Washington. Wayne is arguing. Charles Lee stalks away in a rage; they are going into battle against his advice. Then Washington calls him back. Hamilton is sulking alone by the tent. Steuben can't keep away from the men.

"Mine children—you vill remember . . ."

The sun is just rising. A splatter of light fans the tops of the pines. No wind. Even at that hour of the morning, it is unbearably hot. The smell of powder, of sweating men, mingles with the odour of the pines. We move uneasily and stare at our muskets as if we had never seen them before.

Suddenly, Wayne goes to his horse, mounts, and rides to the head of the line. La Fayette follows him. Lee is calling something after them. Then Lee mounts too, and the order comes down the line to march. Wayne is leaning over his saddle, talking anxiously to a tall Virginian scout. Washington watches us, his face clouded. Lee rides off to one side, speaking to no one, his strange, ugly face contorted in anger. An ugly man, his ugliness burns in him. A professional soldier, he was respected at least for his professional advice until Steuben came. Now Steuben advises battle, and Washington has overruled Lee's plea not to fight. His hatred for Hamilton, for La Fayette, for Wayne is plain enough.

We march quickly, as if Wayne were eager to get into whatever lies ahead of us. It's damnably hot. We thread our way through the pines and then through woods of birch and maple. We go down into a ravine, form again on the other side. Wayne wheels the brigades, and now we march spread out like the broad end of a fan. We are in a wood. As yet, we have made no contact with the enemy.

We go through the wood, a distance on a road, and then down and out of another ravine. The bottom of the ravine is mud. We sink into it to our knees, suck our feet out, claw through. The mud splashes us from head to foot. The brigade commanders call out to each other, and Wayne waves his sword, trying to keep us in battle line. Lee's white horse, streaked all over, is struggling through the mud. He rides without looking back at us, sitting in his saddle wearily and indifferently.

We have been marching for at least an hour now, maybe more than that. I have no sense of time, but when I look up, I can see the sun through the trees. The bottom of the ravine is less hot than the road; the road was a furnace.

I stumble, and Jacob helps me up. He says: "Stay close to me, Allen—we'll get by. Stay close to me."

Wayne's voice, crying: "Powder dry—powder dry—for God's sake, keep your guns out of that mud."

As an echo: "Watch your powder pans—keep your flints clean——"

Our brigade is climbing out of the ravine, men wet to their waists with mud. We stumble up through the trees, and hear a flurry of shots.

It means that our scouts have come into contact with the British rearguard.

As we are, on the slope, with the ravine full of mud to our backs, we're in a trap. The body of the army is beyond us, perhaps a mile to the rear. It comes like a flash of red fire in our brains; we stop; we stare at one another, our mouths open. I think of getting back out of the ravine—only out of the ravine. I guess we all think of that.

Wayne spurs his horse along our front, screaming madly for us to go ahead. "To the top!" he screams. "Climb to the top!"

I wonder dully how we could have come here, who placed us in a trap like this. Like cattle—to be caught in the mud and shot down.

Ely is shaking his head, like a man in a dream.

Jacob is cursing and screaming along with Wayne. He is ahead of the rest of us, clawing his way up. He seems to slide up through the trees—no volition of his own—slide up through the trees.

We go ahead—as if Wayne were drawing us. Stumbling, falling, we climb the hill, come out on top, drag ourselves forward with our muskets and make a line. More and more men. We make a line, and then we see the Virginian scouts running back through the trees, beyond them a glint of red.

The British drumbeat wakes the morning air into waves of heat. It throbs into our heads, pulses through the ground. It turns over and over, like wheels rolling, beats our thoughts into oblivion, seems an incarnation of the heat. Wayne, dismounted, dashes along the line, pleading:

"Hold them here—hold them here!"

Charles Lee, on his white, mud-splashed horse, reins up, cries: "We have to get out of here, General—we have to get out of here. We're like rats in a trap. We have to retreat."

Wayne screams: "Sir—you can retreat—you can retreat to hell, sir!"

"I'm in command!"

"You can go to hell, sir!" Wayne sobs.

The British are less than a hundred yards away now, marching in three columns, their muskets presented, their bayonets glittering in the sun. The drums waver from a marching beat to a light, rippling rhythm, a rhythm of heat laughing at us. They come on steadily.

I try to count them—how many? Their lines are endless. The entire rear of the British army is marching to attack a few Pennsylvania and New England brigades. Where is the army? What kind of fools' sacrifice are we?

We don't know what to do. Lee is in command. Lee has given an order to retreat. La Fayette and Wayne are raging like madmen— screaming for us to hold our lines. Down the line, Scott stands and shakes his head. We are under the spell of the heat. We are still in a dream of the hell at Valley Forge—heat for cold. Hell is hot; hell is cold. Some of the men drop their muskets and bolt back into the ravine. Some of the men let go their muskets and stand watching the British—dumb. We have forgotten how to be an army, how to do anything but suffer.

We suffer now; we suffer in retrospect. We're bound up in ourselves. As a parade across our eyes are the days and nights in the dugouts, the nights in the freezing cold when we stood on sentry duty, the days when we lay like sodden beasts, starving. The dead who were piled like logs in the snow—unburied. The weight of a nation unborn on the shoulders of men— who are no more than men. We have not the power to suffer as women suffer, to give birth out of agony and rise full and new from the bed of pain. We have not the power to see beyond our sufferings, to make dreams from pain. There are no dreams from pain; we're lost men, conquered men.

The British come on, and we hear their officers speaking commands in sharp, clear voices. Strange voices. Accents of another land, another world. They're on parade, the British soldiers, men without fear, men marching to victory.

And a sobbing voice, the voice of Wayne— who understands now, who will no more ask giant deeds from men who are not giants. The voice of Wayne who sees a spectre of Valley Forge rising to overwhelm him. Wayne grows; Wayne is a man without fear, a madman without fear. But bigger than Wayne is a picture of men becoming beasts, men trying to drag themselves out of hell.

We're in hell, Wayne with us, Lee cursed by the doom he brought on himself, the men leaderless.

Fifty paces from us, the British form for the bayonet charge. We can see them very clearly now, each face under the high, pointed hat, the gold on their red uniforms. I can see one man's mouth move as he chews a wad of tobacco. I can see the drummers, spraying their roll. I can see their powder cases flap against their sides as they march. I can see one man's yellow hair waving from beneath his hat.

We begin to fire. Men let off their muskets wildly, without aim, without reason. A few of the British fall to the ground. I see one man clutch at his belly, stagger out of line and sit down with his back against a tree. The rest of them begin to run toward us. Their bayonets flutter like a line of fire, and their red coats are fire beyond their bayonets. Their muskets roar, and they smash out of the smoke.

I fire my musket. For some reason I am surprised at its recoil against my shoulder. Suddenly, I am alone with Ely. Jacob lies on the ground, on his back, a hole in his head. In that instant, I see and understand Jacob. Jacob who lived like a torch, who went out like a torch. Jacob, who was beyond men, beyond Wayne, beyond Washington, Jacob who was the single purpose of revolution. I see others beyond Jacob, there must be others. What Ely meant when he spoke to me, told me there would be no peace, no rest . . .

Ely is pulling me away. The English are almost up on us, their bayonets sweeping like a scythe. A Virginian scout, ahead of us, is cut down, four bayonets in him while he swings with his clubbed rifle. They have no bayonets, the Virginians—only their long, small-bore rifles.

With a great strength, Ely is pulling me through the trees. We run together, blindly, falling, picking ourselves up. There are other men in front of us, naked men, running, crying out like frightened beasts, falling, hurtling into trees—bruised, bloody, panic-stricken men without thought and in the grip of only one idea—to get away from the merciless line of English bayonets, to get out of the path of the scythe.

We come to the edge of the ravine, stumble down into it. There, on the edge, I have one brief picture of Wayne, a man on a horse—sobbing. He cries out: "What does it mean? What does it mean? Where are my troops? My men?"

We roll down the slope, crash against trees. We struggle through the mud. The morass is full of men—filthy, panic-stricken wretches. They mill around blindly. I am as blind as any; I try to make for the farther bank, but Ely pulls me back.

The British have formed on the top, and they

are shooting mercilessly, picking off the men as they come out of the mud and try to scramble up the farther bank. In spite of that, hundreds of them break through. I point, I cry to Ely:

"We'll go that way, Ely!"

Ely drags me through the mud, down the ravine. I see one man, just ahead of me, pitch forward, as if struck by a hammer blow on the back. He tries to steady himself, wavers, falls, and sinks into the mud. I watch fascinated as bullets strike the mud, splash. I know this place; I have been in Inferno before.

Down the ravine, a few hundred men stand waist-deep in the mud, Pennsylvania brigades. Somehow, they've gathered there, and the officers are trying to beat them into a sort of order.

We go toward them, merge ourselves in their ranks. It gives me a feeling of security and order to see men standing around me and firing their muskets.

The rout goes on before our eyes, as if we were an audience and a stage of fear-maddened men were set before us. Step by step, we retreat down the ravine, our steps to the tone of the brigade commanders:

"Load—wipe your pans—clean your flints—load easy and fire."

I ram my musket. All of a sudden, I am calm, as if a great fire inside of me had stilled itself. I stand there, wondering why I should have run before, why I should be afraid of anything. What can hurt me? What can bring me pain? Death is rest. There's no other rest for me. Inside, I am cold as ice, in spite of the hellish heat.

Ely says to me: "Jacob's dead." He says it dully, as if he didn't quite understand.

"He's dead," I say coldly. "He wouldn't have lived through this. It's the way for him—to be dead."

"God rest him . . ."

"There's rest for Jacob now."

I load carefully. It's almost terrifying, the calm that has come over me. I load as if I were on parade. We are still moving down the ravine, close—I don't know how many of us, maybe three or four hundred. Muller is there—two more officers. Muller stands out in front of us, cool. The man has courage.

The British attempt to cross the ravine, but we sweep them with our flanking fire. I see the red coats stain with mud, fall, bubble down through the mud, try to crawl out of it. The ravine fills with smoke, and men move through that smoke like ghosts. From above, the British snipe us, but they are not good shots. Here and there a man groans, falls in the mud, struggles to bring himself up, struggles against the mud that is choking him.

I load like a machine, aim carefully, trying to find a target in the smoke, trying to pick out a red or a green uniform. I wonder about the army. Have they deserted us? Forgotten us? Have they lost us? Don't they hear the sounds of the battle? Where is Wayne? Where is La Fayette—Charles Lee? Where are Steuben and the artillery? Where are the thousands of militiamen?

Was it too much for Wayne and La Fayette to see that they made a mistake, that men are only human, that men are not beasts to kill one another without fear, without compulsion? Was it too much for them to understand what Valley Forge did to us?

We fight our way down the ravine. Time has no meaning any more. For an eternity, we draw our feet out of the clinging mud, put our feet down again, load until the muskets burn our hands. The heat is unbearable—a clinging, solid wall of heat, heat taking form.

The sniping goes on. The British hang onto

us like flies, and their bullets patter into the mud. Muller is only a few feet from me when a bullet strikes him. I see Ely go to him, attempt to raise him. He shakes himself loose, cries: "I'm dying, damn you! Can't you see?"

I watch him settle into the mud, thinking vaguely that there will be no burial—no stone or bit of crossed wood to mark his place. No rhyme to tell his virtues, whether he lived a good or a bad man. Nothing. After a while, not even a memory in the minds of others. He went alone.

We keep on, desperately, guided by the strange, purposeless drive that animates men sometimes. We come to the end of the ravine, make our way out onto solid ground. The firing has fallen off round us. Some of the men wander off, aimlessly. I call them back—surprised at the sound of my own voice. I beat them into line, and they obey my commands. Ely stares at me, oddly. I tell him:

"Keep them together! Can't you see we have to stay together?"

He nods, dully. I lead the men through high grass, along a hedgerow. The roar of the battle is off to our right—a huge sound, rising and falling, nearing suddenly and then retreating from us, a sound interspersed with the booming of cannon. The cannon are sharp and clear, the roaring of angry beasts.

It's hot out here, much hotter than it was in the ravine. Nothing to shield us from the sun; the sun is part of the enemy. I look behind at the men trailing after me, a few hundred exhausted men—hot, filthy, listless. I wonder why I'm leading them. Where are the brigade commanders? I saw Muller fall; Muller is dead. But there should be others. I look for them. I ask Ely:

"Where is Captain Dean—Marcy?"

He shakes his head.

"Gainbroe?"

He keeps shaking his head.

There is an orchard ahead of us, an old barn and an apple orchard. There are men there—half-naked men like ourselves, hundreds of them, crouched over their guns.

"Rhode Island men," Ely says.

"They're waiting for the attack," I think to myself. "They're waiting like that. They don't know what an attack is—so they're waiting."

I see a man come riding toward us, a man covered with mud and blood. I tell the men behind me to halt. They stand there, dazed, staring at me, their mouths open, their breath coming hard.

I cry: "Sit down—damn you, sit down and rest! Talk! You're not dead!"

The man dismounts, and through the mud I recognize Wayne. He says: "What men are these? Who are you?"

"The Fourteenth Pennsylvania, sir—what's left of it. The rest are Pennsylvania men too, I guess."

"How did you get here?"

"We fought through the ravine—after the retreat. We came out there—through that wood."

"Where are your officers?"

"Dead——"

"Who led you out?"

"After they died, sir? I led the men. There wasn't a lot of leading to do."

Wayne stares at me, nods. He says brokenly: "You're my men—all my men. You fought out of there alone—alone. Christ! I rode off with a retreat, and you covered it. Where are your officers, sir? Tell me!"

"They're dead."

"What's your name?"

"Allen Hale."

I can see him searching his memory. He's sick with heat. He keeps rubbing his eyes, and his hands are full of blood. He shakes his head. "Allen Hale—you were tried for murder——"

"I was tried for murder."

"I know," he whispers. He looks at the men, sprawled out behind me. He says: "Take the brigade——"

"I don't want the brigade, sir."

"God damn you, do you think I want you for an officer? I said take the brigade. I brevet you captain. You'll lead those men—or I swear to God, I'll kill you where you stand."

I looked at him, stared into his bloodshot eyes for just a moment; then I nodded.

I said: "I'll lead the brigade, sir. I'll lead them into hell, sir."

He repeated it, tonelessly: "You'll lead them into hell." He said: "Form them behind that stone wall at the edge of the orchard. Go over their guns. They'll address you as Captain Hale—you'll command that. Prepare to resist any attack, as long as you have a man left."

"Yes, sir."

He held out his hand, but I didn't take it. I stood there watching his cold, blue eyes.

He looked at me a moment, turned on his heel then and walked to his horse.

I went to the men. They had heard Wayne. They were studying me curiously. Ely kept his eyes on me. His face was the face of a man who is in a dream—who knows that he dreams and that he'll never wake out of that dream. I said evenly:

"You're to form as a brigade. I'm in command of you. You're to address me as Captain Hale."

Nobody answered. Some of them nodded.

"Brigade—attention! Form in fours!"

They climbed to their feet, formed in line, dragging their guns. I marched them over to the stone wall and showed them their places behind it.

"You will load—prepare to return fire. I'll give the command to fire."

I go over to Ely and sit down on the wall. The rocks are hot. The sun is dropping pellets of flame. The sweat runs off me, grooving lines in the dirt that covers my body. I look out over the field to where the battle is going on. Our main army is still behind us. The British will have to sweep us out of the way. I think of all that, and yet my thoughts are something apart from me. Inside I am cold and empty; my thoughts come out of that emptiness.

Ely says: "So they've made you a captain, Allen."

"They've made me a captain."

There is no emotion inside of me, but I find that I am crying. I taste the hot salt tears with my tongue.

24

THE morning passes, and we wait. They will attack some time—or never. Behind us, across the Wenrock Brook, General Greene has massed the army to throw off any attack. But meanwhile we are to hold off the British. We are to hold them off until they have exhausted themselves upon us, and then we are to let them roll over us—to be defeated by the massed Continental army, when it forms. We are a thin line of men behind a hedgerow and a stone wall. We have been fighting all morning —fighting in hell. We have sweated out all the water that is in us. We are bone-dry, fleshless, naked men. We are weary to death. We are three brigades formed into one, and God only knows what we will be tonight.

We lie behind the stone wall, in the burning sun. The men crouch close to the wall, seeking shade, but the sun is almost directly overhead, and there is no shade. They plead with me to let them go to the brook and drink.

I hold my musket and say: "I'll kill any man

who moves from this wall." Yet I wonder who is saying it. Who is Allen Hale? Ely looks at me, almost with fear; but had he expected anything else? Hadn't he known? Hadn't he formed me for this, destroying himself? Now Jacob was dead. At the beginning—with a bloody round hole in his head. There are two men left, Ely and myself; and there is no rest for me.

The battle rolls toward us. We stare at the long lines of redcoats, at the Hessians in their green uniforms. A play that we are watching.

I count the cannon shots. I try to study the field. I don't allow myself to remain still, to fall into the dull apathy that precedes sleep. I walk up and down the line, looking at muskets, feeling the powder pans, warning men to keep their wet hands from their flints. I speak out, and the words are strange to me as they come from my lips:

"Don't handle your flints. Keep your muskets in the sun. Keep your muskets dry. Let your powder bake in the sun. Hot powder is better than cold. Loosen your ramrods—loosen your ramrods."

Ely watching me—always watching me—his eyes never off me for a moment. I have an impulse to say to him: "Why, why don't you understand? For the love of Christ—if you don't understand, who will? Must I be alone—like Jacob, like Washington, men crying out in their loneliness, men impelled by fire and letting no man touch them for fear they will lose some of the fire? You're left—you're the only one! You planned this for me! Jacob's dead."

But I say nothing to him, and it comes to me that I'll never speak to Ely again. I've left Ely. I've left him behind, and there's no going back to him. As Wayne understood us this morning, when he saw his picked corps—his beloved Pennsylvanians—melt away like a pack of frightened deer, in that way I understand Wayne now. I understand Washington. There's no joy in that, no achievement. I'm cold inside —and empty.

They form for attack. Afterwards, I learn that these are the Royal Fusiliers who are attacking us. That they are picked men, the sons of the noble families of England, the finest soldiers in the world. That they are men without fear.

I don't know that now. I see a column of English soldiers marching to sweep us out of the way. They have detached themselves from the main body, and they come across the fields, boldly and bravely. They hold their muskets at salute, and they march the way men march on parade. I have never seen such marching, and I recognize the perfected thing which Steuben tried so vainly to teach us. But we are not soldiers, and we will never march like that. We are farmers, naked, filthy man-things. I cry it to myself; I speak it to myself the way I would sing a song I loved: we are not soldiers. We will never march as they march. We are farmers. We are free men, and we know fear—we know hate and suffering. We are weak the way men are weak. We can fight only for what is ours, only for what is ours.

I notice how the men are staring at the English column. It has a fascination for them. It is unreal, lifeless. It has no association with life. We are a part of life, and we know only things that are a part of life. But this is no part of life, this column of men marching into the face of our guns with perfect precision, with drums beating and with fifes playing. I recognize the tune they play—"Hot Stuff"—the tune they played when they marched up Bunker Hill.

For myself, I destroy the fascination, the illusion. There's enough ice inside of me to destroy it. These are men—men out of the other world—to be destroyed. Ice inside of me to destroy them. I walk up and down our line, speaking softly:

"Hold your fire—hold your fire. No man is to shoot until I give the word. I'll kill any man who leaves the ranks. Keep down; keep out of sight. Don't watch them."

I see a boy, no more than a boy, a lean farm lad, rising to his feet, staring with his mouth wide. I crash my open hand into his face.

"Get down! Behind the wall! Don't watch them! Keep under the wall."

Wayne is behind us, sitting on his horse, smiling a little, a man of ice—a man who is all ice. He bends his head at me, but I don't want his praise. I turn my back on him, stand behind the wall watching the English.

They are very close to us now, still they have not moved their muskets from parade position. With each step, the long line of bayonets sways, a crop of shining, shimmering steel. A drummer walks at one end of the line, his hat pushed back on his head, his head moving to the rhythm of his drum. He carries a high, English military drum, gold bands at top and bottom, a crown and lions on the side of it. He has a broad grin on his face, and he struts as he plays his sticks.

Their officers march out in front, sabres bared. They turn sometimes, glancing back at their men, as if they were reviewing the column on parade, swinging on their heels.

It seems that for a moment the battle has paused—to watch this, to watch a single regiment of young, fearless fools sweep a lot of farm louts out of their way.

I say to myself, This is England—this is all of Europe. This is what we are fighting, this crass contempt of man, this laughing contempt of the life of man, of the soul of man, of man's right to live, to know simple things and to be happy with simple things—to have no man over him. I say to myself, This is what we shall be fighting always, time without end. The fight will go on, and there will be no rest. We are life. Naked, starving, dirty farmers are life. They, out there—they are a laughing contempt for life. I tell myself that.

They are very close to us, none of them much more than boys—laughing, flinging jokes at each other with a twist of the head. They show their teeth, hold their heads high. Their clean-shaven, clean-cut faces laugh contempt at us, contempt at death, contempt at life. They've lost life; they've lost fear. They've lost the power to suffer and endure and exist. They're of the past. They are magnificent, but their magnificence doesn't touch me. What is that to me, who have spent a winter in hell, who have seen men die, men who were the blood and soul of me?—Kenton Brenner, who died in shame so that I might live; Charley Green; Aaron Levy—a Jew who had come five thousand miles to die with a dream that some day men might be free; Jacob Eagen, a man of flame and selfless in that flame; Edward Flagg, a farmer who went because he believed in something. The Fusiliers are to be pitied, but I don't pity them. How can I pity them? I walked into the log hospital at Valley Forge and saw a thousand men dying in hell; and the hell was theirs before ever they were dead. I saw nameless men piled in the snow, because the ground was frozen like iron. They were meat for the wolves that roamed the camp, and they didn't die smiling. They died clinging to life, wanting life. They were the blood of men who had always clung to life, who recognized the life of man, the free, beautiful life of man as the one holy thing on God's earth. They died crying out for life. They didn't throw life away.

One of the officers, marching in advance, turns, shouts a command. The field of bayonets sweeps to a horizontal position. The laughing boys break into a run . . .

I cry out: "Now—now—give them hell!"

The Pennsylvania farmers rise up—naked, mud-streaked figures. Their wide-bore muskets belch fire. The hedgerow and the wall burn with a sheet of fire. A blasting, crackling sheet of fire that mingles with the screaming of men. The red line of Royal Fusiliers is a tangled mass of screaming, dying men. Their laughing voices are hoarse with the agony of death. They claw at their bellies and retch blood. They stumble, try to run. Their line is broken, shattered. They give back and back, distorted broken figures through the smoke. Or they crawl forward to the wall where the Pennsylvania farmers brain them with clubbed muskets.

I scream: "Load—load again! Stay behind the wall and load again! Stay behind the wall! Load again! Dry your flints!"

I hear Wayne's voice, as from far off: "Reload—prepare to fire!"

The smoke lifts. They are standing out there on the field, beyond the wreckage of shattered bodies. Their officers form them into ranks. The drummer, half his drum shattered, beats a dull roll. Their courage is beyond reason, beyond life. They form calmly, and again they are on parade. One of their officers walks towards us, stepping backwards until he is no more than thirty yards from the stone wall. He addresses his men in clipped English tones, his voice trembling between rage and pride.

We hear his words clearly: "—peasantry—do men of blood turn their backs?"

They come toward us again. The sun is burning down. We run sweat. I can see how our men are sweating. There is no moisture left in their dry, lean bodies, yet they sweat.

I beat them down under the wall. "Don't look—don't look. No man show his face!"

They are on parade, forcing themselves to smile. They swing their feet and kick up the dust. They laugh. They are glorious, but we have seen death that is not glorious—too much.

Their officer walks ahead of them until he is within ten yards of the wall. Then he stands there, his sword at salute, looking at me and smiling his contempt. I don't hate him. I feel a thrill of savage pleasure in that—in the fact that I am beyond hate. He is part of what must go. I know only that, that he must go. He and all his contempt of life and suffering must go. Their insane, stupid courage must be destroyed. They must be taught that life is good, not to be laughed at.

They advance as before—thirty paces, twenty, fifteen. Their bayonets flash for harvest and they dash toward us.

I cry again: "Now—now!"

The farmers rise up, and the fire rages through the Fusiliers. They go down as before, men screaming in the contorted agony of death. But the Pennsylvanians can't be held now. They've seen what they have never seen before—British regulars shattered to pieces by their fire, on the open field.

They are over the wall, playing Steuben's game. They drive forward with their bayonets, slashing, thrusting, destroying with all the pent-up fury of the winter months of hell. They are hell now—all the slow, kindling hate in them let loose. These are the men who took their city, who kept them in the snow, starving.

I am with them. Life doesn't matter. Death doesn't matter. Nothing matters but that we should clear them out of our path. Destroy them. They were sent to destroy us. They laughed at us. They laughed at country bumpkins hiding behind stone walls. They laughed at a rabble without uniform. They laughed at naked men, filthy, emaciated. Their laughter still burns in us.

I drive my bayonet into a fleeing man, tear it free and leap past him. I am a machine to kill —ice inside. I am no longer a man. I have discovered Jacob.

We stand, panting. Bloody, grimed spectres. We have destroyed the Royal British Fusiliers. We have destroyed the picked troops of Europe, wiped them out in hand-to-hand battle. They are strewn over the rocky field, dead, dying— the blood of England wetting the ground of America. There is an America born out of blood and out of death. They are our blood—but no longer us. A world is ours, made here, made out of a winter of hell and the blood of the Fusiliers.

For a moment we stand that way, weary, victors on a field of battle. We look around us and wonder at what we have done. We are not soldiers. Maybe it comes to most of us then— that we are not soldiers, that we have done this thing once. Forget. A cool place to lie down and sleep. A long sleep to forget. A long, long sleep.

Wayne is riding among us, calling for a retreat. I stare at him dully. Some of the men drop where they stand, their bodies tried beyond endurance. We look at Wayne. Haven't we done enough—held them?

The British army is advancing. We stare at that great horde of men moving down on us, and shake our heads. We are a few hundred men in the path of an army. They come in long lines of green and red, Hessians to the front, bayonets set. A field of bayonets. We try to retreat. We stumble out of the way. I call the men to follow me, call my body to run. My feet move slowly, as in a dream. I fall once—pick myself up. The musket fire is a raging blast in our ears. Nothing can live in that, nothing can exist. It is an eternity before we reach the stone wall, climb over it. I look round, and half the men are gone. Somewhere back there—with the Fusiliers. Dying in a moment that encompasses all the sorrow of winter.

The musket fire of the advancing British seems to sweep the world clean—clean of life. We try to run, twist, get out of that musket fire.

We reach the brook, and the men fall flat into it, soak their heads, gulp the water.

It's like a wave of life, the water. I gulp it in, feel it run through my body. I stand up and order the men to go ahead. Ice inside of me. I walk through the water and give commands calmly, coolly, as if this moment the world were not going mad. The men file past. Greene's regiments are lying ahead of us, waiting behind their entrenchments. Waiting.

One of the men remains in the brook. I say to him: "Get up there, you damn fool!"

"My brother's back there, Captain Hale."

"He's dead. Get out of here."

"He's not dead. I saw him move when he fell."

"I tell you, he's dead. Get out of here."

He walks on, looking back over his shoulder, shaking his head. Wayne passes me, his horse grinding water from the brook. Wayne is lost in the battle, a madman shrieking his battle-cry.

I look for Ely. He didn't pass me by with the men. I look for him to come, and I see only the rolling mass of the British attack.

I say to myself: "Ely's dead. He's back there —somewhere, and he's dead."

Walking toward our lines, I hear men shrieking in warning. The attack is coming—behind me. I try to think, to cut the rushing, blasting sound of fire out of my ears. I must think. I must kill the emptiness inside of me and think about Ely. I must understand what has happened to Ely—who was with me all my life, who stood outside my house with my father when my mother gave birth to me, who heard my mother scream with agony. Where is Ely? Why have I lost him?

Ely's dead, and why does his death mean nothing? They are all dead—and I am the last. I'm alive, and all the rest of them are dead.

I'm running. I must live. I can't rest.

I break into the Continental lines. What's left of the Pennsylvania men are there, sprawled and half-asleep over their muskets. It's a New Jersey line, men fresh for the battle and waiting. It's hot. It's too hot to think, but not hot enough to kill the cold inside of me. I'm in command of men. I must tell them to load and shoot, to dry their flints. My head is aching, bursting with pain, but I must tell them to dry their flints. I wake them. They want to sleep, but I won't let them sleep. I drive them into a battle line.

The British are attacking. A great wave of them roll down to Wenrock Brook. My voice is lost in sound, a solid wall of sound. I see the Hessians sprawling into the brook. They die in the brook. The American front is one solid wall of flame, thousands of men shooting together. A wall of sound and a wall of flame. A pain in my head—bursting it apart. The brook runs red with blood. The British officers, horses shot under them, roll on the ground. The attack falters and gives back. Grapeshot tears the front to pieces. The brook is red; the whole world is red. The blazing sun of day is beginning to set, leaving a red world behind. The Pennsylvanians sleep over their guns. They are no more a part of battle. The crash of sound does not awaken them. A long, long sleep.

A long sleep—to forget. Sleep to forget about Ely. Ely is dead. A good company—a great, fair company. They sleep in peace. No sound can wake them, no sound that the world makes can ever wake them. A deep peace and a deep sleep, without heat and without cold, without trouble, without longing. A rest as sweet as the heart of Ely—a great golden heart.

A heart for man. Man is a holy thing, and

his body is a holy thing. Man is made in the image of God, in the holy image of God.

Smoke out of the battlefield and a sighing that is not sound. They have turned the water of the brook red.

The British retreat. Their retreat turns into a rout, and broken columns flee the field. The Hessians, who bore the brunt of the first fire, can no longer endure the weight of their heavy uniforms. They stagger, sprawl and roll over. The field is dotted with little green heaps of their bodies. They lie in and out of the brook. We stop firing, but the dull booming of the cannon goes on. A wall of grapeshot between them and us.

They splotch the field with red and green patches. They try to form as they retreat. They leave their dead behind them. They leave us the field, the dead and the dying.

Time has been lost. The only measure of time is weariness, and how long have we been weary? Tonight, we'll sleep.

The sun is low. There is almost a breeze, a movement of air that sends the powder smoke into curling tendrils. A curl of smoke from the muzzle of my musket. Like a machine, I have been loading and reloading, firing. The musket is hot as fire in my hands. The bayonet is bent. I try to think how I bent my bayonet. I touch it gingerly. Dry blood—the life-blood of man.

Like the blood of Ely. Ely sleeps. All round me, men are dropping to sleep over their guns, dropping to sleep where they lie. The officers try to wake them. Why? Why? The battle is over. They've earned their sleep—a long sleep and a deep one, a sleep to forget.

But I can't sleep. The pain in my head increases, a beating, rushing pain.

I stand up and watch the retreat. The haze of twilight has fallen over the fields. The British columns are moving slowly, dragging themselves off a field they lost. A cannon booms, again and again. From somewhere in the distance, there is the crackle of musket fire.

There is a wisp of white cloud in the sky in the east, and the setting sun stains it—a pink and then a blood-red. As if the groaning pain of the battlefield had gone into the sky.

The cannon booms, again and again. Gradually, other sounds die away. The cannon booms out in a great stillness.

Why don't they stop firing?

The British columns lose themselves in a haze of twilight. Green and red merge with the brown and green of the ground. I wait for the cannon, but it doesn't come.

The sun has set.

The army sleep. Sprawled over their guns, sprawled in long lines behind their breastworks, the men sleep. The dead sleep beside them, but they are not afraid of the dead. It's a long sleep.

A sighing wind in the trees. I stand there, staring at my musket, which lies at my feet.

I step over the breastworks—begin to walk. Each step is pain, but I have to walk.

A man challenges me.

I say: "Captain Hale—the Fourteenth Pennsylvania."

The man says: "It's hell on guard. Let them have the dead. I'm going to sleep."

I walk on. Wounded men are groaning. A doctor and some stretcher bearers pass me by. "A man needs some sleep," the doctor is muttering.

A wounded man clutches at my foot. I call to the doctor.

"Christ—I'm one man! How much can one man do?"

The dead and the living lie together, naked, sleeping. I stumble on. Cold inside—cold as ice. Ely knew.

I walk through the brook, walk among the bodies of the British dead. It is quite dark now. How long ago was it that we fought a battle?

Somewhere—out there—is Ely. I could explain to Ely. He would understand. He understood how it was with Jacob.

I walk toward a tree. There are two men sprawled under it. They are speaking. I make out the voice of Washington; I would know that voice anywhere. The other is La Fayette's.

I walk toward them. I walk on until I stand under the tree where they are.

"Who are you?" Washington asks.

I am laughing in spite of myself, laughing while my head bursts with pain. I answer:

"A deserter—a murderer. But Wayne made me a captain. The brave General Wayne made me a captain—to lead my men into hell. Do you know what hell is? I was there. I led my men into hell today. Ask Wayne. Ask him. He made me a captain."

"Mad," Washington mutters. "No wonder —the heat and what we've seen today."

"I'm not mad," I say calmly. "I know when a man is mad. I'm not mad—only tired and wanting to sleep."

"Then go and sleep."

"I'll go and sleep," I say.

I walk through the apple orchard, looking at the faces of men. I find Ely at last, lying near the stone wall. Even in the dark, I know him.

I bend over him and whisper: "Ely—it's Allen Hale."

The wound is in his breast. I try to fold his hands over it. I close his eyes. His face is not tired any more. His face is the peaceful face of a man who has given out of a great heart.

I lie down next to him. I whisper: "I'll sleep now, Ely. I'm fair dying to sleep. You know how it is with me. You have a heart for understanding."

Sleep comes slowly, but the hot pain in my head goes. I lie there, next to Ely—listening to the sighing of the wind through the trees of the orchard.

25

THE next morning, I bury Ely. There is much burying to be done—British and Hessians and Americans. Most of the Americans are naked, and we wrap them in the green coats of the Hessians. It's not good that a comrade should go into the earth naked. Stripped and dirty, the Hessians lie in a row. They go into a trench, and no stone marks their graves.

I bury Ely where he fell, in the apple orchard. Close to the stone wall, where there will be no ploughing. And when the sun is low, the wall will shade him. Grass grows greener in the shade, and the grass will grow over Ely's grave.

The farmer who owns the orchard stands there watching us. A tall thin man, he curses under his breath and speaks of money to be paid for damage done. He stops his cursing to stare at his apple trees, stripped and shattered by the rain of shot. Then he begins to curse again, yelling:

"Bury them deep! I'll turn them in my ploughing!"

Some of us look at him, and then he's quiet. We haven't washed; we are bloody, filthy figures, but victors . . .

I want a sword for Ely. A sword to place by his side, and regimental colours to cover his face. Our regiment is gone and there are no colours. Ely never wore a sword, but there are swords on the field.

I walk among the Fusiliers. They have not been buried yet, and some of them lie on their backs, their eyes open. Most of them are boys, and even in death they manage to look gallant in their red coats. I would pity them, but there is no pity in me for anything, not even for Ely.

I find a slim dress sword. I find a blue flag. Blue is a good colour, cool. I cover Ely with the flag, and the sword I place by his side. Dirt falls on the flag, and then there is a little mound to show where Ely lies. I mark the grave with a bayonet—a rusty, bent bayonet that is no use to anyone. It will stand for a little while.

Ely is dead. Jacob is dead.

I walk aimlessly. The field is death, but death doesn't move me.

It is not so hot as yesterday. The sky has a

few scudding clouds that throw shadows along the ground. I sit down under a tree and stretch my legs out. A long rest . . .

A man comes over to me and stands waiting.

"What do you want?" I ask him.

"I can't find my regiment, Captain."

"Why do you call me Captain?"

"You led us yesterday."

He stands waiting.

"Well?"

"You led my brigade."

"That was yesterday."

"Shall I report to you, Captain?"

"That was yesterday," I whisper.

I go to the brook and wash. There are other men there—naked, rolling in the cool water. I lie in the water with them; I lie on my back and let the water ripple over my body. It is very cool and very pleasant. I watch the clouds tumbling across the sky.

There is talk about what we will do now, where we will go. They talk as if the war were over. The British have been defeated; France is our ally.

They talk of going home, and the talk makes me uneasy. There is no place for me to go, no life for me except this. What was my home once is a dream now; the reality is here—with the revolution.

I dress myself. No shirt; a pair of torn breeches and my musket.

I walk back to the orchard, and I see Wayne. He is sitting on the grass, and Steuben stands next to him. Wayne is talking eagerly and quickly, smiling, and Steuben, frowning, tries to follow his English.

I go up to them and stand waiting. Finally, Wayne looks at me; as he looks at me, I see that he remembers, and he smiles.

"Allen Hale," he says.

"Yes, sir."

He nods at Steuben. "This is the man——"

In German, Steuben says: "You are a very brave man."

I shake my head. The brave men are dead. I say to Wayne: "My brigade is gone; my regiment is disbanded."

"Who disbanded them?"

I point to Ely's grave.

Wayne rises and gives me his hand.

"You refused my hand once before," he remembers.

I nod.

"Where are the rest of you—the New York men?"

"Dead, sir."

He is silent for a while. Then he says: "I brevetted you captain. You commanded a brigade."

"There is no longer a brigade, sir."

"Nevertheless, I'll have your rank confirmed."

I nod, salute, and walk away. I pass Ely's grave. Already, the bayonet has lost its grip in the soil. It will not stand long.

We paraded before we marched away. We lined up on the field of battle. Front and centre, there was the Pennsylvania line, militia mostly, but in every company of militia a few enlisted men who had been through the winter. But only a few.

We stood in our ranks with the hot sun over us, with green twigs in back of our ears, with our hot muskets in our hands. The generals reviewed us and praised us. The beggars were an army, standing on a victorious field. The beggars had proven their right to exist.

That is written.

Ely lies on the field of Monmouth, with

Jacob. The others are at a place called Valley Forge.

In the summer, Valley Forge is green and lovely. In the winter it is never so cold as that winter—never so cold that the ground will freeze deep to where they lie.

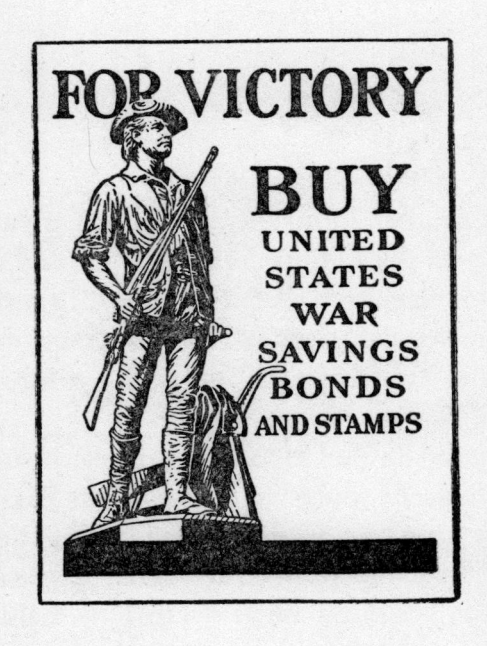

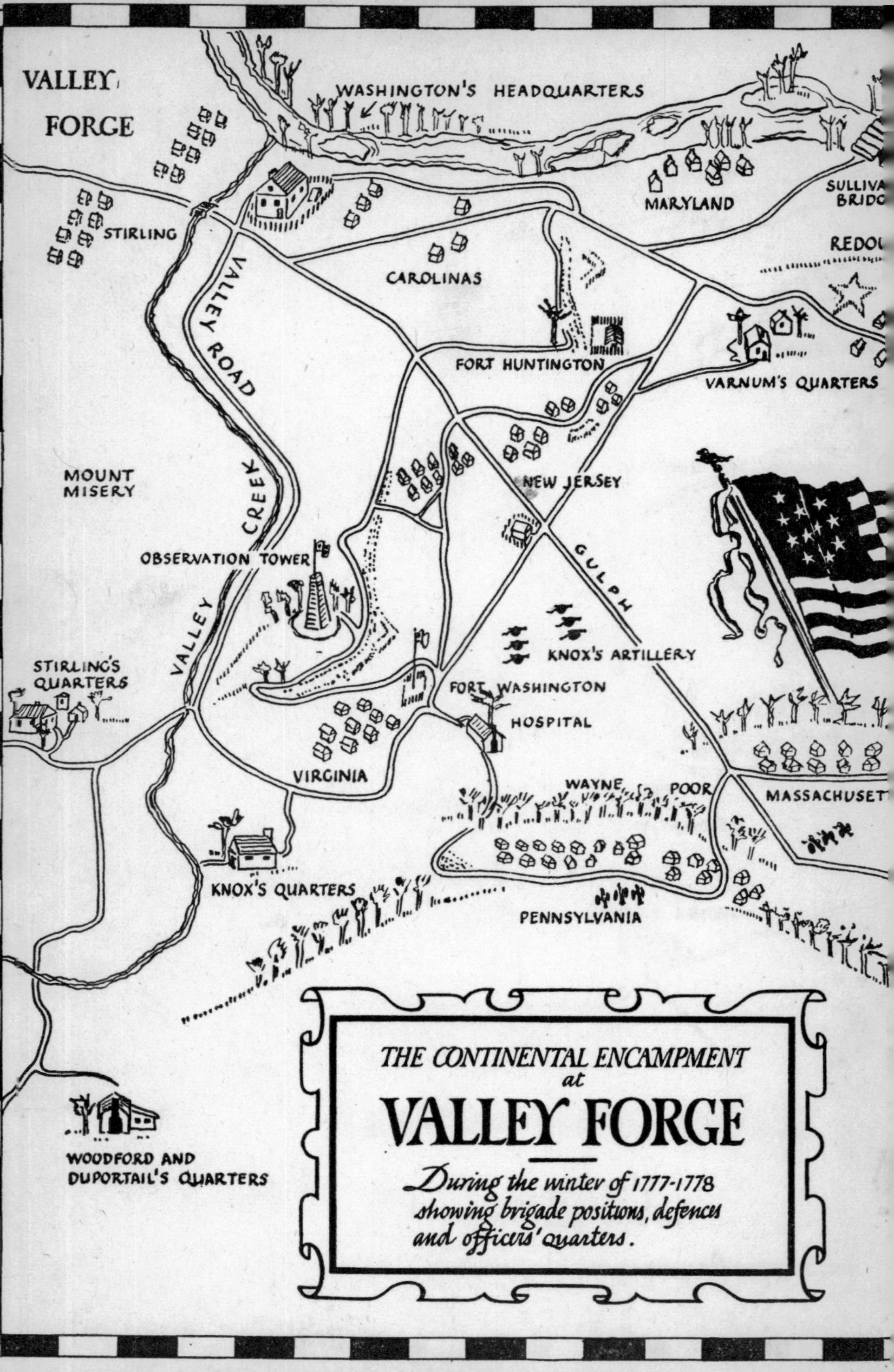
VALLEY FORGE
WASHINGTON'S HEADQUARTERS
STIRLING
MARYLAND
CAROLINAS
VALLEY ROAD
FORT HUNTINGTON
VARNUM'S QUARTERS
NEW JERSEY
MOUNT MISERY
VALLEY CREEK
OBSERVATION TOWER
GULPH
KNOX'S ARTILLERY
STIRLING'S QUARTERS
FORT WASHINGTON
HOSPITAL
VIRGINIA
WAYNE
POOR
KNOX'S QUARTERS
PENNSYLVANIA
WOODFORD AND DUPORTAIL'S QUARTERS
THE CONTINENTAL ENCAMPMENT at
VALLEY FORGE
During the winter of 1777-1778 showing brigade positions, defences and officers' quarters.